From a sassy meet cute, to hilarious shenanigans, this sweet romance will keep you turning the pages. If you love Hallmark movies, you won't want to miss this Cinderella tale.

— TARI FARIS, AUTHOR OF THE RESTORING HERITAGE SERIES

I love a small-town romance, especially when I get to travel back to one of my all-time favorite fictional small towns—Deep Haven, MN. If you're a fan of Susan May Warren's Deep Haven books, then you will enjoy seeing favorite characters pop up in *Can't Buy Me Love*. With this fresh take on the Cinderella fairytale and heart-warming romance, *Can't Buy Me Love* is a wonderful sweet read for a snowy afternoon.

— LISA JORDAN, AWARD-WINNING AUTHOR FOR LOVE INSPIRED

Andrea Christenson has added to the Deep Haven Collection series with a wonderful and well-written book that is just a delight. She gives us characters that are so well fleshed out they seem real. That is a big deal to me when I read a book. I need to connect with characters and I did here! Well done!

— SUSAN S., GOODREADS REVIEW

CAN'T BUY ME LOVE

A DEEP HAVEN NOVEL

SUSAN MAY WARREN
ANDREA CHRISTENSON

sunrise
PUBLISHING

A NOTE FROM SUSIE MAY

I love a great retooled fairytale, and when I read Andrea's unique and delightful story about a modern-day housekeeper and the prince-slash-billionaire who falls for her, I knew they belonged in Deep Haven.

Sure, they weren't the typical Deep Haven-ites, but we love all kinds up in the north. And Ella, with the help of the Christiansen family and a few other locals, learns to fit right in.

I also love stories about billionaires who are trying to find their one true love. And Adrian, with his fast car and big dreams, is no different. The fact that he ends up "doing time" with Ella is fantastic. And the rest is pure fun.

I invite you to dive into this story about two outsiders who are looking for a place to belong...and who find it inside the town of Deep Haven.

Thank you for reading the next installment of the refreshed Deep Haven series. I know you'll love this story as much as I do!

XO,

Susie May

To Macy, my favorite fan,
Anna, my favorite editor,
and Eric, my favorite

CHAPTER 1

*T*hese shoes were going to be the death of her.

Ella wiggled her toes and waited for the elevator to arrive, refusing another glance at her watch. Yes, she was late, but what did they say about being fashionably late?

Just down the hall and through the lobby, music spilled out of the bar area of the Century Hotel in downtown Minneapolis. Elegance dripped from the high-hanging chandelier of the foyer, the deep blue and gold carpets, and the massive floral arrangement on a center table. Through the glass ceiling that arched over the lobby expanse, the night sky had turned to diamonds, while just below it the breath of the underworld pumped out of the massive vents in the sidewalks like a dragon aslumber.

It was a fairytale night.

A fairytale she didn't belong in. Ella *should* be at home in Deep Haven in her flannel pajamas instead of freezing to death in this skimpy ice-blue satin dress. Colleen Decker, her former college roommate, had loaned her the dress, an ankle-length ball gown that hugged Ella's slim curves before flaring out at the knees. The neckline dropped to just below her collarbone in the front and just below her shoulder blades in the back. The shoes —Manolo Blahnik stilettos that Colleen had found on eBay— would probably cut off all feeling from her toes by the end of the night. She should have worn her pink Converse.

The price she paid for her dreams.

She inventoried the contents of her tiny handbag for the third time in as many minutes. Lip gloss? *Check.* The 3x5 note-cards for her pitch? *Check.* Thumb drive with a backup copy of her pitch? *Check.* Shareholders' Gala invitation with "Ella Nicole Bradley" embossed in gold across the front? *Check.*

She squeezed the clasp back together. If only Colleen would have let her bring her own normal-sized purse along. That bag had been relegated to the same pile as the flannel and jeans. But she probably wouldn't need the Kleenex, sewing kit, hand sanitizer, Band-Aids, granola bar, and other supplies she usually kept fully stocked in her oversized purse.

Probably.

Ella adjusted the white faux mink stole Colleen had thrown across her shoulders at the last moment.

"You're going to need something warm," her friend had said earlier that evening. "It may be nice outside now, but it's still winter in Minnesota. The weatherman said we may get a late-March snow tonight."

"No way." Her conversation with Colleen drifted back to her as she watched the elevator lights crawl down from the twenty-first floor. "That dress is way out of my comfort zone." She turned to look at the back of the borrowed dress in the mirror.

"Nonsense. This color is perfect with your blonde hair, and it will bring out the blue in your eyes. You want to knock 'em dead tonight. After all, you might meet the devastatingly hand-some and irredeemably rakish Adrian Vassos." Colleen had given her a wink. "Did you hear he drove his car into the nearly frozen Lake Kellogg a month ago? Silly man. He should know that the ice wasn't going to be thick enough this late in the winter. He's lived there all his life. Good thing that boy is hot. He can get away with things like that." Colleen fanned her face with her hand, pretending to swoon at the thought of Adrian Vassos.

Adrian Vassos was the last person on Ella's mind tonight. He could drive into as many lakes as he wanted, woo any girl he came across, as long as he stayed out of her way. He might be the son of the owner, but her goal was a face-to-face with the man at the top of the food chain.

Her last chance to salvage the life she hoped to create.

The lights dinged at floor fourteen.

"A good pair of shoes make all the difference." Colleen had reached to the back of the closet and pulled out a shoebox. Nestled under the lid inside a few sheets of tissue paper lay a pair of pale blue slingback heels with tiny crystals sewn in a star pattern across the toes.

If only they fit. Her feet screamed, even after only ten minutes. Why hadn't she stuck to her Converse sneakers?

"Over my dead body! Girl! You don't wear Chucks to the party of the year."

So, yes, she'd tried on the shoes, a little mesmerized. Maybe these shoes would bring the confidence she so desperately needed.

"Fine, I'll wear them, but if I fall on my face and die, I'm coming back to haunt you."

Colleen had grinned at her. "Haunt me all you want. I'm on your side. Want to practice your pitch one more time?"

"Let's just get going. Wouldn't want to be late to the party of the year."

The drive from Colleen's apartment in Robbinsdale to the newly built Century Hotel in downtown Minneapolis passed more quickly than Ella would have liked.

"I don't think I can do this," she'd confessed as they pulled up.

Colleen had waved her words away. "Nonsense. You can and you will. You have months of research under your belt. No one could be more prepared than you."

"They will know I don't belong here. They'll know I'm just pretending."

"Why do you hold so tightly to the idea that you don't belong? The party is for shareholders, and *you are a shareholder.*"

"Colleen, I have one half of a share. *One half.*" Ella's palms grew damp. She clutched the edges of her seat to keep from wiping her hands on the satin of her dress. "They'll see right through me the second I walk through that door. I'm just a housekeeper, a glorified maid."

Colleen pulled up to the valet stand and put her car in park. "Ella, look at me. No, look me in the eyes. Ella Girl, you are the daughter of a King, and no one can look down on you."

"I *used* to be the daughter of a king." It was true. Her dad had been Michael Bradley, the King of Clean, owner of the Helping Hands cleaning empire. But all that came to a screeching halt when he died two years ago.

"That's not what I'm talking about. Do you believe you are a child of God? He's the king I mean. You are every bit as worthy as the people inside this hotel. Not because you have half a share or a thousand, not because of your job or anything in your bank account." Colleen had been so earnest, Ella couldn't stop herself from nodding.

Besides, Colleen was right—she *had* studied for months, practicing and perfecting her formulas as well as her sales pitch. It was time to take Essentially Ella to the next level. All she needed to do now was convince Mr. Vassos to listen to her for five minutes. Surely he'd give that much time to the daughter of an old friend. And then, hopefully, he'd love her idea.

"You got this. Go in and knock 'em dead."

Right.

Now, Ella shifted again in her too-small shoes as the elevator dinged to the lobby.

"I can do this," Ella murmured. "I am prepared. I am ready. *I can do this.*"

The doors slid open.

Oh no.

The curving back of the tiny elevator was a clear pane of glass, a window to the world. Supposedly these glass elevators were elegant and classy, offering riders a view of the sprawling city below...but the open look across the high vista of downtown Minneapolis sent a shiver down Ella's spine. It was easier to pretend she wasn't up so high when she didn't have a constant reminder of the distance. The elevator seemed to be designed to make passengers feel like they were soaring into the clouds.

Maybe she should take the stairs instead.

She took a step back and nearly stumbled. Nope. In these shoes the elevator was the only real option.

Ella wobbled inside, grabbed onto the brass handrail, and hit the button for the twentieth floor. She would just face forward, breathe deeply, keep her eyes on the wall panel, and watch the numbers go up as she rose higher and higher. She would be fine.

Probably.

After all, the odds of plummeting to death in a catastrophic elevator incident were about one in 10.5 million.

Above the number panel was a poster for a charity event happening tonight on the twenty-first floor. Buy-in was listed at three thousand dollars. Apparently it was an opportunity for rich people to prove to their rich friends how charitable they all were.

Checking her reflection in the mirrored surface of the elevator wall, Ella noticed one of her blonde curls escaping the updo she and Colleen had labored over earlier. She reached a hand up to re-pin the wayward piece of hair. This whole outfit was beginning to feel like a costume, a mask that Ella put on to accomplish her goal.

Her stomach grumbled, lunch with Colleen a distant memory. See—she *did* need her regular purse. At least then she'd have snacks.

This had to be the slowest elevator in the world.

The doors finally started to slide shut when she heard a shout.

"Hold the door!"

Ella rolled her eyes but stuck her hand against the door to keep it open. A tuxedoed man slid in, bringing the spicy scent of cologne. The delicious, heady fragrance washed hints of pine and summer rain over her. He carried a purple stole in his hands.

One of the upper crust, heading to the upstairs party. She knew the type.

"Thank you. Floor twenty-one, please," Tuxedo said as he stood slightly to the left.

Yep. She hit the button, stole a glance sideways.

Goodness. The man was possibly the most handsome human being she'd ever shared a small space with. His tuxedo stretched across broad shoulders, and dark, wavy hair skimmed the back of his neck, nearly to his collar. His green eyes sat over a Grecian nose. Suddenly the heights weren't the only thing making her blood zing through her veins.

Oh brother. She hadn't come to the party to swoon over the men.

Focus, Ella, focus. You have one night to make this happen. One night to change lives.

No distractions allowed.

She risked another glance at him.

~

This night would change his life if only Adrian could get his date to lighten up.

He fingered the fabric of the purple wrap he'd retrieved from the car. High-maintenance women baffled him. Next time his cousin Athena tried to fix him up—with a blind date, no less —he'd turn her down. Tonight's presentation at the Shareholders' Gala was supposed to be all about his new start. He needed to be focused on that, not on fetching things from the car like a pet poodle.

Adrian checked his watch—7:27. Good. He still had over an hour to schmooze the shareholders before his presentation at the annual meeting. Plus, he really hoped they served those little spanakopita he'd taste tested the week before. The Greek spinach pastry emblazoned with his family insignia impressed even Costas Vassos, his notoriously hard-to-impress father.

He checked his watch again. "Slow elevator, eh?" He didn't know why he'd said that—maybe because he always had trouble with silences. Still, the woman next to him seemed to bristle at his words.

Perfect. One of those women who suspected every man of misbehavior. He stepped away from her, even as he glanced her way.

She was pretty. Wore a blue dress that shimmered like a waterfall. It looked a little chilly for this time of year, but it pulled out the blue of her eyes. Golden blonde hair, piled up, with a few escaped curls framing her face.

Okay, *very* pretty. "Going to a party?"

She nodded, her jaw a little tight.

The elevator jerked as it started to ascend, and she grabbed the railing.

"You okay?"

"I'm fine," she said after a tiny gasp, a swallow. "Statistically, an elevator has a zero-point-zero-zero-zero-two chance of getting stuck."

The lift smoothed out as it ascended. "That's one in every five thousand," she added.

He quirked a smile. "Yep. I think we'll make it."

He turned his back to the panel and stared out the window. What a view. He'd visited the Century just after it opened, when they were choosing a meeting space for this year's event. But he'd taken a service elevator to the top. This was a much better choice.

The city dropped below him, an array of bright lights against dark sky, and overhead, the moon puddled light across the skyline. From the top, the metropolitan spread turned glorious with the glitter off the Mississippi River and the dazzling lights of the Stone Arch Bridge at St. Anthony Falls.

The perfect setting for him to wow his father with his proposal for expansion. The hotel and water park he had planned for Deep Haven would win over the board—he knew it.

The elevator jerked again, and even he reached out to steady himself.

Behind him, the woman yelped and stumbled backward. He turned just in time to catch her, using both hands to steady her as he grabbed her arms.

She caught her hand on his arm. "Sorry—sorry!" She gave a tiny, high, and maybe a little terrified laugh.

"What's that math again?" He smiled at her and had to amend himself once more. No, not just really pretty. She was a *knockout*. Curves, and the dress clung to every one of them, and a shapely mouth, not too much makeup, but enough to pull out her high, almost regal cheekbones.

He sort of wished he was going to *her* party.

"Thanks," she said, and when she smiled, something happened to his insides.

Or maybe it was just the jerk of the elevator. It hiccuped again, and this time he braced his hand on the glass as the woman fell against him.

"These stupid shoes!" she said, but she sounded almost near tears.

He wanted to argue that maybe it wasn't the shoes—

The elevator shuddered, and just like that, dropped.

She shrieked and he didn't know how she ended up in his arms, but in a second he was holding onto her with one arm, the other gripping the elevator bar as the car fell.

It dropped ten feet, then more, and he bit back the urge to shout.

God, please don't let us—

It stopped with a shudder.

He'd barely taken a breath when she pushed away from him, leaping to the door. "Let me out!"

"Um, I don't think—you can't—"

But she was wide-eyed as she turned to him, breathing hard. "We're going to die!"

"Nope." He held up his hand. "Shh. We're going to be okay." But his hand shook. He made a fist.

She was looking past him, through the glass, her face turning pale.

"Hey." He grabbed her arms. Met her eyes. "Breathe."

Nothing.

"Look at me and breathe."

Her blue eyes shifted to meet his. So much fear inside, but she nodded.

He couldn't move, caught in the fear, the sense of her trying to right herself.

In a way, it calmed his own racing heart.

"You're right." She pulled in a deep breath and then pushed away from him. "You're right. I'm sorry. It's just—" She looked past him again.

"Hey. C'mere. Sit down." He sat, his back to the glass, just to urge her to do the same.

9

She considered him a moment, then reached down and pulled off her shoes.

He patted the floor next to him and she took a breath, nodded once, and joined him, positioning herself a little in front of the window.

"Sorry about that," she said finally. "I have an irrational fear of heights."

"It's not irrational when the elevator decides to fall twenty or thirty feet on its own. Plus, I kinda like having beautiful women leap into my arms." And he didn't know where that came from. For the first time, he noticed her appealing smell. Lemon, surprisingly sweet, with a hint of something else, a spice his mother used to use when she cooked. Rosemary?

Interesting.

"What do you think happened?"

"I'm no elevator expert, but we seem to have come to a stop. Somewhere between..." He looked out the rounded glass at the world outside. "I'd say the tenth and twelfth floors."

"Ha ha, funny man." She glanced at her watch. Her hand still shook too. "How long do you think we'll be trapped? I have to be somewhere."

"Me too." Oh, the last thing he needed was to miss the shareholders meeting.

She stood up. "Let's see if we can get the doors open."

"I don't think we can pry them open."

But she was already jamming her fingers into the crack between the elevator doors. What did she think she would accomplish? But he rose to help her, reaching his arms around her to push his fingers into the crack also.

She was grunting in her efforts, and he hid a smile at her wrestling with the door in her fancy dress.

The interior doors creaked open with a groan.

"We're getting it!" she said and redoubled her attack. He had to give her points for tenacity.

At the midway point the panels halted and refused to budge. "End of the line." He reluctantly stepped back from her.

"What do you mean?" A few strands of her hair had fallen in her efforts. "We still have the outer doors to push open."

"I hate to be the bearer of bad news, but there's no way they are budging. And there's nowhere to get our fingers jammed into the outer doors." The outer doors were tightly shut, the crack between them nearly invisible.

Her mouth tightened, a line of frustration. "Stupid Colleen."

He pulled out a handkerchief and wiped a black smudge from his hands. "Who is Colleen, and what does she have to do with all of this?"

"Colleen is my so-called friend who wouldn't let me bring my own purse. If I had my stuff, we wouldn't be in this mess." She accepted his proffered handkerchief and wiped at her hands.

"What good would lipstick and old Kleenex or whatever you girls pack in your purses do? Would you wipe the door open?"

She shot him a withering look and handed him back the cloth. "If I had my purse, I would have my multi-tool. If I had my multi-tool, I would have my screwdriver. I could fit my flat-head into that space. That would give us enough leverage to get those doors open. As it is, I have nothing. My cell phone wouldn't even fit in this tiny scrap of a purse."

Huh. He'd never met a woman who carried a multi-tool. "Let me try phoning for help." He pulled out his phone to try 9-1-1 and realized his cell phone battery was down to three percent. Perfect.

Thankfully, the elevator emergency phone chose that moment to ring.

She fairly leaped for it.

He listened to her explain their predicament, all big gestures and hyperboles. But there was something about her, a sort of energy that radiated off her, like the surface of the sun, hot and light, and he didn't hate it. Little Miss Sunshine was a refreshing change from his elegant and uptight date upstairs.

A light rain had started, pattering against the window. Outside, the air had felt chilly enough for the rain to turn to snow before the night ended.

He wondered where Sunshine was heading.

"They said they're assessing the problem." Sunshine hung up the phone. "But it could be a while. The elevator technician is coming up from Apple Valley."

"We may as well get comfortable then." He shook out his date's wrap and laid it on the elevator floor. "M'lady, your couch awaits." He spread his arms wide. Inviting her to sit. She quirked an eyebrow.

"Do you always travel with purple stoles?"

"What can I say? I like to be prepared." They sank down onto the soft fabric, their backs to the glass wall. He noticed she never looked over her shoulder. The small elevator floor was a tight fit and their knees kept brushing each other. Not that he was complaining.

"When I planned out this night, I did not factor in getting stuck in an elevator." She crossed her arms. "I hope this doesn't ruin my chances."

"Chances for what?"

"Pitching my product to Mr. Vassos."

"*Adrian* Vassos?" Oh man, did his voice just squeak?

"Um, no. Not that irresponsible playboy. No, I need to pitch to someone who can actually make a difference. Costas Vassos, Adrian's father."

Irresponsible playboy. The words dug into him. Would he ever outgrow who he'd been in high school? Not if the media had anything to say about it. "I don't think Adrian is that bad."

"You call dating anything that moves and crashing his car into Lake Kellogg not that bad?"

Hey. He was picky about who he dated. Usually. Still,

"Maybe he's just misunderstood. Maybe those women took advantage of the situation. Maybe that street weirdly ended in the lake instead of going around it like a normal street." At her look, he quickly added, "Hypothetically, of course."

"Irresponsible playboy or not, I don't really care. It's the father I'm aiming for. He's the real decision maker of the family. Or maybe the older brother, Alex. If I can just meet with them for a few minutes, I can save lives."

Save...*lives?* Whoa, this girl was intense, but he could have guessed that after her attempt to free them.

"I'm Ella, by the way," Sunshine said, reaching out a hand.

"Oh, um, I'm...Roger."

Sunshine—Ella—quirked an eyebrow at him again. "Not sure about that?"

"I wish it was more exciting, but I'm just plain old Roger." And now he'd just doubled down on the lie—*half* lie. A lot of people went by their middle name, and, let's face it, after what she'd thought of him, he wasn't about to embarrass himself. Or her. Besides, the anonymity of this elevator felt good, and he wanted it to last forever if possible. Well, that wasn't really true either. He did want to give his presentation at the meeting, and he wanted, possibly even needed, this project to get a thumbs-up. Maybe then his life would be worth something. Maybe then he could actually put his training to good use.

But there was something of good fun in remaining anonymous to this strange, beautiful woman in the elevator. Really, what did it hurt?

"So, what does talking to the owner of a chain of hotel water parks have to do with saving lives?" he asked, his voice easy. "Bear Creek Resorts are already number one in safety. They've never had an accident, and all their rides are triple-checked for problems before anyone ever rides one." Listen to him, sounding like a walking, talking Bear Creek Resorts brochure.

"They can do better. I don't think Costas Vassos realizes how deadly chlorine can be. Not to mention all the chemicals he is using in his cleaning products in every hotel room every day."

Now that was laughable. "Chlorine? Dangerous? I'm pretty sure no one has died because their bathing suit got a little bleached out."

"I'm not talking about bathing suits. I'm talking about chlorine poisoning. I'm talking about toxic chemicals getting into the air and into the water. With all the new advances in clean water technology right now, the Vassos empire could do better. They could really change the face of hotels and water parks across the world."

She was passionate, he'd give her that much, but *come on*. "Toxic chemicals, really? Chlorine poisoning?"

Bright red spots appeared on her cheeks.

Her next words were spoken through clenched teeth.

"My mother died of chlorine poisoning."

And, he was the world's biggest jerk. "Ella. I'm so sorry. I didn't know. I didn't think that was possible. After all, they let little kids swim in the stuff all the time."

She speared him with a look. Oh, right. Thus the danger.

A beat passed between them, during which he glanced up at the number lit on the button panel, suddenly debating another go at those doors. "I forgive you," she finally said. "You didn't know. No one realizes it."

"Thanks."

"Anyway, that's why I have to get upstairs. I need to talk to Costas Vassos about my ideas."

"What about Adrian? What if you could talk to him?" He didn't know exactly why he'd said that, but—

"Are you kidding me? No. He's the last person I want to talk to."

Talk about a gut punch. How could she hate him so much when she didn't even know him?

But, maybe...maybe this was his golden chance to prove

himself without the tabloids and headlines. If he won her over, perhaps she wouldn't hate him when she found out who he really was.

"Wait, how are you planning to speak to Costas Vassos? Maybe you don't know this, but he has a really big meeting tonight."

"I know. I'm going to it." She motioned to herself. "That's why I'm in this getup."

"No, it's shareholders only. They won't let you in without an invitation."

She stiffened. "Why do you think I don't have an invitation?"

He paused.

"Why would a girl like me be a stockholder, right?"

He opened his mouth. Hoo boy, he'd really stuck his foot in his mouth this time. Of course she was a shareholder.

"Besides, how do you know all of this?"

"I'm heading there too."

"Then why are you going to the twenty-first floor?"

"The party is on the twenty-first floor…" He let his words hang a moment as her body stiffened. The rain outside the windows turned to heavy flakes of snow as the temperature dropped.

"No, it's on the twentieth floor." This through clenched teeth. "It says so right here. On. My. *Invitation*." She pulled out a creamy white square of paper from her minuscule bag and shoved it at him.

He stared at the invitation, at the indictment, and sighed. She was right.

"Listen, Ella, I'm really sorry. I seem to keep saying the exact wrong thing. Can we start over? I'm not usually this much of a dunce. I've had a lot on my mind." He gave her the best smile he possessed, the one that won hearts and influenced people and made him the key negotiator for Bear Creek Industries. "I'm a shareholder in the Bear Creek Resorts business, and I'm heading to their party and business meeting, which is clearly on the *twentieth floor*. It's nice to be stuck in this elevator with you."

It took her a moment to catch up as she just stared at him. Then she released a breath, and her face softened. She shook his hand. "Hi, Roger, I'm Ella. *Also* a shareholder. Sorry to be so uptight. The truth is, I only have one half share, so I kind of feel like an imposter. I guess I need to be less touchy about it." Her face colored a little and she dropped her eyes to their clasped hands. He suddenly noticed again how tiny this elevator car really was. If he just moved to the right a little, her head would be right near his chin. Just a dip of his head and...

The elevator phone rang again. And, frankly, just in time because *what was he thinking?*

Ella jerked her hand away as if burned. Adrian reached around Ella and answered.

The voice gave him an update, and he hung up. "They said the technician arrived. It should be less than an hour and we will be home free."

Now he just had an hour to convince Ella that he wasn't the playboy she thought he was. Less than an hour to prove that she could trust him.

Less than an hour to win her vote for the one thing that could change his life.

And probably he should do it without thinking about kissing her.

CHAPTER 2

*T*hank goodness for ringing telephones. If it hadn't been for the elevator technician, Ella suspected she would still be holding Roger's hand.

Thankfully the phone interrupted any other foolish ideas she'd been having.

Ideas like shifting closer to him and tipping her face just so. She certainly hadn't expected their corny reintroduction handshake to set every one of her nerves on fire. She still felt tingly. What was wrong with her? Nearly kissing a stranger. It must be the way her stomach took a dive every time she caught a glimpse out the back of the oh-so-high elevator. Her fear of heights, not Roger. Because anything else would be...

Crazy. Just like these shoes. Just like this night. Just like the idea that she'd actually be able to pitch her business proposal to Mr. Vassos.

It would be easier if Roger would kindly step out of her airspace, taking his delicious spicy scent and manly physique with him.

So much for keeping her eye on the prize.

"How did you manage to get a half share of Bear Creek?

That's an odd amount to own." Roger crossed his legs in front of him and leaned back against the glass wall. Keeping his hands to himself.

Bummer.

No, no, bad Ella!

"My dad used to be friends with Costas Vassos. He always said he knew Mr. Vassos in another lifetime." Ella traced a flower on the wrap they were sitting on. The silken fabric warmed her fingertips. "My dad was starting a commercial cleaning business when Mr. Vassos bought his first hotel. Right before Mr. Vassos opened the Bear Creek Resort, my dad and mom cleaned the place from top to bottom. None of them had much money back then, but Mr. Vassos gave my dad a share of his company."

"That accounts for the share, but what about the half?"

"My mom died, and about ten years later my dad remarried. Then he died. In his will, he left half of his share to me and half to my stepsister. Maybe he thought that would cause us to become best buddies or something. I don't know." She shrugged. "I don't think anything can do that. She doesn't like me and never has. Now she resents me because she thinks she should have the whole share. Or, at least, her mother thinks so."

In fact, Jackie Kent-Bradley wanted everything that had ever belonged to Ella's father. She felt it was owed her. Jackie still had trouble believing that the half share in Bear Creek Resorts stock and a pink VW Bug were the only two things Ella had left from her father.

Ella, on the other hand, had trouble believing that her father had lied to her all those years. Lies like, *"I will pay your college bills."* False. He had taken loans out in Ella's name, leaving her with debt up to her eyeballs. Good thing she'd attended the University of Minnesota instead of someplace spendier like St. Kate's.

Two years after his death and she was still trying to climb out of the black hole of debt.

"I'm sorry. Family is tricky. I have an older brother and he never stops lording over me that he is better in every way. Even if it's not true. I earned my place fair and square." Roger passed a hand through his hair, but one wayward lock flopped back over his forehead.

"Apparently there's something magical about elevators that makes us spill all our secrets." Ella made the mistake of looking into Roger's eyes at that last statement.

Her mouth dried, and then she stupidly licked her lips.

His gaze dropped to her mouth.

Her breath caught. If she just leaned forward a little, she...

Her gaze fell on the snow falling outside the glass beyond Roger's shoulder.

A thousand miles above ground.

And now came the nausea. She took a deep breath.

No good.

Ella closed her eyes and did it again. Better. Opening them once more, she caught Roger's concerned look.

Shifting away so she no longer looked directly at Roger, or the glass, she opened her purse and retrieved her lip gloss. Slicking it on, she recapped the tube and dropped it back.

"What else do you have in there?" Roger wore a small, irritatingly cute, smile.

"Unfortunately, I don't have much." While the contents of a woman's purse ought to be strictly confidential, this was certainly a safer topic than others they had already broached. "Just my 3x5 cards, my lip gloss, a thumb drive, and my invitation."

He chuckled.

"What? Why are you laughing?"

"It's just the way you said '3x5 cards' as though it's the most natural thing in the world to carry around in a tiny little purse." His grin was so adorable she couldn't help returning it.

"Why? I wanted to be sure I had all the information for Mr. Vassos right at my fingertips." Not that she would ever get that opportunity now. *Please, God, don't let this elevator mishap ruin my chances.* Although, she wasn't really sure if God was even on her side. He'd been pretty quiet lately. "Right now I wish I had packed a granola bar instead. Or insisted that I carry my own purse."

"Your friend Colleen must be very persuasive."

"She kept going on about how I needed to look the part. I needed to be well put together if I wanted Costas Vassos to take me seriously." Now she just felt like a fool. A girl dressed up in someone else's clothes, who was way out of her depth.

"She's probably not wrong. Costas Vassos is a hard man to please."

"You sound like you've had a run-in with him."

"You could say that."

"Hard man or not, I may never get the chance to talk to him now."

"Why didn't you just make an appointment with him through normal channels?"

"I tried, but apparently his secretary didn't think I was worthy of having a conversation with the big man. I tried dropping my father's name but that didn't help either. I guess having a formerly famous father doesn't count for anything." Not that it counted for anything in Ella's book anymore either. Most times she would rather not remember her connection to Mike Bradley.

"I don't know if she even mentioned my many calls to Mr. Vassos. I like to think that he would have remembered his friendship with my dad and granted me even a short inter-view. In fact, I was counting on that very thing tonight. Ambush him at the party, bring up my dad, and then convince him that my products work and would be great for Bear Creek Resorts."

"Ambush him. How very Navy SEAL of you."

"That's me. Just call me Rambo."

"He wasn't a...never mind. Back up a second. Famous father?"

Oh, she could kick herself for bringing that up. "My dad was Mike Bradley, the King of Clean. You know, the one with all those billboards." She felt her face getting hot. Once upon a time she was proud of those billboards with her dad's cheesy tooth-filled smile stretching six feet wide. Now she saw it for what it was—a twenty-foot lie designed to make her believe in miracles. She was so over that.

"The King of Clean, eh? That makes you a princess."

He smiled, but she couldn't match it.

"Yeah, well, that was before he lost all his money to gambling debts and his friends all abandoned him. Truthfully, he must have struggled with gambling for a long time, probably since my mother passed away. I didn't see it then. I was just a kid and believed everything my father told me. Looking back now though, I can see when he must have been high on a win and when he probably had suffered some losses. We moved around a lot and I'm finally putting two and two together."

Listen to her, rambling on about her dad. She hadn't talked this much to one person in a very long time. Even her phone calls with Colleen were brief updates on her non-life. She'd moved to Deep Haven to escape the specter of her father, but in her six months there she hadn't really built much of a new life. She didn't know why, but Roger's acceptance and under-standing felt like a lemon mint balm to a part of her heart she hadn't known was sore.

"Anyway, now I stand on my own two feet and try to be prepared for anything."

Although, maybe not an elevator breakdown in heels. She

suppressed the urge to check the time on her watch. She was either going to make it in time for her hoped-for ambush or she wasn't.

"Tell me more about your business plan. Maybe I'll buy in." Roger folded his hands in his lap and shifted against the glass.

The snow outside had turned back to rain, and the droplets on the window looked like Christmas twinkle lights around his head.

"Do you have millions of dollars you're just waiting to invest in organic cleaning products?" she teased. "Maybe you just hang around in elevators waiting to be trapped with a girl who has an idea you can profit from."

He glanced at her, a smile on his lips. "Maybe I'm a prince who is waiting to join kingdoms with the right princess in a fight against evil empires."

Ella laughed, but *what?* The sudden thought of having someone on her side swept through her, filled her throat. Thumped her heart.

A prince waiting for the right princess—

Oh, for Pete's sake! She'd been stuck here too long—maybe they were low on oxygen.

"This princess is battling the overwhelming army of toxic cleaning supplies." She held up a hand to stop whatever response he had. "Before you think I'm some hippie-dippie, crunchy, earth lover, give me a second to explain. Most of us just accept the various chemicals in our lives because we don't know any better. But science is beginning to show that the way we are using some of these chemicals isn't good for us or the groundwater." Now she was in lecture mode. Time to scale it back before his eyes started to glaze over.

"I don't think that sounds hippie-dippie at all. In fact, I think it's noble that you want to do good for so many people." An errant lock of hair fell over his face again. She pushed down the urge to brush it back behind his ear, dragged her mind back to what he was saying. "Clean water and healthy living are important goals."

"It's not just about that." She sighed, not sure—

Okay. Something about the intimacy of this elevator car pressed the words forward. "I told you my mother died." She stilled when he reached out and took her hand.

What?

But his forehead crinkled in sympathy.

Okay, yes. "When I was about seven, she and my father were cleaning at a hotel. They still aren't quite sure what happened, but she was getting some supplies from the pool equipment room—you know, where the pumps and stuff are?"

He nodded, his eyes on hers.

So much attention could steal a girl's breath, so she looked away as she continued. "A shelf fell over and she was trapped under it. Unfortunately, a jug of chlorine for the pool was also on that shelf and it cracked open right on the floor next to her face. Every breath she took was laced with that toxin. For normal people this might not be a problem, but my mother had asthma. They think she must have had an attack. By the time the paramedics arrived, there was nothing they could do."

"Oh Ella," he said softly.

Her eyes burned, though she wasn't sure why. She'd lived with her mother's death for nearly two decades.

"I'm sorry," he said, making it worse. "That is horrible. No wonder you hate chemicals so much."

Her breath trembled out. "I don't hate chemicals. After all, everything is made of chemicals. It's just the unnecessary ones we use that get to me. I want to make the world a safer place for families, you know?"

She finally looked over, met his eyes. His were kind and so impossibly blue she could hear her heart thunder.

"Sure sounds like you are on a noble quest, m'lady. I'd love to hear more about it. That's why I'm involved with Bear Creek—

they're in the business of making happy, safe places for families."

She believed him. She didn't know why, but suddenly, looking at him, the way he still held her hand...

Maybe she had met her prince right here in this glass carriage.

In front of her, the elevator doors they had forced open began to shut.

"I think this is it." A pang of regret curled through her.

"I think so," Roger said.

She couldn't place the expression on his face.

Then he got up, and she slipped her too-tight shoes back on. He helped her up and they faced the door. The elevator lurched and started climbing. Somehow Ella found Roger's hand folded around hers.

"Thanks," she said quietly.

"For what?" he said as button twenty lit up.

"For being the right guy to be trapped with."

His hand squeezed hers as the elevator came to a halt and the doors slid open.

A small crowd stood in the hall landing. A number of women in evening gowns, a few white-gloved waiters, a maintenance man.

And at the front—what? "Sophie?" What was her stepsister doing here? Except—right. She owned the other half share.

Sophie wore a white evening gown, a pair of deep purple shoes, and of course looked every inch the princess Ella's stepmother expected her to be, with her long brown hair swept up, a pair of diamond earrings at her ears, a glittering necklace at her neck.

Probably here to catch the eye of the most eligible—and richest—bachelor in town.

Roger dropped Ella's hand.

"Sophie?" Ella said again as she stepped out. "How did you

know I was trapped?"

Sophie just looked at her, frowned, then swept her gaze past her. "Seriously, Adrian? What took you so long? And why—" She brushed past Ella. "Why are you *standing* on my Gucci wrap?"

Wait. What? *Adrian?*

Roger scooped up the purple fabric from the floor.

Ella stood frozen as the louse—the liar!—Adrian shot her a look full of apology and walked out to Sophie. "Sorry," he said. "We needed something to sit on. I'll have it dry cleaned and sent to you."

Sophie's dark look melted. "It's okay, darling." She leaned in and gave him a kiss on the cheek.

Ella couldn't move.

But she must have spoken or made a sound, because Sophie backed away and looked at her. "And what are you doing here?"

She opened her mouth, but Roger—Adrian—spoke for her. "She's a shareholder." He offered a sheepish smile.

Ella looked at him, her entire body on fire. Was he *serious?*

But she turned to Sophie. "Yes. And Adrian and I were talking about...business." She clenched her jaw, willing herself not to cry as she stared at those blue eyes.

Liar.

His mouth tightened as if he could read her mind.

"Oh, what do you know about business?" Sophie said. "You're just a housekeeper. C'mon, Adri. Let's get some champagne."

"Adri" swallowed, and Ella cocked her head at him. Raised an eyebrow. And refused to run.

"I'm sorry," he said quietly.

She held up a hand. "No. I'm the fool here. You and your games are way out of my league." Then she walked past him into the party.

But in her mind she was throwing off her shoes, ripping off

this stupid dress, and running down all twenty flights and out into the cold.

Where she belonged.

The last thing Adrian needed was to let Ella get into his head. Sure, she did have a point—he had lied to her about his name. But there was nothing he could do about it now. He had to get his game face on and concentrate on presenting his proposal.

Sophie tugged on his arm. "We have enough time to grab a champagne before the meeting if you want."

Champagne was the last thing he needed. "No, thanks. Let's just get to the meeting. I need to make sure my presentation is loaded." He glanced at Ella again, her back stiff and straight as she disappeared into the meeting room across the hall.

One thing at a time.

He'd deliver his proposal and then figure out how to untangle the mess he'd made.

People were streaming toward them out of the ballroom into the hall now, and most were making a sharp left into the boardroom his father had rented for the business meeting. Adrian's brother, Alex, stepped out of the ballroom doorway and looked his way before taking the few steps across to where he and Sophie stood near the elevator.

"Hey, man." Alex held up a glass in mock salute. He was wearing a suit Adrian hadn't seen before. Adrian always suspected his brother asked the tailors to cut his suits down a size in order to emphasize his muscles. People told the brothers they looked alike, but Adrian didn't see it. Alex kept his hair short, and it was darker than Adrian's. He also had a shorter, wider face—the face of their father, the bulldog who knew how to make deals and get the job done. Except for his nose, Adrian looked like his mother, his features more European, less Greek.

"Glad you made it in time. I've been trying to warm people up to your idea, but they all want to see your pretty face. You've always been better at schmoozing than me."

Adrian checked his watch again. Ten minutes to showtime. "Tonight I hope they see that I have good ideas, too. This project could be a game changer."

"Sure, bro. Break a leg up there." Alex slipped into the crowd funneling into the boardroom.

Sophie tugged on his arm again. "C'mon, Adrian. I saved us some seats at the front of the room. The meeting starts soon."

Adrian followed Sophie across the hall and into the boardroom. The sleek room, decorated with black and white and the occasional splash of deep blue, buzzed with the voices of a hundred shareholders.

"You made it!" Costa Vassos said as Adrian and Sophie approached the door. Costas Vassos wore a fitted tuxedo and his most charming smile. His dark hair waving around his face was turning gray at the temples. His gaze went to Sophie and he offered Adrian a wink.

Perfect. Just what he wanted—his father to think something was happening behind the scenes with this girl. Worse, briefly, Ella was in his head with her disdain. *Irresponsible playboy.*

His mother stood beside Costas, wearing a pink dress and her favorite diamond necklace.

The pair looked like a cake topper. If the cake was for two middle-aged millionaires who couldn't stand the sight of each other.

Adrian let go of Sophie and gave his mother a kiss on the cheek. "You look beautiful, Mom. This shade of pink suits you."

"Thank you, Adrian. Glad to see you made it out of the elevator and were able to rejoin Sophie. I had the pleasure of getting to know her while you were gone. She's such a sweet girl."

He smiled, not sure what to say after the way she'd treated

Ella.

"I was happy to get to know your parents, Adri." Sophie took his hand. "I'm just sorry you had to get stuck for so long."

Perfect. The last thing he wanted was Sophie "getting to know" his parents. They'd start having her over for dinner and then family events. If he knew his mother, he'd wake up one day and the wedding invitations would already be printed. Maybe bringing a blind date to this event wasn't a bright idea.

"Especially since you're supposed to be the man of the hour." Costas slung an arm around Adrian's shoulder and turned to say directly into his ear, "Don't forget you need at least seventy-five percent of the vote for your proposal to go through. I'm giving you a second chance on this thing, but I won't tolerate failure."

"Thanks, Dad. I won't let you down." He gave his father a forced smile. Still, his plan was a good one. He'd spent countless hours shaping it until he was confident it would make money for the company and be successful. He was more than a pretty face. He wouldn't allow his past failures to haunt him.

His father turned to greet an older couple walking through the doors, and Adrian did the same.

"Mr. and Mrs. Carlson, so good to see you here tonight," Adrian said, reaching out to glad-hand the older couple. Mid-sixties, they were his parents' closest friends.

"We've heard some rumors about the new plan of yours," Mr. Carlson said. Portly man, whitened hair, gold rings on his pinky fingers. His wife wore her dark hair—clearly freshly dyed—up.

"That's right. I will be giving a formal presentation in a few minutes. I know you'll love it." Adrian left them and walked into the room.

Seventy-five percent of the votes meant he needed to do some work. He stepped up to an elegant woman in her mid-forties. "Ms. Harris, I'm glad you could make it."

"I couldn't stay away. Wild horses and all that," Ms. Harris said, laughing. She wore a necklace that should probably come accompanied with a small military protective squad.

"You're who I thought of while designing the spa. State of the art. The plans include a sauna." Adrian winked at her as he walked away and spotted another investor.

"Roscoe! Good to see you, buddy!" He caught the hand of a local basketball star, clamping him on the shoulder. "When this hotel is built, I'll see you in the indoor basketball court for another round of one-on-one. If you still think you can take me."

Roscoe laughed. "I'll do my best."

Jace Jacobsen, one of the coaches of the Blue Ox hockey team, walked up. Adrian reached for his hand. "Jace! Great season."

"It's not over yet. We still have the playoffs." Jace lifted one shoulder and Adrian kept his smile.

"You'll do great. You're five up over the Predators. You'll smoke 'em."

Jace smiled and glanced over at his pretty wife, Eden, who was chatting with a female stockholder Adrian didn't know. Yet.

Adrian dropped Sophie off at the front row of seats and climbed the few steps to the dais and the table for the board members. He shook hands with each one and had a brief word with his dad before joining Sophie in the front row.

I won't tolerate failure. Not exactly a pep talk, but it didn't matter. Adrian knew he could do this. He was ready.

The chairman of the board called the meeting to order and there was a general rustling while everyone found their seats. As the financial secretary droned through the year-end report, Adrian took the time to mentally run through his presentation.

Focus on the benefits—the money, but also the families. Most of the shareholders had families, had invested in the company because of the growing trend toward resorts. He had to appeal to their pocketbooks and their hearts.

No problem. He was born for this.

His father ceded the floor to him and Adrian took the stairs to the platform two at a time. His presentation flashed onto the big flat-screen. He'd asked the design team to put together a 3D mock-up of the plans he'd drawn.

For a second, his gaze snagged on Ella. She sat halfway back, arms crossed.

Focus, man, focus.

He started with a smile. "Friends, we have an opportunity to build something beautiful together. Not only will we provide endless fun for families traveling to the area, but we will also revitalize an area of Deep Haven that is becoming run-down. The small community is great for family vacations. It's ripe for development."

He clicked to a slide of the Westerman Hotel. He'd found the site on his way to Canada for a fishing trip a year ago. It was a hollow wreck, a blight to the community, and he'd get the property for a song.

"We will tear down this old eyesore and build a sleek, fun resort fit for families who want to combine adventure with the Great North. Families like yours, Mr. Carlson. Your grandkids will love it up there. Your family too, Ms. Harris. Those boys of yours will find tons of things to burn their energy on. The resort will feature two swimming pools, plus one more fitted with basketball nets—I put that in for you, Roscoe..."

Roscoe grinned.

And now, Adrian purposely ignored Ella.

Instead, he looked at his father. Costas sat in the front row, nary a smile on his face. Ah, but Adrian had a slide for him too. "Now, before you start wondering just how much this will cost us, don't worry. I've run the numbers, and projections have us making back our investment in three years. *Three.* That's unheard of in this industry."

He ran through the numbers on a series of slides, then ended with a photo of a boy going down a slide with an expression of pure delight.

"I'm really excited about this project and I know you are too. Let's build this dream together."

The room erupted in clapping, and more than a few shareholders stood up.

Ella was lost in the crowd.

His father climbed the podium next to him. "Okay, you've heard the proposal. Now, before we vote, is there any discussion?"

The crowd hushed. For a space of ten heartbeats, the room was quiet.

"Excuse me." Ella's voice rang out in the silence. She stood from her spot halfway back, her hair still a little disheveled from the elevator. And, stupidly, her efforts to open the door, the way she felt in his arms swept in, and Adrian nearly missed her words. "I don't believe that building a water park in that area is necessary. There is plenty to do up there already. Things like hiking, canoeing, and camping."

She looked right at him when she spoke, and he took a breath, fixed his eyes on Mr. Carlson as he stepped to the microphone again. "Yes, there are plenty of everyday activities. But people don't want the everyday—they want something new and fun. And research shows that tourists go to Deep Haven to *escape*."

People nodded along with Adrian, smiling.

"Let's vote," his father said and asked for a show of hands.

Adrian walked off the stage to the water table and filled his glass. Turned his back to the vote. He gave a sideways glance into the audience and spotted Ella, her hand up with the nays. But even his quick math as he listened to the count told him that his proposal had passed.

Still, more people must have been swayed by Ella's argument than he expected.

His father took over the meeting and Adrian headed out the side door.

Movement down the hall caught his attention. Ella had escaped and was hustling to the elevators. Those fancy shoes didn't seem to be bothering her now.

"Ella!" He took off after her.

She ignored him as she reached the elevator and jammed the down button.

He caught up to her before it could open. "You didn't get enough of the elevator tonight?" He tried for a bit of levity and lifted his hand to touch her elbow but stepped back when she rounded on him.

"How could you, Adrian?" She used his name like a spear, voice dripping with scorn. "After all those things you said to me in the elevator, I thought you *listened* to what I had to say." Bright red spots appeared on her cheeks.

"I don't get it." He reached for her again, but she moved a step back, looking at his hand like he had some toxic disease.

Fine. So whatever they had in the elevator had died. But it didn't mean she had to kill his idea, his future. He kept his voice down as a couple approached and stood waiting for the elevator. "Why do you care about a new water park? Expansion is good for the company. A company needs to grow to remain healthy."

"I care because you're building that toxic and germ-infested chemical cesspool in *Deep Haven*. In *my* town."

Whoa, he didn't see that one coming. She lived in Deep Haven? Wasn't it only outdoorsy, camping types up there? At least, that's the kind of person he'd run into during his research trips. With Ella's sleek dress and fancy updo, he couldn't imagine her in a backwoods anything.

Also, *wait a minute.* "Germ-infested cesspool? I don't think that's fair."

"Didn't you listen to *anything* I said in the elevator? Water parks are the worst offenders. Afraid of making your guests sick? Just throw in more chlorine. A little chemical soup never hurt anyone, right? Don't you even remember how my mother died? I should have known better than to tell a stranger that story." She punched the down button a few more times. "Is this thing even working?" A tiny growl came on the last word, and Ella wheeled around. She stalked toward a door at the end of a corridor.

As if she was taking the stairs.

Oh, c'mon. "Ella, wait. Stop a minute. Let me explain."

She jerked the door to the stairs open and began stomping down. He started down after her.

"You can't go down all twenty flights in those shoes."

"Leave me alone. You don't need to worry about me and my shoes. Go back to your party. You have guests waiting. They'll all want to congratulate you. Besides, I'm sure Sophie is wondering where you are."

How *did* she know Sophie? This night kept getting more confusing. "Ella, will you please stop a minute and talk to me?"

"Fine. You want to talk? Let's talk." Ella came to a halt on a landing so abruptly that he almost ran into her. He put his hand on the wall to steady himself. The cold of the concrete brick seeped into his palm.

Her stormy gaze warned him to take a step back. "Let's talk about how you lied to me in the elevator, *Roger*. Let's talk about how I thought you were a good guy. Let's talk about how you're trying to ruin my town with your poisonous plan. Deep Haven has plenty of fun things to do. We don't need your toxic water park. And let's talk about how you're dating my stepsister."

Her stepsister?

She turned and kept walking down the next flight of stairs.

"Ella—"

"Serves me right." Her voice echoed up to him. "I spilled my guts in that stupid elevator and I didn't even get a chance to speak to Costas Vassos. Who, as it turns out, is your father. Maybe we should talk about *that* little detail!"

He was three steps behind her now, so she didn't exactly need to shout. "I'm sorry I didn't tell you who I was in the elevator—"

Ella cried out, a gasp of pain, and clutched the railing.

"Ella!" He reached her step and put his arm around her.

"Stay away from me." She took another step and stumbled.

This time he did grab her before she plummeted down the remaining ten flights of stairs.

"Let me go!"

He drew in a breath, but did as she asked. Ella gripped the railing, then bent over and, hopping on her right foot, pulled off her left shoe.

And threw it against the wall. "These stupid shoes and this terrible night."

Oh. Wow.

She hopped around as she pulled off the other shoe.

"Ella, c'mon—"

She rounded and held up that shoe as if she might throw it at him.

Adrian held up his hands.

"Stay away from me, *Adrian* Vassos. It's liars like you that are what's wrong with this world." Ella pivoted and continued down the stairs, bare feet slapping the concrete beneath her.

He sank to a stair and put his head in his hands.

"Adrian?" Sophie's voice echoed from somewhere far above him. "Are you down there? Come back up to the party."

He got up. Gave one last look at the door.

And wished he was just a guy named Roger.

CHAPTER 3

"Seriously, I'm going to go a little crazy if you don't tell me what happened tonight," Colleen said through the bathroom door. "I'm getting worried. How do you manage to go to a party and lose one shoe?"

Oh. Right. Probably best not to tell Colleen that Ella had also lost her thumb drive after running into an older gentleman and spilling everything onto the floor when she'd finally made it to the shareholders meeting. She'd been so flustered by Roger—Adrian—and his little presentation that she must not have gathered everything up afterward. "I'm sorry about your shoe. I'll pay you back, I promise."

"Ella, I'm not worried about the stupid shoe. I got them on eBay for a steal. I'm worried about you."

"I'm fine!"

Or close to it. At least back in her clothes, Ella would finally feel like herself.

She shoved her arm into her flannel shirt. The soft fabric lent a warmth to her body, but the heat didn't reach her heart. The icy grip around her chest still remained an hour after leaving Adrian standing in that stairwell. After the sparks in the elevator, she should be glad for the cold filling her veins. No, check that, she *was* glad for the cooling off.

Strange men who lied to her shouldn't be allowed to warm her heart.

"Everything okay in there?"

"I'll be out of your hair in a minute." Ella finished her last buttons and opened the bathroom door to the hallway. Colleen stood just outside with two mugs.

"I still think you should stay here tonight. It's late and I'm not sure the rain is going to continue to hold off. If the temps drop again it could start snowing for real."

"Thank you for coming to pick me up early." Ella ran a hand through her damp curls. Her updo had become a tangled mess while standing in the rain outside the Century Hotel waiting for her friend. "I could have just taken an Uber."

"That would have cost you what you saved on not parking downtown. Besides, that's what friends are for." Colleen held out one of the steaming mugs. "Friends are also for giving hot chocolate to their bedraggled houseguests and making them spill the gossip. So spill, already."

The warm cup in Ella's hands amplified the comfort of her flannel shirt, and the aroma of chocolate wormed its way down to her nearly frozen core, thawing her the tiniest bit. "Fine, fine. Let's go sit. I can spare a few minutes before driving home. I have a job tomorrow I can't miss. Besides, you've already helped me a ton."

They sank into Colleen's overstuffed sofa, Ella managing to not lose her grip on her cup. She sipped a mouthful of the hot drink and closed her eyes in appreciation. Colleen made a mean cup of hot chocolate.

The calm in the tiny apartment living space untangled even more of the knots between Ella's shoulders. The room would have been right at home next to the sea with all the aquas, greens, and blues woven through the decor.

This little oasis looked out over a park in a quiet neighborhood in Robbinsdale, just a few miles from the hospital where Colleen worked as an emergency department nurse. Colleen had done well, making her small space feel like a real home. The type of place Ella longed for. A place that felt safe, secure. Lasting.

"I'm ready anytime you are." Colleen looked at her from over her mug. "What, did Adrian Vassos proposition you?"

Ella's wide-eyed expression probably gave her away.

Colleen set down her mug. "Seriously?"

"I don't even know where to start."

"Just do like Julie Andrews suggests and start at the very beginning," Colleen said in a singsong voice.

Ella pulled her feet under her, cozy in woolen socks. "It all started when the elevator broke down, trapping me in the car with Adrian Vassos for over an hour."

"What?" Colleen sat up straighter. "That must have been terrifying."

"You have no idea. It's funny though, how fear can fade after a while." No need to tell Colleen the embarrassing truth of how often she'd slipped and ended up in the circle of Adrian's strong arms.

"I suppose being trapped with a gorgeous man helped a little." Okay, maybe Colleen had guessed some of it after all.

She shoved the image of Adrian's concern out of her head. His quiet, *We're going to be okay.* Better to dwell on the part where he totally betrayed her than to think about how he'd seemed like a good listener or how great he'd smelled or how she could feel his heart beat as he'd leaned over her to reach for the emergency phone. Nope, the man was a liar. His good-guy routine in the elevator was all an act.

"He sat there, listened to my story—I even told him about how my mother died—and he still had the gall to propose to the shareholders his ridiculous plan for a water park in Deep Haven. A *water park* in Deep Haven? Can you even imagine?"

Colleen laughed. "A water park in Deep Haven isn't the worst idea. But you're right, that sleepy little town certainly doesn't need something like that."

"Not to mention he lied to me about who he was. Roger indeed." She adjusted her grip on the mug of cocoa. "Remember when you brought me up there for the weekend our sophomore year of college?"

"My parents loved you."

"And I loved them. And Deep Haven. Quaint. Quiet. The perfect getaway. And Adrian wants to destroy it all with a germ-infested cesspool of a water park. Not to mention the garish hotel he plans to build it in."

"Wow. You *have* had quite the night." Peering over the edge of her mug, Colleen gave a wide-eyed innocent look. "I just have one question—is Adrian Vassos as hot in person as he is in the paper?"

Ella's cheeks heated. She avoided looking directly at Colleen. "I suppose so. I mean, he's good looking for a snake."

"Liar! I can see it on your face. You think he's cute." Colleen's grin was infectious.

"Fine. Yes. He's very hot."

"You know you're the envy of nearly every red-blooded girl this side of the Mississippi, right?"

She took another sip of cocoa. "Too bad his good looks are lost on me. It would have been better if Sophie had been trapped in that elevator."

"Methinks the lady doth protest too much." Colleen paused. "Wait—Sophie? Your *stepsister*? What does she have to do with all of this?"

"Oh, did I forget that part? Adrian's date tonight was Sophie." Another gut punch. Not that he could have known, but it still rankled. "I guess she was there on the strength of her half share."

"Whoa. Ella, I'm sorry. Maybe I shouldn't have encouraged you to go." Colleen picked up a bowl of candy kisses from the side table next to her and handed them to Ella. "Here, chocolate. You need as much as you can get right now."

Ella reached for a kiss. "No, you were right to push me. I just wish I hadn't missed my chance with Mr. Vassos. No telling when I'll get an opportunity again." She peeled the silvery wrapper away and popped the candy into her mouth.

"What are you going to do about it?"

"My business idea? Probably nothing. I need to get home and regroup. Maybe I'll start pursuing a different hotel company. There's a market for my products—I just need to find it." Either that or find another way to make money. She really wanted to show the world that her Essentially Ella products worked, but she *needed* to pay back the student loans her father left behind, and she needed to be able to hold her head up on her own. The money she made cleaning houses paid the bills, but she wanted more security than that.

"Not about the business. I know you'll figure something out there. I meant what are you going to do about Adrian's water park?"

Ella set her empty cup on the coffee table in front of the couch. "Nothing, I guess. What am I going to do against someone like Adrian or a corporation like Bear Creek? They have tons of money and I have nothing."

"You could always try to talk to Adrian about it. Maybe now that he knows you, he'll listen to you."

"No way. I never want to see him again, let alone have a heart-to-heart." She looked out the window. Outside, the barren trees rattled in the wind. "I've got nothing."

"Not nothing. You know the town and you know the people.

Besides, you were always the smartest one in all our classes in college. Surely there's something you can think of."

"I've only lived in Deep Haven six months. I moved into town not long before the first snowfall, when everyone went into hibernation."

"Yeah, it's hard to get to know anyone in the winter. People lock down and stay at home. It's easier in the summer."

"Right. So, I'm not likely to rally everyone for a protest. I suppose I could lie down in front of a bulldozer…"

Colleen smiled at that, but it didn't help.

Ella pulled a throw pillow out from behind her and cradled it to her chest. "I'm such a failure. Nothing ever goes right."

"What? Why?"

"I had *one* goal for the evening. One. Get in, talk to Costas Vassos, and get out. Now everything is ruined. My dream is a corpse."

"Okay, that's a little overdramatic—"

"No, it's not. Adrian will probably tell his dad not to talk to me. Not that I will ever have that opportunity again. I wish I could rewind this night and start over." She put the pillow behind her head and leaned into it. "I'd start by taking the stairs."

Colleen got up and reached for her empty cup, which Ella handed over. "Well, you can't get a do-over on the night, but one thing I do know for sure. Deep Haven is a great place to start over."

"I used to think so. It was the perfect place to get away after Dad died and his business went bankrupt." And at least on Lake Superior's North Shore, she didn't see one of those ridiculous billboards every time she turned around. Most of the signs were gone, but every once in a while, she'd be startled by one that hadn't been papered over. The huge smiling face of the King of Clean rubbed salt in each of her wounds. How could her dad have lied to her all those years?

Colleen walked to the kitchen. "Is Jackie still giving you a run for your money?"

Ella heard the sink running as Colleen rinsed out her cup.

"No, she's backed off. I don't know why she thought I was hiding money anyway. If Dad had had any, he would have spent it. She should've figured that out after two years of living with him. I don't know why she hates me so much."

"She's probably just jealous. Is it possible she's right about your dad hiding money? He always seemed to do just fine for himself."

If only. A hidden stash of money could be used to pay off the debts her father had left behind in Ella's name. But, no. The only thing her dad had left her besides the pink VW and the Bear Creek half share was an overwhelming desire for stability. The kind she hadn't felt since before her mom died.

"Nope, not a possibility. It was all smoke and mirrors with him. Nothing we ever had was real. Or really very stable."

"I'm glad you're finding some stability in Deep Haven, then."

Ella turned and put her arm over the back of the sofa, watching Colleen fix her another cup of hot chocolate. "That's why I need to head back tonight. I have a job scheduled for tomorrow and I don't want to cancel. Your mom got the church to hire me to clean the sanctuary after services."

She also needed to get home so she could recover any pride she had left. All her preparation had gone to pieces. Maybe she really was just a cleaning lady.

The life her dad had built had turned out to be a sham, so why did she believe hers would be any better? God never cared before. Why had she thought tonight would be any different?

Colleen gave her a weird look. Oops, that last bit must have slipped out.

"Ella, I don't have all the answers. I'm still trying to figure it out too. But one thing I do know is that God cares very much. He wants good for you, not bad."

"Then why does everything in my life always end in such spectacular failure?" Everything except maybe for her schooling. She'd worked hard and earned top grades. Her almost-degree from the U of M remained the only positive thing to happen in her life. That and this friendship with Colleen.

"Like I said, I'm still learning too, but I think that a verse my pastor talked about last week might help you." From the bookshelves lining one wall, Colleen plucked a notebook and Bible. The pages made a crinkling noise as she searched for her spot. "Psalm 46:1. 'God is our refuge and strength, a very present help in trouble.' I love that part about him being present in our trouble. God wants to come alongside and help. He wants to be our refuge and strength."

The words pierced Ella. God wanted to help her? She wanted to believe it, except, where had He been all this time? Why did it feel like the only person she could trust was herself?

No, God wasn't on her side. It was up to her to fix this mess and to take charge of her life.

And the first thing would be to forget this night—and the man who had betrayed her.

The sooner this night ended, the better.

The snow and rain from earlier had tapered off, leaving the streets wet and gleaming. The temperature hovered around freezing in the late-March night. Adrian turned the car's heat on full blast.

"I don't understand why we had to leave the party so early." Sophie sat in the other seat, arms folded, chin jutting out. His tuxedo jacket was wrapped around her shoulders. She'd needed something to cover her after the mess he'd made of her wrap in the elevator.

He just couldn't dance with her when he kept hearing Ella's

words in his head. *It's liars like you that are what's wrong with this world.*

Yeah, maybe he deserved that. "I have a headache."

"It was that fight you had with my stepsister, isn't it? What happened in that elevator, anyway?"

He drew in a breath. *Everything.* "Nothing."

"You should have let Alexander drive me home. He was so nice while you were stuck in the elevator. If it wasn't for him, I wouldn't have met your mother."

Yes, maybe. His brother was probably back at the party, glad-handing all the shareholders, taking Adrian's place as the hero of the night. Sure, the vote had squeaked by, but he'd hoped for a unanimous approval. *We don't need your toxic water park.* Ella's words rang in his ears.

"I'm glad you had a good time even if I wasn't there to introduce you to anyone."

"Don't worry, Adri. I didn't have too much fun without you." Sophie put her hand on his arm. "I was just trying to make a good impression on your family. Athena told me how important they are to you."

Shoot. He hoped his mother hadn't gotten too attached.

Adrian pulled into Sophie's neighborhood, a trendy block in Uptown populated with young professionals in recently renovated houses. He parked at the curb and walked around to open the door for Sophie. She got out then put her hand on his.

He extricated his hand and, making sure her dress was free, shut the car door. "Good night, Sophie."

"Aren't you going to walk me up to my house?" Sophie pulled his tuxedo jacket tighter around her and brushed past him. Adrian bit back a sigh. The walkway to her front door was dark, and her roommate apparently had forgotten to leave the porch light on. A gentleman walked a lady to her door, and he had a little redeeming of himself to do tonight. He followed behind a half step.

Sophie fumbled in her purse for her keys then put the key in the lock. As her keychain swung back and forth from its place in the door, she took off his coat and used both hands to drape it back over his shoulders. She slid both hands down his arms and leaned up to him.

Oh no.

He tried to step back, but she kept her grip and raised up on her tiptoes, eyes closed. At the last moment, Adrian turned his face so Sophie's lips missed his and landed somewhere near his left ear. She held them there a moment and then whispered, "Thank you for a lovely night. I'm glad Athena set us up. I'll have to send her some flowers in the morning."

Maybe he really was shallow and an irresponsible playboy if the person who knew him best in the world—his cousin Athena —thought Sophie would be a good match.

Good grief, the girl was trying to kiss him again, turning her face up to his. He took what seemed to be the safest route and dropped a brief kiss on her forehead and then extricated himself from her grasp.

"Do you want to come in?" She pushed open the door.

"No, it's late. I need to get going." And he wasn't interested in that sort of an invitation. Not anymore. He saw the hint of the pout beginning around her eyes. "I'll send you your wrap when it gets back from the cleaners." With each word, he put a step of distance between them.

"Okay then. See you soon!" Sophie waved two fingers at him, her bright smile replacing the half pout.

He declined to answer that with a promise of his own and forced himself not to run to his car. And he waited until Sophie was safely inside and had shut the door before taking off. He wasn't that big of a jerk.

Silence surrounded him on the drive back to his apartment in Kellogg. His thoughts drifted back to the elevator. To the girl who'd sat in his arms, afraid of heights. The woman who'd told him her story and trusted a man named Roger.

Yeah, he was a jerk. He could send Ella flowers and apologize.

Or, he could leave her alone, as she'd requested.

He pulled into his neighborhood in Kellogg. Right after college, he'd purchased a bachelor pad in a renovated hundred-year-old warehouse building. The architect in him appreciated the history of the building, but the practical part of himself wished the plumbing was more reliable.

He took the stairs up the two flights to his apartment. No sense chancing the elevator. Pushing open the door, he saw the lights were already on. What? Maybe Alex hadn't stayed for the party either.

"Hey, it's the Golden Boy. Everyone's favorite. I wondered if you'd come home tonight." Alex sat on the leather couch in Adrian's living room, feet on the coffee table in front of him. He'd kicked off his dress shoes and pulled off his tie, loosened his shirt, his jacket hung over a chair.

Adrian kept walking past him to the left into the hallway that led to his bedroom. He didn't have time for his brother's insinuations tonight.

"Where are you going? I thought we could have a drink and talk over the night."

"You know I don't drink anymore." Hadn't, in fact, since he'd been stupid in college and nearly gotten himself and Athena killed. Just thinking about that party after homecoming made him shudder. Nope, he wasn't going to risk that ever again.

"Fine, not that kind of drink then. Just a soda or something."

Maybe a half hour wouldn't hurt. Adrian shrugged out of his jacket and then moved back into the living room. He sank into the recliner across from his brother and popped the footrest. "What're you doing here? Did Therese kick you out again?"

Alex spread his arms wide. "Can't I just want to spend some time with my favorite brother?"

"Not likely. That'd be a first. C'mon, bro. It's late and I'm tired. Can you just be straight with me?"

"Fine. Fine. Yes, Therese kicked me out." Alex tucked his hands behind his head, leaning back. "She said she wanted space. I can never figure out how to keep that woman happy."

"Maybe you should propose. I can't believe she's stuck around this long as it is." Adrian noted an overnight bag dropped by the sofa. Oh, that was what was happening. "Or maybe you should bring her around to some of your dinner parties. I noticed she wasn't there tonight."

"Like I said, I can never figure her out. She says she wants to spend more time together, but then when I ask her to come, she says my work is boring and that I don't pay attention to her at those things anyway." Alex shrugged. "What can you do? Women are unfathomable. Okay if I crash here for a few nights? It's so humiliating to go home to Mom and Dad's."

"That's why I gave you the key." Although, maybe he should rethink that.

Alex got up and poured himself a drink in the kitchen. "Want something?"

Adrian heard him open the fridge. Something crinkled.

"Water, with lemon." He sank back farther into his chair. The interior of his apartment looked far different from the dated brick exterior. His mother had insisted he use her regular interior designer. The designer had filled the living space with firm, black leather couches, sleek black cabinets and bookshelves, glass tables, a marble fireplace at one end—installed after the fact—and a huge flat-screen over the mantel in place of a photo gallery. A white rug covered part of the dark wood flooring. The kitchen and bathroom followed the same motif, plus a gray-veined granite for countertops. The designer's only concession to color was in the bedroom, where Adrian had been adamant about breaking the monochrome with some yellow. He'd always been partial to yellow.

Alex returned and handed Adrian a tumbler of water with a lemon wedge added to the side. He held a tall glass of root beer and an ice cream sandwich for himself. "So, you really knocked it out of the park tonight. I wasn't expecting that from you."

"Thanks. It means a lot knowing my own brother doesn't believe in me." Adrian moved the lemon into the water and took a drink. He winced at the sour residue left on the glass rim.

"Maybe it was the influence of that chick you were with— Sophie, right? She was a looker. I didn't mind playing the gentleman while you were stuck in the elevator."

"Can't I have just done a good job? Does it always have to be about a girl with you?"

Alex swirled his drink. "Oh, it doesn't always have to be about a girl, but it sure is nice when it is. Women are good motivators. Where'd you find Sophie anyway? Is she a friend of Mom's? The two of them certainly were chummy. Of course, Mom always approves of the girls you date."

Great. Now his mom would be after him to set up another date with "that nice girl from the party."

"Athena set us up. I guess they're sorority sisters, but she's not really my type. Mom will have to be disappointed." Adrian drained his glass. Set it on the side table.

"Oh, I get it. It's about the *other* girl, the blonde you were trapped with. What was her name?"

"Her name was Ella, and she has nothing to do with this. If you want to bunk here, you'd better consider your next words."

"You don't have to get testy. All I'm saying is that I wouldn't mind getting trapped with her for a couple of hours. Wasn't she the one that spoke up against your big proposal? That time in the elevator must have been a real trip." Alex drank the last of his root beer in one quick movement, tipping his head back like he was taking a dose of medicine.

47

"There's a nice hotel down the road."

"Hey. Take a breath. We're just having a conversation here."

"I'm not liking this conversation." Adrian stood up.

"Adri! What's got you so hot?" Alex stood up too. Setting his glass on the glass coffee table, he blocked Adrian's path to the bedroom. A slow grin slid up his face. "Wait. You wanna fight? Burn off a little steam?" He raised an eyebrow. "It's better than driving into the lake."

Adrian stared at his brother for one beat. Two. Finally, "No. I'm fine. I just had a lot riding on tonight."

Alex lifted a shoulder. "Fine." He sat back down. "Besides— and no thanks to your elevator girlfriend—it looks like your proposal squeaked through."

"I really thought the vote would be higher. And she's not my girlfriend." In fact, he doubted he'd ever see her again.

"What's the big deal? You got what you wanted so now all you have to do is get that Deep Haven permit." Alex put his hand on Adrian's shoulder. "That part shouldn't be hard. Just do what you're best at—charm the yokels of Deep Haven with your good looks and you're home free."

"I'm not so sure charming the locals will be as easy as all that. Maybe they'll feel the same way as Ella."

"Forget the girl. I'm sure it won't be that hard to figure out some way to convince the folks of Deep Haven that they will love a new hotel and water park. You'll think of something to get the board begging to approve your project. Like Dad says, whatever it takes, right? Don't let your last failure get into your head."

Right. When Alex put it like that, it sounded so simple. Head north. Get the permit.

And, most importantly, forget the girl.

CHAPTER 4

*E*lla refused to wallow in her defeat.

She needed to get home and form a new plan. Something that didn't depend on wearing satin dresses and pretending to be a princess.

Ella checked the clock on her dashboard—3:00 a.m. Colleen's full-court press to get her to stay the night had nearly worked, but no, thank you.

Ahead, the twinkling lights of Deep Haven shone out a welcoming glow. Tiny snowflakes drifted down, turning the town into a snow globe. The tight knot curled in Ella's throat unraveled just a bit. Coming into town felt akin to coming home. Huh. Maybe Colleen's words about Deep Haven were true. This could be the place Ella finally, truly, put down roots and found her security.

She turned onto her street and parked in front of her rented house. The tiny cottage nestled on its scrap of a lot, surrounded by a white picket fence. Late snow lay piled here and there in the yard where the sun hadn't reached it. When she'd moved to Deep Haven six months before, this place had caught her eye and she'd signed the month-to-month lease within a week. Sure, her landlord wasn't incredible, but she'd gladly trade that for a white picket fence.

As she grabbed her overnight bag and purse from the passenger seat, she considered the box nestled beside them. The dented cardboard box, sealed tightly with packing tape, had traveled in her pink VW for years. Ever since the day her dad had packed it up. Perhaps it was time to bring the box inside, unwrap the tape, and see what it contained. She reached toward it.

No. She wasn't ready to go down that road. Better to leave those demons undisturbed.

She trudged up the walk and then the steps, aware of the thickening snow—usually Deep Haven, four hours north, got twice as much snow as the Twin Cities did. At Christmastime, it was magical. Not so much when it was supposed to be springtime.

Oh, her entire body wanted to drop right here on the porch, and she could almost feel the warm blankets on her old double bed. She'd sleep for a year, or at least until noon. Okay, maybe until nine o'clock—she shouldn't be late for church and her cleaning appointment. Maybe she'd even find some of that refuge and strength Colleen had talked about.

At her cottage door, Ella fitted her key in the lock and turned. The lock refused to budge. She slid the key out and tried again. No luck. Piece of junk doorknob. The landlord outdid himself this time.

While it would be untrue to say that her landlord was a slumlord, he was most definitely a stingy, money-grubbing corner cutter who didn't much care for the people who were paying him rent. If it weren't for the low cost of her month-to-month lease, Ella would have moved. As it was, however, she'd learned not to bother Ed Hansen with the things that broke down in her house, and instead she fixed them herself.

This doorknob must be the latest example of his money-saving ventures. A cheap knob replacing the one she'd complained about several times in the past. She had taken the old one apart so many times to adjust the mechanism she could see it in her sleep. At least he'd finally replaced it, but couldn't he have given her a warning, or at least keyed it to fit her current key?

Ella shivered as she dug in her oversized purse for her multi-tool. Prying out the screwdriver function, she broke the doorknob. *Sorry, not sorry, Mr. Hansen.* She walked inside, flipping on all the lights as she went to the kitchen for a rag to stuff into the hole left by the doorknob. Fixing the lock could wait until later that morning. It's not like Deep Haven was a hotbed of crime.

She moved one of her heavy living room chairs in front of the door. There. She would at least have some warning before nonexistent burglars broke in to steal her scraps of a life.

Remembering her promise to Colleen, she pulled out her cell phone and dialed her friend's number.

"Hey, sorry it's so late. I made it back."

"I'm glad you called." Colleen's voice emerged gravely and low. "Was the drive okay?"

"Yep, went just fine. I had to break into my place though."

"What?" Colleen was fully awake now.

"I guess Ed Hansen forgot to tell me he was fixing the lock." She rubbed her hands together. The cold air in the room seeped into her skin. Was the heat not working again?

"At least you got in. And he didn't leave the door unlocked so people could steal your stuff."

Speaking of stuff. As she had flipped on the lights, she'd noticed that boxes lined the wall near the front door with all of her soapmaking supplies tossed inside. What in the world?

"Colleen, I'll have to call you back later. There's something strange going on here. All my stuff is boxed up." She wandered back into the minuscule, galley-style kitchen. On her left, against the breakfast bar for two, several more boxes held her few kitchen items. Mr. Hansen had a lot of explaining to do.

"Maybe he's finally planning to spruce up the paint in there."

Colleen had a point. It was possible. Hopefully he picked something better than the avocado green currently on the walls. "Yeah, that's probably it. I'll have to sort it all out in the morning. Good night, Colleen."

Heading to the bedroom and ignoring the boxes stacked there, Ella tugged on an old T-shirt and a pair of flannel pants and crawled into bed. Things had to look better in the morning, didn't they?

She added another blanket and then fell hard into slumber.

Three hours later, a shaft of light peeked through her bedroom curtains and burned into her eyes. As she opened them, her breath formed in the air.

Perfect. Had her furnace gone out, too? She pulled her covers up over her head and groaned. Tracking down Ed Hansen and giving him a piece of her mind held top spot on her to-do list for the day, but that didn't mean she was looking forward to it.

A loud knock banged on her front door. "Deep Haven Sheriff's Department. Is anyone in there?" The front door rattled against the chair butted up against it.

"Just a minute, I'm coming." Ella threw back the covers, steeled herself against the cold, and grabbed her bathrobe.

Ella cracked the door to find two deputies—a man and a woman—standing in the cold, both wearing their uniforms, along with gloves, wool jackets, and stocking caps. She shoved the chair out of the way and held the door wide. "Can I help you?"

The two officers exchanged a look.

"Miss Bradley?" the male deputy asked.

"Yes, that's me."

"I'm Deputy Cole Barrett and this is Deputy Gail Morgan. Ma'am, you are under arrest. Please grab a jacket. I'm afraid we have to take you down to the station."

Wait, *what?* "Under arrest? For what?"

"Breaking and entering." This time it was Deputy Morgan.

"Um, where am I supposed to have committed this crime? And come to think of it, *when* was I supposed to have committed this crime? I was out of town until late last night."

The two officers exchanged a look again. Yeah, that wasn't annoying at all.

"Breaking and entering. Here. Last night."

"That's ridiculous. I *live* here. This is my house. I didn't break and enter anything."

Deputy Barrett shot a pointed look at the missing doorknob. Oh.

"Look, I know it appears that I broke in here, but really it's just that Mr. Hansen changed the doorknob and didn't bother to key it correctly. I'll give him a call and we'll straighten this right out." Ella reached for her phone, in her pocket where her coat hung on a kitchen chair.

"Stop." The male deputy moved his hand to rest it on his gun holster.

She froze, held up her hands. "Um—"

"Miss Bradley, it was Ed Hansen himself who called in the complaint. He's down at the station right now filing charges."

The words didn't register. "He's...what?"

Deputy Morgan took a step toward Ella. "If you could just grab a jacket. Don't make this harder than it has to be."

"This must be a mistake. Why would Mr. Hansen want to have me arrested?"

"You can put your hands down, Miss Bradley," Officer Morgan said. "We'll get it all sorted out at the station."

Unbelievable. This whole weekend kept getting worse. "Can

I get dressed first at least?" Her flannel pants and ratty T-shirt suddenly felt more revealing than her slinky dress from the night before.

The female officer walked her down to the bedroom and did a quick scan around the tiny room. Ella grimaced at the sight of her unmade bed and half-spilled overnight bag, the boxes lining the wall. Granted, the hastily packed cardboard boxes weren't her doing, but still, seeing the mess from someone else's eyes was sobering. Finally Deputy Morgan waved her in.

"I'll be right outside."

"I promise not to climb out a window." Ella tried for humor, but it fell flat. She quickly pulled on a clean pair of jeans and an oversized U of M sweatshirt. She shoved her feet into her trusty pink Converse and opened the door.

"Ready when you are."

It turned out that being booked into lockup was a long, tedious event. The fact that she didn't do the crime made it that much worse. She sat at Deputy Morgan's desk and read the complaint a third time. Ed Hansen claimed that Ella's rent check had bounced and under the terms of her rental agreement he had the right to evict her immediately in the case of unpaid rent. He said he had another renter ready to take her place, several in fact, so when her check bounced he'd boxed up her stuff and changed the locks.

"This is crazy," she said. "I have money."

Deputy Morgan handed her a cup of coffee.

Ella drank it down black and bracing, hoping she might wake up, and fast.

After being fingerprinted, photographed, patted down, and questioned repeatedly about her actions over the past twenty-four hours, Deputy Barrett escorted Ella to her new home, a 5x8 cell in the back of the station.

"She shoulda called me." Ella overheard Mr. Hansen

complaining to the officer helping him with paperwork as she passed by. "I woulda let her in to get her stuff. Now, I have no choice but to hold onto it until she pays me back."

He wore grimy jeans and a filthy canvas jacket and an orange gimme cap over his balding head. Ella gave him the dirtiest look she could muster. The snake. He must have been waiting for any opportunity to get her out of that place. After all she'd done to keep the appliances running, he should be thanking her for being a model tenant—not pressing charges.

Ella turned to Deputy Barrett. "Again, please listen. I paid my rent. I have proof. If you just let me go back to the house, I can show you."

He seemed like a nice guy, especially with the face he made. "I'm sorry, not my call."

"Hey, speaking of call, aren't I supposed to get one?" Ella felt her face heating. She needed to call and let Mrs. Decker know that she wouldn't be making it in to clean the church after all. How quickly would her other jobs dry up once news of her jail time circulated around town?

"I'll look into it." He had the decency to look regretful as he slid the bars into place. "Lunch will be in a few minutes."

Great. Just great. She'd gone from princess—or at least pretend princess—to convict in the space of less than twenty-four hours.

Ella plopped onto the shiny gray metal bench lining the cement wall of the cell and looked around. The chilly room resembled every crime show she'd ever watched, minus the strung-out druggies. Another bench lined the other wall, and everything was painted a shade of gray that defied description. Kind of a "depression meets hopelessness" shade.

Who would ever take her seriously now? She could never look a potential investor in the eye. Not after mismanaging her own finances.

She shifted on the bench. How had her check bounced? After making a double payment on her loans, she'd carefully added enough to her checking account to cover all her bills. This couldn't be happening. There must be a mistake. She could not be turning out to be just like her father.

"Sorry this is so late. We had to order in from The Loon Cafe." Deputy Barrett held a paper bag through the cell bars. "I hope you like turkey."

Ella accepted the bag from his grasp and then returned to her seat on the bench. "How much longer am I in for?"

"I talked with Ivy, our county prosecutor, and she's trying to get the judge to sign off on releasing you on your own recognizance."

"Don't I get a defense attorney?"

"Yes. But the DA won't be up until tomorrow."

Perfect.

Barrett handed her a bottle of water, minus the top. What, did they think she'd try and choke on it? "Do you have anyone who could vouch for you? I'd hate for you to have to spend the night in here."

Yeah, she would hate that too.

"If I could get my phone call, I can ask Annaliese Decker to come in." At least she hoped Mrs. Decker would come. Despite being friends with Colleen, Ella didn't know her parents that well. She had been surprised when Mrs. Decker called to ask her about cleaning the church. Most of her other acquaintances in town were clients for her housecleaning business.

"I'll see what I can do." Deputy Barrett turned and went back the way he came.

Ella dug into the turkey sandwich but gave up a few bites in. It tasted like defeat.

An eternity later, a jangling sound came down the hall. Deputy Morgan walked toward her cell, flipping a set of keys in her hand.

"Ivy went to bat for you. The judge agreed to let you out if Mrs. Decker vouches for you. You're getting that phone call." Deputy Morgan unlocked the door, slid the bars back. "You'll still have to see the judge tomorrow. If you fail to show, there will be a warrant issued for your re-arrest."

Ella stepped out of the cell, hearing it clink behind her, feeling bedraggled, grimy, and now, oh joy, homeless.

What was that verse Colleen had quoted? Something about God on her side? He'd sure picked a funny way of showing it.

Driving along Lake Superior's North Shore in his Porsche in the darkening twilight of late March may have been risky, but Adrian had refused to rent a bigger vehicle. The black Porsche had never let him down before, and he wasn't leaving it behind now. So far the roads had been clear and dry. No problem handling the sports car in these conditions.

Handling his dad was a whole different thing.

He didn't know how his mom had put up with him for so long. Earlier that day she had come over to the apartment to rehash the evening before.

"I was so proud of your presentation, honey," she'd said. "The investors loved your new ideas."

"Dad seemed less than thrilled." Had told him as much during the after-party.

"You know your dad and I don't always see eye to eye, but your father is not a bad man, just driven. He wants to see you succeed. That's why he pushes you so hard."

"Yeah. Maybe."

His mother had crossed the room to where he stood. Put her hand on his cheek. "You have to remember what things were like for him. He struggled hard to get where he is now. When we met, he had just started his first business." She'd taken his hand. "Shortly after we married, that business failed and we had to move in with relatives. He vowed then to not let that happen again. He studied hotel and travel trends until he was an expert, then got into the hotel business."

"He never talks about his failure."

"He uses those memories to fuel his determination. I think he wants you to do the same thing. One little failure in the past doesn't define your life. But, ultimately, you need to care more about how God sees you than your father."

Adrian had let go of his mother's hand and turned toward the fireplace. "Mom, it wasn't a *little* failure. I can't forget it, and neither will Dad."

She'd put her hand on his cheek again, waiting until he met her eyes. "You can't dwell on that. Focus on what your heavenly Father thinks about you. He loves you for yourself, not for what you can do for Him."

"I don't know how to do that."

She'd smiled. "You'll figure it out. I'll say a prayer for you at church tonight."

"Thanks, Mom. I'm heading up to Deep Haven this evening. I want to get started right away in the morning."

Believing his mom had been a lot easier while standing in his own living room. Now, on this shadowed highway, he couldn't keep his dad out of his head.

I won't tolerate failure. His dad's words from last night wound their way around Adrian's heart as he pushed the dial button on his steering console.

His father's voice came on the car speaker. "Where are you, Adrian?"

"I'm heading up to Deep Haven."

"Tonight? I thought you would wait until tomorrow when Joan had a chance to make your arrangements."

As much as he appreciated Joan Miller, his dad's long-time

assistant, Adrian didn't need her help on this one. "I didn't think I needed to bother her. I can handle it on my own."

Papers rustled on the other end of the line. Adrian imagined his dad at his desk, refusing to go home until the mahogany surface was cleared of work. "Okay, if you're sure."

"Dad, I'm capable of renting a hotel room for a few nights." He popped open the glove box and confirmed that he had remembered to grab his wallet. "I'll give you a call in a few days."

"Joan could help you get things set up with the mayor too. She's good at what she does. You're not used to working hands-on."

True, he was the guy who smoothed the way for the heavy lifters, the closers. He was invited into meetings when the other party needed a little charming. But he wanted more.

He wanted the world to look at him like they did his father.

I need to pitch to someone who can actually make a difference.

Yeah, that had stuck a knife in his chest.

"I can handle it, Dad. I know what I'm doing."

"Just get the job done. Call me if you have any problems."

There was no way Adrian was calling his father with problems. His voice was tight as he repeated, "I'll call with a progress report in a few days." He cut the connection and looked down for a split second to hit the speed dial for Athena.

His car beeped at him, signaling he was drifting off course. Adrian refocused, moved back into the center of the lane, and waited for his cousin to answer her phone.

Rats. Voicemail. "Hey, Cuz. Just wanted to let you know I'll be in Deep Haven this week. Someday soon we're going to need to have a chat about Sophie Kent. I'm not sure I'm looking for any more blind dates." He hung up.

Tapping his hands on the steering wheel, he hummed a few bars of a Beatles song. The GPS in his dash told him Deep Haven lay just one mile ahead. He pushed the gas pedal a little harder. A few more minutes to his destination.

SUSAN MAY WARREN & ANDREA CHRISTENSON

Check that, a few more minutes to his destiny.

Blue and red lights flickered in his rearview mirror. He checked his speed. A respectable 68 mph. The officer must need to pass to get to an emergency. He drove onto the shoulder and put his car into park, then leaned down to rummage through the bag he'd tossed on the floor on the passenger side. He'd left a granola bar in there somewhere. No luck. He tugged on the bag to move it to the seat when he noticed that the flashing lights were still behind him.

Huh?

In seconds, a sheriff's deputy complete with the distinctive hat stood outside his car window, shining a light into his face.

Adrian rolled down his window. "Good evening. What's the problem, Officer?" He squinted at the deputy, tall and muscular, his brown uniform looking crisply ironed. Aw man, was that a sheriff's badge on his shirt? Perfect. "I mean, Sheriff …?"

"Sheriff Kyle Hueston." The sheriff cocked his head. "Going a little fast there, don't you think?"

"Uh. No. I was going sixty-eight."

"The speed limit is forty-five. And, you swerved back there. I'm going to need to see your license and registration."

"I didn't swerve." C'mon. His little off-the-center-of-the-lane moment had hardly constituted a *swerve*. And wait, forty-five? "The speed limit is sixty-five, isn't it?" Shoot. He hadn't seen a speed limit sign—must've missed it while talking to his dad. He probably shouldn't mention he'd been on a phone call.

Adrian leaned over to get his license and insurance from the box. In the wan light, it tumbled onto the floor. He swept his hand over the floor, trying to grab it.

"Sir, have you been drinking?"

Whoa, what? "No. Sheesh." He handed his license over, as well as the paper insurance confirmation.

"This is expired."

"What? Let me see that." He reached out for the paper, and the sheriff took a step back.

"Hey, there." His small-town demeanor seemed to slide away. "Just stay in the car." The sheriff went back to his vehicle and got in. Perfect.

Adrian sat shivering in the early morning cold, the window down.

The sheriff returned. "You need to get out of the vehicle, sir."

Oh, brother. Adrian sighed and got out. Small-town law— trying to flex its muscles. The sheriff stepped back as Adrian shut his door.

The chilly night air worked its way through him, and Adrian quickly zipped up his jacket.

"I haven't been drinking." Confusion masked his normal politeness, gave an edge to his words. "So why am I being asked to step out of the vehicle on a speeding violation?"

The sheriff flashed the light over him again. "As I mentioned, you swerved." He frowned. "I'm going to ask you to submit to three field sobriety tests. Do you consent to the administration of these tests?"

"Tests?" It sounded like the tall man in the sheriff's uniform thought he was some sort of drunk driver.

Except, oh man. Probably his five-year-old dropped charge of drunk and disorderly had shown up on his record when the sheriff looked up his vehicle information.

"Yes, three. Do you consent—"

"I heard you." Adrian didn't mean to snap, but come on. "And no, I don't consent." He'd heard plenty of stories of people being falsely arrested on the basis of field sobriety tests to stake his reputation on them.

Besides, he hadn't done anything wrong. Well, okay, apparently he'd *sped*. Maybe swerved a little bit. But never would he drink and drive, not after that incident in college when his dad had bailed him out of a serious mistake.

The sheriff put a hand on his belt. He was intimidating, Adrian would give him that. About two hundred pounds of muscle standing right in Adrian's personal space. He sighed, shook his head. "Fine. Then I'm going to have to ask you to come with me to the station."

And ruin his chances of a good first impression on the town of Deep Haven? Heat flashed through Adrian. "Sheriff, come on. I promise I haven't been drinking."

The radio squawked into the silent night from the squad car, and for a moment, the sheriff turned his head. Something about another DUI stop.

Maybe this was a shakedown, the department trying to fulfill some sort of quota. Well, fine, if Adrian had to walk a straight line to showcase his innocence, he would.

He turned sharply, and his foot hit a patch of late spring ice. Slipping, he fell forward, arms outstretched—right into the sheriff, who stumbled backward with the impact.

He landed on top of the man, his hand unfortunately on the sheriff's holster.

And that was it. Suddenly, Adrian found himself on the ground on his belly with a two-hundred-pound knee in his back as the sheriff slapped on handcuffs.

"Get off me!"

"Sir, you're under arrest for assaulting an officer."

"I didn't assault you!" But now he wanted to, the way the guy was hauling him to his feet. "What is your problem? I was just talking on the phone! And maybe I swerved a little, but—"

The look on the officer's face suggested he was only making it worse. "I'll have someone get your car. Come with me and we'll figure it out at the station."

And then, he read Adrian his rights.

Perfect.

"You've blown this all out of proportion."

Without response, the sheriff directed him to the back seat

of the police car. Looked at him for a moment before shaking his head. He shut the door, retrieved Adrian's duffel bag from the Porsche's front seat, and tossed it into the trunk.

Adrian went hot, then cold, then hot again. Despite what the papers said about him, for the last several years, he'd mostly kept his nose clean, stayed out of trouble. Ending up in the back of a patrol car through no fault of his own was almost laughable.

Almost.

Possibly when he looked back on this event in ten years he would laugh.

Okay. Make that twenty years. Or thirty.

The sheriff folded himself into the front seat of the car before calling in his location. Adrian leaned his head back and closed his eyes. Hopefully no one would read about it in the local police report.

A few minutes later, they pulled to a stop in front of a small, squat building on top of a hill. The brick exterior stood solid in the moonlight pouring from overhead. The sheriff escorted him through locked doors, inside past the administration desk, and all the way back into a room where he was asked to breathe into a hose connected to something that resembled a fax machine.

Ten seconds later, the number beeping on the screen had him sighing with relief. He'd known he hadn't been drinking, but sometimes those machines weren't calibrated correctly.

"See? You can let me go now."

"Let's just take a breath and talk," the sheriff said before leading him to an interrogation room. Adrian sat on a sturdy silver chair, and the sheriff unlocked his handcuffs.

"Coffee?" he asked Adrian.

Adrian just looked at him. "How about a warm meal and a bed?"

"We'll see what we can do." The man raised an eyebrow.

Adrian had the distinct impression they had different definitions of that request.

He left the room. Across the table sat another silver chair. The fluorescent light hanging from the ceiling buzzed in the silence when the officer left.

Another officer came in. A woman this time.

"Deputy Gail Morgan." Curly brown hair was tamed back in a severe bun. "The sheriff asked me to get your statement. Want to tell me what happened out there?"

Adrian tried out his most charming smile. It bounced off the deputy without making an impact. "This is all just a misunderstanding. As the breath test has proven, I was not drunk. But when I tried to walk in a straight line to prove it, I tripped and fell into Sheriff Hudson."

"Hueston." Stern eyes belied the deputy's youthful face.

"Sorry, Sheriff *Hueston*. I was *not* assaulting him. He seems like a nice guy, just doing his job, but he wasn't looking when it happened. The facts are all wrong."

Behind Deputy Morgan in the middle of the gray-green wall was a one-way mirror. Maybe Sheriff Hueston was back there listening right now.

"But were you belligerent to an officer?" She made a mark on the papers in front of her.

"That's not how it happened."

"And did you run into my colleague after leaving your vehicle?"

"I slipped."

She looked at him. "According to the sheriff, you fell and reached for his gun."

"That's not true."

"And now you're being argumentative with *me*." She made another mark on her paper.

"Whatever! What is wrong with this stupid town? Sheesh.

So, I swerved. So I was driving over the speed limit. I fell—" He got up. "I'm outta here."

"Sir—"

And just like that, it happened again. She got up just as he moved past her. And him, being larger than the deputy, slammed into her. She fell back against the wall.

Aw—

The door banged open. The sheriff came in, a fire in his eyes. And again, Adrian was up against the wall.

"I think maybe we need to get you those accommodations," Sheriff Hueston said, a soft edge to his voice.

Adrian was making all sorts of friends.

The tiny cell had a bed with a thin blanket to the left, a metal toilet and gleaming matching sink at the back wall. Guess he could kiss privacy goodbye. Adrian turned back to the sheriff beyond the bars.

"Is this really necessary?"

The sheriff sighed, stepped back. "At this point, I think we'll let the judge sort it out. He'll be here in the morning."

Court. "Wow. I *slipped on some ice*. I'm not a criminal."

"And what happened back there?"

His mouth closed. "This is all a misunderstanding."

"I hope so," Hueston said. "For now, try and calm down. Get some rest."

Adrian just gave him a look as the sheriff left.

Adrian's cashmere jacket shed some dirt from the road as he shrugged it off and tossed it on the end of the metal slab attached to the wall that passed for a bed. He stretched out on the thin mattress without bothering to remove his shoes.

Wonderful. So much for impressing the town council.

Breathe. Calm down. Maybe he had been a little out of line. I *can handle it, Dad. I know what I'm doing.*

Yes, this would be fun to explain.

He closed his eyes, his gut churning. And right then, of course, Ella walked into his mind. *Let's talk about how I thought you were a good guy.*

Yes, let's. He rolled over, pulling the jacket over him. Welcome to Deep Haven where all your wildest dreams come true.

CHAPTER 5

*M*aybe she should have taken Annaliese Decker up on that offer of a guest room after all. Ella closed the door to the bathroom at the Java Cup. She only had a few minutes before she needed to be at the courthouse.

The day before she had been surprised when Mrs. Decker had shown up at the sheriff's department and met her at Deputy Barrett's desk. She had called Mrs. Decker to cancel her cleaning appointment at the church and asked her to vouch for her to be released. Ella had thought it could all be done over the phone.

"You didn't have to come all this way for me," she had told Annaliese.

"Nonsense. It's what I would do for Colleen. Of course I would do it for her friend too."

"I really appreciate it. Please tell the church ladies that I'll clean the sanctuary for them later this week. No charge."

Annaliese waved the concern away. "I'm sure no one is worried about it. We can be an understanding bunch once you get to know us better. I'd like to take you home with me. I have a guest bedroom you can stay in until you get back on your feet."

Somewhere in the central room a phone rang. There were several desks lit by fluorescent lights overhead. Deputy Barrett had left them with the paperwork and promised to be back in five minutes to set her free.

"Thank you, but no. I'll head over to an ATM and get some cash for a motel. I don't want to bother you."

"Oh, it's no bother. We'd be happy to have you."

Ella stood and pulled her jacket on. "Thank you. I appreciate the offer. I really do. But I need to do this one on my own."

Annaliese gave her a gentle smile and a hug. "Let me know if you change your mind."

Ella had left the sheriff's department and headed straight for an ATM. Her balance had shown an overdraft. She checked her online banking app, which also registered zero. What had happened to her money?

Tired and frustrated, she'd ended up sleeping in her car and had woken up with an ache in her back.

Right now Ella would trade anything she owned for a hot shower. Okay, not her last forty dollars—she'd need that to eat for the next few days—and maybe not her car since it appeared that was where she'd be living for the foreseeable future. And she definitely wouldn't trade her pink Converse. Those shoes had seen her through so much, they were practically family.

So, she'd trade *almost* anything she owned. A long, hot shower with sudsy soap wasn't too much to ask, right?

But right now she had to do something to make sure she didn't spend another night in jail. She looked at her reflection in the mirror of the tiny coffee shop bathroom.

Sheesh. She looked just how she felt. Like she'd spent last night in her car and now was trying to repair the damage in a four-by-three-foot cubby. Which, of course, she had and she was. She still wore her clothes from the day before. She tugged out a wrinkle in the sweatshirt and smoothed a few more in her jeans.

Thankfully, she could pull herself together at least a little bit. She dug around in her purse for her emergency toothbrush kit. The travel-sized toothpaste was nearly squeezed dry. She finally eked out a teeny amount onto her brush and tossed the container into the trash. So much for having fresh breath.

There wasn't much she could do about her hair. She ran her fingers through it and then tied it into a messy bun on top of her head. It would have to do. She didn't have time or resources for anything else.

The scent of donuts tickled her nose, and her stomach roared in response. The half-finished turkey sandwich from the day before sounded like a gourmet dinner about now. She packed her stuff back up and stepped out of the bathroom. The idea of a latte full of caffeine was an almost primal pull, but with only forty dollars to her name, she couldn't afford to blow five whole dollars on a coffee.

"Everything okay, hon?" Kathy, the Java Cup owner, was scrubbing down a table near the cash register.

"I'm fine." Nowhere near fine, but she wasn't going to tell Kathy that.

"You look like you could use a donut." Kathy straightened and moved toward the cash register.

"It's going to take more than a donut to get me through this day." Her stomach rumbled again. "Thank you anyway."

"Wait right there. I've got one or two day-olds I was about to throw away. If you don't mind it being a little stale, you can have one of those on the house." The shop owner disappeared briefly into the back, then returned with a sugared cake donut clutched in a piece of wax paper.

"Oh no, I couldn't possibly accept that. I'm fine. Really." Just like Mrs. Decker, Kathy was incredibly kind to offer a hand up, but Ella literally couldn't afford to be in anyone's debt. If she was ever in absolutely dire straits, of course she'd accept the help—she wasn't *that* prideful or stupid. But neither was she that desperate.

Her stomach chose that moment to rumble again. Traitor.

Kathy smiled and handed over the donut. "It's no trouble. Have a nice day."

"Thank you." Clutching her stale donut, Ella pushed open the door. The cold air swatted her face, bringing with it the distinct scent of muddy snow. The flakes from the weekend had turned to slush without covering the dirt along the streets. Gray skies above threatened more snow before the end of day.

Ella slid into the front seat of her car and tucked her donut into her purse.

She turned the car key but the engine wouldn't turn over. "C'mon, baby," she coaxed. "Don't let me down." Taking a breath, she tried again. This time the VW roared to life.

All the way to the courthouse, Ella rehearsed what she was going to say. She knew she had money in her account—she just needed to get to the bank to prove it. She would've done that this morning already except she was due in court before the bank opened. Checking her ATM yesterday hadn't helped. The machine kept saying her account was overdrawn, which she knew wasn't possible. She'd just deposited several payments from her cleaning clients last Wednesday.

A few turns later and she pulled into the back parking lot of an imposing brick building with tall white columns. Once inside, she went through a metal detector and felt like a criminal when an officer made her open her purse.

Because, ahem, she *was* a criminal. Nausea brewed in her stomach at the thought.

The marble floors captured the chill from the outside, and she shivered, although maybe more from the fate that awaited her. Finding a directory, she searched for the location of the courtroom she'd been assigned to, though it turned out there was just one in the building. The rest of the rooms were listed as offices for the various county staff.

Ella checked her phone. Five minutes until she had to meet with the public defender assigned to her case. Maybe she could sneak in a few bites of her donut. A coffeepot nestled in the lobby offered her the caffeine she couldn't afford to buy. She filled a foam cup and added cream and sugar. This day called for plenty of fortification.

Balancing the coffee in one hand and her purse over her shoulder, she bit into the donut. A little stale, but the fat and sugar combo did the trick.

"Ella?"

She turned to the voice.

"I'm Charlotte Hopewell, the public defender assigned to your case. You are Ella Bradley, aren't you?" The beautifully coiffed older woman was tall, dressed in a slim, purple-striped pantsuit. Her short, black hair gleamed in the fluorescent lights of the cavernous room. Ella bet that she had even had a full dose of toothpaste that morning. Ella lifted her hand to shake the lawyer's hand but at the last moment remembered the sugar covering her fingers. She looked around for a napkin then settled for wiping her hand on her jeans.

Real smooth. If she ever needed proof that her pride had totally gotten the better of her, that was it. Compared to the woman in front of her, Ella felt like a bag lady.

"Let's get started." Charlotte led Ella to a table down the hall. Stark white walls angled into a corner area perfect for a private chat. "I've taken a look at your case, but it doesn't look good. I think you should plead guilty."

"But I'm *not* guilty. I paid my rent. I didn't know Ed Hansen had changed the locks to keep me out. I thought he was replacing the doorknob I've been complaining about. Can he really hold onto my things?" Ella sat up straighter in her chair.

"He says your check bounced. I looked over your rental

agreement. It says that he is within his rights to evict you if your rent isn't paid." The lawyer opened a file and pointed at a few lines with her pen. "The rental agreement also says that he can hold onto your things until the damage is paid for." She clicked her pen in a one-two rhythm before flipping the file folder shut and placing the pen on top of it.

"How did my check bounce? I have plenty of money in the bank. In fact, if we can delay this trial, I can get the information from the bank to prove it." This wasn't making any sense. Worse, how would anyone believe her when even the person who was supposed to be defending her thought she was guilty?

"Well, Mr. Hansen has the rejected check and a note from the bank to prove it. Plus, the bank slapped on a hefty fine for the bounced check. So you will need to pay that back as well as the cost for the damages." Ms. Hopewell smiled, her perfect teeth flashing. "I'm sorry, Ella. I really do think your best bet is to plead guilty and pay the fines."

"What if I want to plead *not* guilty?"

"I'll be honest. I don't think you have a good chance of winning. It will take time and money. Besides, I think Judge Mason will be lenient because this is your first offense." Charlotte said this as though Ella ought to feel grateful.

After a night spent in her car, trying and failing to sleep wrapped around her steering wheel, a girl could be excused for feeling quite a bit less than grateful. She didn't even know where she was going to sleep tonight. If it was true that her account was drained, and her emergency money all poured into posting bail, she had nothing to use for a night in a motel, let alone rent money for a new place to live.

Okay, forget the shower. What she needed was a long bath with lavender-scented bubbles and a bar of her lemon-rosemary hand-milled soap. Ahhh.

Ella caught herself before her internal groan became audible. There was *no way* a bath was in her immediate future. Like this morning, she would have to make do with a quick wipe down in a public bathroom after a night spent in her mobile apartment, AKA her pink VW.

"Fine," she said to Charlotte. "We'll play it your way." Because, really, what choice did she have? She certainly didn't have enough money to pay for a court battle.

"Looks like it's almost our turn." Charlotte stood and brushed the front of her impeccable jacket. "We'll go in and sit near the front until Judge Mason calls our case."

The next hour passed in a blur of real criminals pleading guilty. She could barely look at any of them.

When it was her turn, Ella's public defender asked the judge for clemency. "Your Honor, this is my client's first offense. She has a long history of paying her bills. She claims that the breaking and entering was an honest mistake. I don't think a heavy-handed approach is necessary."

The judge checked his watch and turned to the prosecutor's table.

Across the aisle, Ella saw Ivy Christiansen, the Deep Haven Assistant County Attorney, stand up. "Your Honor, I agree with Ms. Hopewell that this doesn't have to be prosecuted to the fullest extent of the law. Ms. Bradley did not harm the residence or steal anything from Mr. Hansen. I recommend sixty hours of community service."

Judge Mason checked his watch again.

Was he even listening? The injustice of the entire thing roiled inside her.

Suddenly, she found herself on her feet. "Your Honor, this is just all a big mistake. If I could just show you my checkbook—"

The judge banged his gavel. "Ms. Hopewell, please control your client. Young lady, sit down, or you will take this from being a misdemeanor to something more. Your lawyer is your voice right now."

Ella sank to her chair and sat, words shucked out of her

when the judge sentenced her to sixty hours of community service. Not to mention the money she would have to pay Mr. Hansen to get her stuff back.

But I'm innocent.

The words died, however, as she shuffled out from behind the defendant's table and turned into the aisle.

Sixty hours. Three weeks of service, four hours a day. Maybe she could do something indoors.

As she trudged up the aisle, her eyes downcast in shame, her peripheral gaze snagged on a figure seated in the far corner of the courtroom.

Dark hair, a Greek nose, his face set like flint.

Adrian Vassos? What was he doing here?

Worse, he'd heard the charges. Seen her pitiful defense. Bad enough that she looked like a homeless person—okay she *was* a homeless person, and had just been declared guilty of a crime— but now her chances with the Vassos family were entirely shot.

If they weren't before.

She just barely stopped herself from breaking out into a run. But as she passed his row, her stomach growled. That half bite of donut from earlier hadn't lasted long.

That did it. She fled the courtroom.

Spotting a vending machine, she rooted around in her purse for enough change to buy some peanut butter sandwich crackers. Yes. A dollar bill, albeit crumpled and a little torn. Smoothing out the wrinkled and stained bill, she tried to insert it into the machine.

The machine spat it back out.

She tried again.

Again, the rejection.

"C'mon!" She nearly hit the machine but took a breath and tried again—

"Ella."

She caught her bill as the machine rolled it back out, and

turned to the voice. Oh no, whatever the petite assistant county attorney wanted, it couldn't be good. Ella tugged her sweatshirt down, wished she was dressed more professionally. "Thanks for what you did in there, Mrs. Christiansen."

"Call me Ivy. Listen, I just have a few minutes—the judge called a lunch recess." Ivy brushed a red lock of hair out of her eye. "I'm sorry you got sentenced at all."

"You were doing your job." She turned to the machine and tried feeding the dollar again. After a grinding noise, the dollar came right back.

Even the Deep Haven vending machines didn't trust her.

"No. Well, I mean, yes, I was just doing my job, but I still feel bad," Ivy said. "It's obvious the breaking and entering was an honest mistake. Unfortunately, I had to prosecute."

"It's just my life right now. Don't worry about it."

Ivy put her hand on Ella's arm. "But I do—worry about it, that is. Worry about you. My sister-in-law Grace says you've been here for a few months, but it's hard to meet people in the winter. Too cold to show our faces." She laughed. "But Grace speaks highly of you and your cleaning products."

"Really?" She'd only worked for Grace and Max Sharpe for the past two months, after they'd moved to Deep Haven permanently. Ella liked Grace and her positive outlook despite her husband's disease. They had a cute little girl too.

"Yes. Listen, do you have a place to stay?"

Ella looked up at her, nonplussed. Swallowed. Found her voice. "I'll be fine. I'm used to fending for myself." She had to be when she grew up with Mike Bradley as her father.

"But I'm trying to tell you that you *don't have to* fend for yourself. I'd like it if you'd stay with us. At Darek's resort, I mean. You know his family owns the Evergreen Resort?"

Of course she did. Ella had heard about the cabins in the woods, wished she might offer her cleaning supplies to them—if she ever got her company off the ground.

"Occupancy is low right now, the winter season is basically over, and the summer visitors won't start coming for a couple months. You could stay in one of the cabins."

Ella sighed. "Thanks anyway, but I'm a little short on cash right now." That was an understatement.

"Sorry, I'm not making myself clear. Maybe I'm hungry. I should grab a sandwich too." Ivy began digging in the Coach purse she had slung over her shoulder. "What I mean is, you could help the family get the cabins ready for the summer season. I know you're a brilliant housekeeper. I've heard about you from others who have been very pleased with your work. In exchange, you could stay in one of the cabins. For free."

Oh. Turning so Ivy couldn't see the wetness in her eyes, Ella tried the dollar again. No luck.

"Ella, here." Ivy held out a crisp dollar bill and traded it for the stained, crumpled one in Ella's hand. "I remember when I was all alone. The Christiansens became my family, even before Darek and I got married. Give them a call. I'll let Darek know to expect you."

Ella fit Ivy's bill into the vending machine. A whir and clunk told her that the vending machine had finally dispensed her crackers. They dropped, and she picked up the package then turned to Ivy. "Okay. I'll give him a call after I finish up my paperwork." She wanted to say more, but it was all balled up in her throat.

"Good," Ivy said. "Hang in there, Ella. It's going to get better." Ivy stepped up to the machine. Stuck Ella's dollar bill in.

The machine gobbled it and dropped a sandwich. Of course.

Because people like Ella didn't have the luck—or the happy endings.

People like Ella were lucky to get a hot bath.

~

Adrian slunk a little lower in his seat. Maybe the bulk of the officer sitting next to him would shield him from sight. The one person he had hoped to avoid, or maybe impress, here in Deep Haven had found him in the last place he wanted to be seen.

So much for forgetting the girl.

Around him the courtroom buzzed as the court took a lunch recess.

Maybe Ella hadn't seen him. She had been hustling by at a rather quick clip. And why not—the stupid judge had barely listened to her.

He'd just about stood up himself to plead her case. Probably should have.

Instead, he'd sat there wishing his family's lawyer would call him back. As it were, he was probably going to have to throw himself on the not-so-abundant mercy of the court.

The wood-paneled room was larger than he had expected, but it wasn't that big. And even though his Loro Piana jacket and designer jeans were wrinkled from the narrow cot-not-a-bed in his jail cell, he did stand out from the others in the crowd. Apart from the lawyers, everyone here seemed to think that court was a big slumber party. Most of them were in varying styles of leggings, sweatpants, and flannels. Thankfully, the officer who had escorted him in here had removed his handcuffs before they sat down.

"Adrian Vassos?" A tall, slim woman wearing a purple pantsuit approached. "I'm Charlotte Hopewell. I've been assigned to your case."

Adrian shook the lawyer's hand. "This has all just been a big misunderstanding."

"Aren't they all." Charlotte responded without a trace of humor in her voice. "I reviewed your case. Assaulting an officer is a felony offense, but I think I can talk them down to a misdemeanor."

A felony? As in real jail time? "Talk them down? These charges should be dismissed. I *tripped*!" This wasn't right.

"That's not likely, Mr. Vassos. Sheriff Hueston said you were argumentative and you pushed him." Charlotte opened a manila folder, reading through the charges, the report. She absently clicked her pen in a one-two rhythm.

"Oh, for Pete's sake, I was *confused*, not argumentative." Once again, his explanation of the events of the night before was ignored. Great. Just great. "Look, what can I do to get these charges dropped?"

"You're welcome to try to fight this one. But you'd have to hire a different lawyer and it will take time."

Yes, please. But he'd checked—the Deep Haven judge only came to town on Mondays. He might be in the clink for an entire week waiting for his lawyer to sort it out. And that's *if* the guy ever got back to him.

Pen click, one, two. "I recommend we wait and see what the judge says. It could be worth it to just accept the ruling." After another series of pen clicks, she looked him straight in the eye. "Adrian, your best chance is just to hear the judge out. I'm sure you feel you did nothing wrong. I can understand that. But unless you are willing to hire someone else, you're stuck with me."

Great, his whole life hung on the word of someone who, according to her last up to bat, was happy to throw him to the wolves, or at least the wildlife judicial system of northern Minnesota.

"Fine," he said. He'd take his chances with the public defender and make a plan from there. He needed to get moving on his project, not be stuck in the courtroom.

The noise of the room picked back up as everyone returned from lunch and took their places.

All too soon, his case was called in front of the judge.

Judge Mason glanced at his watch. Rubbed a hand over his

face. "Let's get right to it. Ms. Hopewell, what does your client plead?"

"He pleads *Nolo contendere,* No Contest, Your Honor."

Adrian rolled his eyes.

Charlotte stood and placed her hands on the table in front of them. "Your Honor, my client believes these charges are just a big misunderstanding. He claims he fell into Sheriff Hueston and meant no malice."

Claims? Even his lawyer didn't believe him. This sham of a hearing was going to be over before it even began.

"I do have a statement here from Sheriff Hueston regarding the incident. He asked me to be lenient with my sentence. However, I just can't ignore the fact that Mr. Vassos broke the law, both by excessively speeding and by getting into an altercation with an officer of the law." Judge Mason adjusted his glasses and reviewed a paper in front of him. "I'm inclined to sentence Mr. Vassos to community service."

This was unbelievable. Adrian shot to his feet. "Community service? C'mon, Your Honor. It was an accident. These charges should be dropped."

The judge banged his gavel. "Ms. Hopewell, please control your client."

"Sit down, Mr. Vassos." Charlotte pushed down on Adrian's shoulder. "You're just going to make this worse."

He sat. "Can't I just pay a fine or something? I don't even live here."

Charlotte shook her head at him.

"As I was saying, you'll need to complete twenty hours of community service. And since you are so eager to pay the court off, Mr. Vassos, you will also receive a one-thousand-dollar fine." The judge banged his gavel again.

Seriously?

Adrian sat there as the court clerk called the next case.

"Mr. Vassos?"

"I'm just collecting myself after this miscarriage of justice," Adrian said, looking up at his useless defense attorney.

Her mouth tightened.

"Where do I pay?"

She directed him to the county clerk, and he forked out his cash, then shouldered his duffel bag and made his way outside. The clouds from earlier had blown away, leaving the clear sky brilliant and crisp.

Perfect. Somewhere in this town, his Porsche was also in jail. And he needed a place to stay. For much longer than originally intended, thanks to his sentencing. So much for a simple reservation at a hotel in town.

Admitting defeat, he grabbed his phone and dialed Joan Miller, his father's longtime assistant.

"Adrian. How is the beautiful town of Deep Haven?" She'd been the one to point him to the town as a stopover on his way to the fishing resort.

"Joan, I'm afraid I'm calling in another favor. I'm swearing you to secrecy on this."

"Of course, Adrian. You know I will. Unless it involves bloodshed or isn't good for you, I keep your secrets."

Boy, had she. Adrian was pretty sure his dad still didn't know how Adrian had nearly been kicked out of school for the prank he pulled his senior year. After Adrian and some of his football buddies had gotten caught plastic wrapping the school counselor's car, it was Joan who called and sweet-talked the principal out of suspending him. Then when they moved the music teacher's MINI Cooper through the double doors into the school and up the steps to the cafeteria, Joan had arranged for a generous donation to the music department rather than involve his father.

"I've run into a little trouble here in Deep Haven, and I'll need to stay for longer than I thought. Can you book me a room somewhere? I'll need it for the next couple of weeks, maybe even a month."

"No problem, I'll see what options you have. It won't take me long to get something set up."

"Thank you, Joan. I knew I could count on you. Remember, mum's the word."

"Now, Adrian, you know me better than that. Did I tell him about any of your high school shenanigans? Of course I didn't. But you stay out of any more trouble, okay?"

He pictured her in her usual work attire, black skirt suit over a white top, her hair in a tight gray bun at the nape of her neck, flipping through her ubiquitous Rolodex, searching for a contact in Deep Haven to utilize. Prim and proper, Joan Miller was the best thing to have happened to his father's company. To Adrian too. He didn't often see his Grandma Vassos who still lived in Greece, but Joan Miller made an excellent substitute.

Adrian opened an internet browser on his phone. Searched for the address of the impound lot. Located a mile out of town at the city garage. He sighed. It wasn't probable that Deep Haven had a thriving Uber business. Oh well. He looked up walking directions on his phone, then set off down the road.

A sheriff's car pulled up in front of him and Sheriff Hueston got out of the driver's seat. Great. Was Adrian being followed by the local law enforcement now?

He held up his hands. "I don't want any trouble, Sheriff."

"Neither do I." Hueston held out his hand to Adrian. "Look, I want to apologize for last night. It was a mess of bad events, starting with the speeding, and it went downhill from there. We had a recent run of people going too fast for conditions. Last week there was even a bad accident on that same stretch of road. Some college kids were messing around and an innocent driver got hurt. They were carrying a bunch of drugs and generally acting stupid."

The sheriff cleared his throat. "I know we're a small town,

but we have serious crime up here too, and when I saw your record, I wasn't sure what I was dealing with..."

He'd figured. But getting upset for judgment over his past wouldn't do any good. Here was Adrian's first chance to prove to a Deep Haven resident that he was a good guy. He shook the sheriff's hand. "I get it."

"Good. I hope we can be friends. Deep Haven is too small of a town to hold a grudge."

"Sure. No hard feelings, Sheriff," Adrian said. Then he laughed, a sort of half chuckle. "Maybe you could just run in and tell the judge to drop the charges?"

"Call me Kyle, and uh, no. Sorry." Kyle's mouth turned up in an amused smile. "You still deserved it. Going sixty-eight in a forty-five zone is frowned on up here."

So much for clemency. He supposed he did deserve a ticket, even if the speeding had been an innocent mistake. "It was worth a shot anyway."

Kyle nodded. "I can offer you a ride to pick up your car though. I figured you wouldn't want to walk all the way over to the impound lot."

Adrian's cell rang. He excused himself to Kyle and checked the caller ID before picking it up.

Joan.

Her voice came on the line at his greeting. "I did one better than booking you a hotel room. I found you a whole cabin. You'll be renting Cabin 5 at the Evergreen Resort. I'm sending the address to your phone. A family named Christiansen runs the place. They said it would be no problem for you to stay as long as you need. They're in a slow time right now. I put the rent on your usual credit card."

Adrian let out a breath. "Joan, you're a peach."

"Flattery will get you everywhere." Her smile carried through the line. "Enjoy your vacation."

Vacation, ha. That was a joke. The dream of completing this water park project was turning into a nightmare.

Kyle was still leaning against the front of his cruiser. "Did you want that ride?"

"That'd be great. Thanks." Adrian slid into the cruiser—in the front seat this time. "You have a beautiful town."

"Sure do. I've lived here all my life and I still can't get over the views." As they talked, Kyle drove them a mile out of town along the shoreline, where the deep cobalt-colored lake combed a rocky shore. They drove down a road where pine trees lined the road like silent sentinels. Kyle pulled into a lot peppered with cars and enclosed by a chain-link fence. "End of the line. I'll walk you into the office, help you get things sorted with Big Jim."

"Thanks, I appreciate it." What a change from big city life. In Minneapolis he'd have fended for himself.

After paying Big Jim the impound fine and signing a few papers, Adrian held out his hand for his car keys. He flipped them around his finger while following Kyle out to his cruiser and then he walked down the row of cars until he found his Porsche. The black car gleamed in the sunlight and didn't appear to be any worse for its night in the lot.

Adrian got in his car and braced his hands on the steering wheel. Time for a definite plan. First things first, directions to his new home for the next few weeks. He put the address for the Evergreen Resort into his car's GPS.

Once there, he'd build a strategy for winning over Deep Haven.

But first, he needed a shower.

CHAPTER 6

*O*h, this was just peachy. Twenty minutes until her first community service assignment, and her car wouldn't start. The cold snap the night before must have zapped the battery.

Ella leaned her head back on the headrest and groaned. Bad enough she had to even *go* to community service, now she was going to show up late. What else could go wrong? She tried the key one more time. No luck. A click and then nothing. Maybe Darek Christiansen could give her a jump. She always kept jumper cables in her trunk.

We're so sorry for the inconvenience... The words the bank manager had spoken the afternoon before kept rolling around in her mind.

She'd give them inconvenience. Sheesh. After her court disaster, Ella had gone straight to the bank to figure out what had happened to her account. The small-town bank manager had told her that money had indeed been withdrawn, presumably by someone attempting to steal her identity. It was bad enough that she had no money, but now the bank had to outsource the identity theft investigation. *Your account has a $50 immediate protection allowance, but we'll have to wait for the investigation to be completed before we can issue the insurance coverage. I'm so sorry, but our hands are tied. If you'd like, you can take out a short-term loan. Despite the circumstances, I'm sure we can figure something out.*

Fifty bucks. What was she supposed to do with that?

Before Ella could think through the pros and cons of taking out a loan—and thus, getting further into debt—she'd realized the time and had made another appointment before racing off to work. Hopefully they would be able to work something out this afternoon.

To top off an already bad day, two of her clients had called and canceled her cleaning services yesterday. Yeah, that hadn't made her feel better about her time in the slammer.

At least her night in the little cabin at Evergreen had been pleasant. She'd picked up a few groceries and made it back to the two-room haven on the lake just as the sun was setting. She had warmed up some ramen for supper, taken a long, hot shower, then crawled into bed, pulling the quilt over her head, and fallen fast asleep.

She got out of the car, opened the trunk, and pulled out her jumper cables. Her pink VW Beetle looked a little shabby compared to the black Porsche she was parked alongside. She let out a low whistle of appreciation. The sleek Porsche 911 was so smooth she had trouble stopping herself from running her hand along its body. The Evergreen Resort must have some high-caliber guests staying this week. A cabin door opened and a man in a black wool jacket strode toward the parking lot.

Oh no. No, no, no. What was Adrian Vassos doing *here*? She'd almost written off seeing him in Deep Haven yesterday as a trauma-induced nightmare. Of course he'd be in town to file paperwork to get his project going. But apparently the nightmare had followed her to the Evergreen Resort. Ella turned toward her car quickly. Please don't let him see her.

"Ella?" His voice reached out and snagged her.

Oh, this could not be happening. She turned back around. Pasted on a smile. "What are you doing here?" And, of course, he was wearing a jacket that cost more than her car. She recognized the wool overcoat from the cover of a celebrity magazine. His designer jeans and Italian leather shoes confirmed what she already knew—he was way out of her league. She tugged at her ratty U of M sweatshirt. At least it was clean. Mostly.

"I could ask you the same thing." He waved a hand at her pink VW. "Is this your car? It suits you."

She wondered what adjectives he ascribed to her car that *suited* her. Provincial? "You don't know anything about me."

"I know that you appear to be having car trouble."

So those were the adjectives—broken down and in trouble. She wouldn't give him the satisfaction. "I'm fine."

He gestured to the jumper cables still in her hands. "Clearly. Listen, why don't you let me give you a ride to wherever you're headed. I'd like a chance to talk to you."

"I'd rather get a ride from a snake. Oh wait, that's exactly what I'd be doing, riding with a snake." She crossed her arms and glared at him.

His mouth tightened. "Okay, that's a little dramatic, but I deserved it. I'm sorry. Really, I am. I shouldn't have given you my middle name in the elevator. I should have told you who I was right away."

She'd give him points for being willing to apologize, but he wasn't getting off that easy. "Yes. You should have."

"Look. Will you please get in my car and I can apologize some more? We can give your car a jump tonight. I hate to rush you, but I have somewhere to be in fifteen minutes." And, of course, he gestured to the Porsche. Just the car to accent his outfit.

"Fine." It had to be, because what other option did she have? Just finding Darek could take fifteen minutes and then she really would be late for her first day. "I'll need a ride to the courthouse."

She slid into the car without looking at him. The soft leather seat molded to her like a glove. Oh, she could get used to this. Other than the slight fishy smell, nothing indicated this car had taken a swim recently.

He pulled out of the parking lot and headed along the lake toward the highway into town.

"Don't you need directions?" At his silence, she turned to look at him. "Adrian, do you know how to get to the courthouse?"

He cleared his throat. "I'm actually heading to the courthouse, too."

That's right. She'd seen him there the other morning. Of course he knew how to get there.

"I suppose you have permits to file and paperwork to begin." Ella tried to keep her voice light.

Adrian rubbed a hand along the back of his neck as he stopped at an intersection, waiting for a lumber-filled truck to pass. "Actually, I, uh, I have to check in there for community service."

She glanced at him. He looked almost embarrassed. And he should be. "Don't think a little community service is going to trick the Deep Haven population into backing your project."

He turned out onto the highway. Below them, the town spread out around the harbor, the sky turning the lake a deep, mysterious blue. The sun ate away at the barest edging of snow covering the boulders stacked up along the harbor. It could be a glorious day.

If she wasn't going to serve her time.

"No," he said to her accusation and cleared his throat again. He cut his voice so low that Ella had to lean in to hear his next words. "Community service as in 'don't go to jail' community service."

What? "You were in court because you were *arrested*? Please."

"It was all a misunderstanding."

"Sure it was. What'd you do? Accidentally rob a bank?"

"Ha ha, funny girl. I got pulled over for speeding. I didn't know the speed limit changed before coming into town."

"That's it? You got community service for *speeding*? Why didn't you just pay the ticket? I thought guys like you just paid fines without blinking. Better to spend some cash than to say you're sorry."

"Guys like me?"

She didn't look away when he glanced at her. Raised an eyebrow.

His mouth tightened. "That's where the misunderstanding came in." He swallowed. "The sheriff ordered me to get out of my car. I didn't know how icy it was, and at one point I kind of slipped and fell into him. Sheriff Hueston thought I was trying to escape or something and arrested me for assault."

"You were arrested for assaulting Kyle Hueston?" She shook her head. "I've heard the guy is a total softie."

"He didn't seem like a softie when he wrestled me to the ground. But it *was* a misunderstanding. I swear. There was an icy patch."

Ella put her hand up to stop him. "I don't know why, but I believe you. Plus, I know something about being misunderstood." After all, her own court date was due to a big misunderstanding too.

Her words settled between them as he slowed, coming into the town limits.

"Ella, I really am sorry about how things played out the other night."

His tone wheedled inside, a sincerity to it. "Okay. I'm listening."

"I didn't mean to lie to you in the elevator. I don't even really know why I did it. It was nice to be out of the spotlight for a few minutes. Then when you came out saying what a horrible person Adrian was, I kind of froze."

Ella sighed. She *had* been a little hard on the Adrian she didn't really know. "I should apologize for that—even though I didn't know it was you. I guess I was a little harsh."

"A *little* harsh?" He glanced at her, a hint of a smile on his mouth. "I believe your words were *irresponsible playboy*."

She winced. Oops. "Yeah…"

"Don't worry about it. Truly. The look on your face is enough of an apology." Adrian laughed. "How about a truce?"

"All right. Truce." She paused. "But I still don't agree with your plan to build a water park in Deep Haven. It's dangerous and I intend to talk you out of it." And it occurred to her that she would have plenty of time now that he was stuck in town doing community service.

He said nothing.

And in the silence, the words just bubbled out. "How do you know Sophie?"

Oh, she wanted to cringe. But for some reason, she just had to know.

"I don't."

Ella raised an eyebrow.

"Okay, that didn't come out right. Yes, I obviously know her. But only because my cousin Athena set us up. She knew I needed a date for the gala so she set me up with Sophie."

"You two appeared pretty cozy for only knowing each other for one night." Oh, stop. So what, they went out. He could date whomever he wanted.

He glanced at her, and this time his eyebrow went up.

"Not that I care."

He suppressed a smile. "She isn't my type. I don't plan on seeing her again."

They pulled up to the courthouse and parked. Adrian checked the clock in the dash. "Looks like we made it with a few minutes to spare."

Adrian followed her into the courthouse, and she found the office. The community service officer stood inside handing out assignments to the small group of wrong-doers congregated in the room. Ella and Adrian checked in.

It felt strange to once again be in trouble alongside him like in the elevator. As if they were, weirdly, in this together.

The officer turned to Ella, then Adrian. "You two are scheduled to work on the highway crew. There's a van parked at the side door. They'll give you more instructions on the way."

"We're working *together?*" Ella leaned over to look at the list, but the officer pulled it out of sight.

"On the work crew, yes. Everyone coming in today is on either road cleanup or on the park crew. You'd better hurry. Carol doesn't like stragglers."

Ella and Adrian made their way to the crew van where Carol, a heavyset woman with short dark hair and the demeanor of a prison guard, assigned them yellow highway-crew jackets.

Perfect. Now she looked like a criminal, as well as felt like one. Adrian didn't seem any happier about his attire.

And frankly, the yellow jacket seemed a little silly on him.

They piled in, and she sat next to a younger woman with long stringy brown hair wearing such a surly expression that Ella almost wished she'd taken the space next to Adrian. Almost.

The van pulled out, taking the chain gang to the cleanup spot.

A short distance outside of town, the van parked alongside a barren, muddy stretch of highway, and the group piled out. They assembled in a loose formation around Carol. She also wore a yellow vest over her canvas jacket, and a stocking cap and boots.

"My name is Officer Carol Lang. We'll be cleaning this half mile of highway on each side. This isn't a PTA meeting, a coffee break, or a stroll in the beautiful north. I expect you to work. No shirking or you will get written up. I'll be watching."

Ella caught Adrian looking at her. He widened his eyes and mouthed the word *shirking*. Oh brother. Did he think this was funny?

"I'm authorizing each of you to use one of these." The leader held up a pole with a grabber claw fixed on its end. "If you break this deluxe trash picker, you will be fined. These are not toys."

Adrian had moved closer. "Cue the soundtrack from *O Brother, Where Art Thou?*," he whispered out the side of his mouth.

"Shh!" she hissed and hid a rebellious smile. "I'm trying to pay attention."

"Prepping for the pop quiz?"

"Maybe." She couldn't afford to get written up or time added to her sentence. Not with her pocket cash dwindling.

The leader handed out a trash grabber to each of them. "You will be paired up, two per garbage bag. When your bag is full, bring it back to the van and you will be issued a new bag."

Adrian grabbed a bag. He gave a slight bow, bending at the waist. "Will you be my bag buddy?"

She rolled her eyes.

Armed with a trash picker each, the two walked a short distance from the van.

The road was edged with a hump of blackened snow, the ditch muddy and soft. Debris of all kinds was wedged into the snow or lay trampled in the mud. She picked up a coffee cup and dropped it in the bag Adrian held.

"How does someone lose one boot?" she asked, spotting a man's Sorel boot a few feet into the ditch. She hiked down and tried to use her grabber to pry it out of the muck.

"Probably took it off with his one glove," Adrian said, holding up a dirty, torn glove with one finger missing.

She slipped, the boot breaking free, and nearly fell.

"You okay?" Adrian asked.

She gave him a narrow-eyed glare.

"Maybe you need another hand?" He held out the glove on the end of his grabber.

"Funny." Ella dropped the boot into the bag. "Listen, I don't want to get in trouble for goofing off."

"Aye, aye," Adrian said, mock saluting with the glove.

She hid another smile. Oh, he was hard to stay mad at.

The bright morning sunshine poured over them like a soothing blanket, glinting off the patches of snow along the road. Through the trees, she caught glimpses of Lake Superior, its waves alternating azure and iron gray.

Ella stole a glance at Adrian. In his designer hip-length jacket, dark jeans, and Italian leather shoes, he was the best-dressed trash picker she'd ever seen. His dark hair ruffled in the wind. If it got much longer he'd need to pull it back with an elastic to keep it out of his face. The best-looking chain gangster she'd ever met.

Suddenly she realized he was watching her watch him. Her face heated as she went back to picking up a candy wrapper, then an empty water bottle.

"These grabber things are too much fun," Adrian said, as if trying to ease her embarrassment. He held out their garbage bag, which he'd managed to snag with the pincher. "Got trash?"

She tossed in a soda can and then a plastic grocery bag. "Do people just not care about littering?"

"Maybe they don't think about it," he said, adding a Styrofoam container. "Or they think it doesn't matter."

They worked in silence for a while.

"You're pretty good at this," Adrian said.

She risked a look at him. He was no longer staring at her. "If there's one thing I know, it's cleaning."

"Right, the Princess of Clean. I remember."

"Please, don't remind me."

He shrugged. "Okay, how about a different topic. Where did you go to school?"

"High school or college?"

"High school."

"My dad's company had a cleaning contract with St. Peter's Academy in Minneapolis so I got a scholarship there."

"That's a great school. I think we played them in football a few times."

Of course he did. Was probably the team captain. "The education was great. But when the girls found out that I was the daughter of the King of Clean, I earned myself the nickname Princess Toilet Scrubber. It got worse when they discovered I was on scholarship. That was the end of any friends I made there."

"I'm sorry. Kids can be so cruel."

"Being lonely was great for my grades. I studied hard and took advantage of the advanced curriculum. How about you?"

"I went to Kellogg Prep."

She could have guessed that. "I'll bet you were pretty popular." He had prom king written all over him.

"I was until junior year when I tried out for the football team. I made it on the squad, but for some reason everyone started ignoring me. I thought they didn't like me, but then I found out that my dad had made a huge donation to the school during the team tryouts. I guess they all figured that's why I made the team. I'll never really know if I was good enough or if it was my dad's influence that got me on the team."

Huh. She'd assumed someone with his looks and money wouldn't have any trouble making friends. She picked up a fast-food wrapper and put it in the bag.

"I fit in by being funny. If you're making people laugh, they want to keep you around." Adrian added an empty pop bottle to their bulging garbage bag. "How about college?"

"The good old University of Minnesota. Majored in biology and environmental science. I was almost finished when my dad passed away. How about you?"

"MIT. Studied architecture and design with a minor in engineering. Turns out there's not really a school for water park building."

MIT. Of course that's where he would go.

The van drove up beside them, and she glanced over to see Carol looking at them. Ella offered a tight smile and held up her grabber, a piece of newspaper on the end.

Carol kept driving.

Adrian shifted the bag to his other hand. "So, you never graduated?"

"Couldn't afford it. Dad was broke. I hadn't fully realized that we had basically lived paycheck to paycheck for my whole life." She put the paper into the bag. Stared out at the expanse of water, the sunshine, the greenery. "There were times we'd live in such beautiful homes and condos. I found out later they were empty properties my dad had been hired to clean. I think we need a new bag."

Adrian closed up their bag and they headed down to where Carol had parked the van. "That's a lot to work through, your dad dying and then figuring out the mess he left behind."

"Yeah, it's been a long couple of years."

"I'm sorry. That must be rough."

"My dad was all smoke and mirrors. I didn't know it as a kid, but I couldn't trust him at all. The only house he owned was in Minnetonka. He bought it after he landed a big cleaning contract. I loved that house. It looked like something a movie family would live in. There was even a pool in the backyard."

She picked up a potato chip bag and carried it along toward the van.

Carol handed Adrian a new bag, cast a look at Ella, then smiled up at Adrian. "Let me know if she's bothering you."

Seriously?

Adrian said nothing and walked back to her. "Stop bothering me." But he smiled, winked.

"Maybe I should leave you two alone," Ella said, grinning back. "I hate to get in the middle of true love."

That swept the smile off his face. He picked up what looked like the pieces to a car's rear taillight. "I used to waterski on Lake Minnetonka. Which house was it?"

"A rambler on St. Albans Bay." And maybe it wasn't a big house, not to his standards, but she'd loved it, until... "When I turned thirteen I had all my friends over for a pool party. While we were eating pizza, the cops came to evict us."

He had stilled, and she didn't look at him, her throat inexplicably tightening. What was it about Adrian that made her dig into her secrets and spill them out?

"That's terrible."

"One of the worst days of my life, actually. That was when I learned that life can turn on you and you always have to be prepared."

She knew it sounded jaded, but really, maybe it was a lesson he could learn too, out here picking up trash with her.

"I'm really sorry, Ella."

"It gets worse. One of my dad's associates told me at his funeral that Dad had defaulted on his loan and had basically been squatting in the Minnetonka house until they forcibly threw us out. My dad was always a dreamer and a big talker. After my mom died, he didn't have anyone to keep his feet on the ground. She was his biggest cheerleader, but she also watched his back. I wish I had someone like that, someone to be my safe place. But since I don't, I have to take care of myself. Try to be prepared."

Beside her, Adrian had stopped walking. He was looking past her, down the road. She followed his gaze.

Both sides were littered with trash for half a mile.

"At least we know what we're getting into," she said.

He considered her a long moment, then nodded. "Yep." Then he went back to picking up trash.

And she had the strangest feeling that she might survive her walk on the wrong side of the law.

Things could be worse.

So what that he was wearing a garish yellow jacket, the word Convict practically written on the back. Or that his Italian leather shoes—the only shoes he'd stupidly packed—might be wrecked. Or that the chill in the air had found its way down the back of his wool jacket.

Or that he was probably missing a half dozen calls from his father.

He'd almost rather be here, picking up trash with Ella, the Princess of Clean, who lived up to her name by rooting out every errant piece of litter along their little stretch of highway.

Her father would be proud—except he suspected that wasn't a compliment she'd want to hear, not after her brutal story.

Costas Vassos might be a hard-edged tyrant of a father, but at least Adrian had never been saddled with his father's mistakes.

No wonder she worked so hard to start her own business. She was digging herself out of a financial grave. And Adrian had messed up her chance to pitch to his father.

He was putting that together as she talked, seeing through

her words to a woman who was both a hard worker and a dreamer.

If it were possible, he liked her even more than he had in the elevator.

Shoot. If only he hadn't blown it so badly. Even if she had forgiven him, she didn't seem like the kind to turn around and trust him again. Not with all of her scars.

So, yes, he knew what he was getting into. And he was ready for the long, littered road ahead.

In fact, he didn't hate being a prisoner if he could serve his sentence out in the sunshine with Ella.

She worked ten feet away from him, down in the ditch, digging out what looked like the rubber from a tire. She'd put down her grabber and was digging at it, working it out of the dirt.

"Hold on, Ella, I'm on my way—"

Her scream broke the air. She stumbled back, then fled up the ditch and stood behind him freaking out.

"What?" He realized he'd lifted his grabber like a man at bat.

She stood frozen in place, wide eyed, her hand over her mouth.

"What is it?" She didn't look hurt.

She pointed down to the tire in the weeds. "Snake."

He squinted at the tire. There—as if blended into it, a fat, dark racer snake. All three feet of it lay curled on the hot rubber, as if sunning.

The snake lazily lifted its head, tongue flicking from its mouth.

Oh boy. He wasn't afraid of snakes, exactly, but he did have a healthy dislike of anything that slithered.

"Be careful!"

"I don't think it's poisonous," he said, but what did he know about snakes, except for a once-a-year visit to the snake barn at the Minnesota State Fair? "Maybe we just leave it?"

"But that tire is just going to sit there and rot and contaminate the soil and—"

"Okay, okay." He should have known that would be her answer. As smoothly as possible, Adrian reached out with the grabber. The snake turned his beady eyes at the movement, and Adrian froze.

"Don't move," Ella said.

"Thanks for that."

When the snake seemed uninterested again, he took a step forward, and then another.

He took it back. He *hated* snakes. Taking a deep breath, Adrian reached out again with his tool, then lunged forward for the last foot and closed the grabber end around the snake's middle.

The fat body squirmed and he almost lost his grip.

Ella gave another shriek.

Yeah, him too. But he ran toward the woods and whipped the snake as far as he could. The snake flew end over end until finally crashing into the trees far beyond them.

Ella stood on the side of the road, watching, her face pale.

"You okay?"

She nodded. And he had the craziest, probably wrong, urge to put his arms around her.

"You know what sounds great right now? A sauna. I always take a sauna after defeating wild animals. I spotted one at the Evergreen Resort. Would you be up for taking a sauna with me after we're finished up for the day?"

She opened her mouth. Closed it. Then, "I have an appointment, but after that I'm interested."

Right then Carol pulled up in her van. "Shift is over," she said through the open window.

He got into the van and Ella slid in beside him this time.

So, there it was. Finally he'd done something right.

They turned in their equipment, the little yellow jackets, and he offered her a ride back to the Evergreen Resort.

Oddly, she said very little. And when she got out of the Porsche, she headed up the path to her cabin with just a quiet *thank you.* He didn't even have a chance to offer to jump her car. Huh.

He liked the Evergreen Resort. The cabins were small—his cabin had two tiny bedrooms with a quaint kitchen and a main room with a gas fireplace that he'd left burning when he left. The entire place looked out over a pristine lake. A row of evergreens planted along the edge of the property created a sense of seclusion, and the piney scent in the air suggested springtime and escape.

The resort boss was standing on the steps to the main lodge. A big man, dark hair, burly shoulders, the kind of guy that belonged in the north woods. No Italian leather shoes for him, and Adrian felt silly walking up to him in his city clothes.

"Darek, right?" Adrian said, holding out his hand.

Darek shook his hand. "Been out hiking?" He indicated Adrian's muddy wingtips and dark pants.

"Volunteer work," Adrian said. "Unexpected."

Darek raised an eyebrow but said nothing. He glanced at Ella, now entering her cabin. "You two together?"

Oh, he wanted to nod, but, "No. I just gave her a ride. We're sort of..." Aw. "Okay, I got picked up for speeding and have to do some community service for a couple weeks."

"Ah," Darek said. "You're the one."

Adrian raised an eyebrow.

"My wife talked about a guy who got in a tussle with Kyle—"

"It was not a tussle. I slipped—aw, it doesn't matter." Adrian shoved his hands into his pockets, needing that sauna badly, with the chill deep in his core. "I'd call it a misunderstanding."

"You're overdressed for your misunderstanding," Darek said.

"If you want, we have some extra clothes we often lend out. Boots, coats, hats…work pants."

Adrian must have worn relief because Darek grinned.

"Check in the closet across the hall from the office."

If he was going to live here for the next two weeks and possibly longer, he'd definitely need to dress the part. As long as he could still drive the Porsche.

CHAPTER 7

*A*t this rate, she'd never climb out of her financial hole. Ella had cleaned up after community service, gotten Darek to help jump-start her car, and made it to the bank two minutes before her appointment. Her quick face wash and hair combing had done little to rinse the morning out of her mind. But she couldn't think about that now. Not while trying to get a handle on her finances.

And now she waited as Mark Bammer, the bank manager, hunted and pecked his way across his computer keyboard. The interior of the bank oozed money, from the heavy cherry wood furniture to the pastoral paintings on the wall. The place reminded her of a tour of a lumber baron's parlor she'd once taken back in Minneapolis. The light filtering in through the windows did little to add warmth or charm.

Or maybe it was her own sense of poverty. Whatever it was, she really just wanted to get up and run from the bank. But she had nowhere else to go, really.

She couldn't help but think she was walking right back into her father's mistakes.

"Okay, as we discussed yesterday, we have limited options, Miss Bradley. Part of the problem is that we usually need at least a year of history banking with us before we offer loans. But we could offer you five thousand dollars, at thirteen percent interest, payable over five years." He showed her the figures on his computer.

"That's over two thousand dollars of interest!"

He made a face. "Sorry. That's where your numbers land."

Probably she should be grateful for any loan, but really... "This isn't my fault. Someone stole my identity, and I'm waiting on the insurance to repay it."

"I don't think there is much else we can do for you." Mark folded his hands on the desk. "I'm sorry."

"You're...sorry? That's it?"

"I'm not sure what else we can offer."

"How about my money back? In the *supposedly* secure bank I put it in!" Oh, she didn't mean to raise her voice, but—

"Ella, what are you doing here?"

She turned and, sure enough, Adrian stood behind her, his hair slicked back, damp and lightly tousled. "This is the appointment I mentioned."

Mark held his hand out to Adrian. The two men shook. "I'm just finishing up here, Mr. Vassos. I'll be with you in a moment. Please, have a seat." Mark pointed to the dark wooden chairs arranged around a low table a short distance from his desk. "I'm so sorry, ma'am, but until the identity investigation is completed, this is the best we can do."

"Really? Thirteen percent?" Oops, that echoed louder than she had intended. But still. "That's highway robbery!"

"Is there some way I can help here?" Adrian had re-materialized next to her.

No. But yes, it would be nice to have someone on her side. "Probably not. I need a loan, but the rates are crazy high. I don't have any money until the identify fraud investigation is completed—"

"I'll loan you money, Ella."

Uh, no. The last thing she needed was Adrian offering to bail her out, like he might be her knight in shining armor. And maybe he saw her answer on her face, because he turned to Mark and said, "What can we do to speed up the investigation?"

"I…it's outsourced. We don't have those kinds of resources here."

"Fraud and internet security resources?"

"That's right."

Adrian reached into his back pocket and pulled out his wallet. "Call my office. We have our own internet security department. Maybe they can help speed this along."

Mark took his card. "Okay, we'll see what we can do."

"In the meantime, I'm happy to co-sign a short-term loan for her. I'm sure we can work on that interest rate, right?"

"No, Adrian. I can wait until the insurance kicks in."

He considered her. Looked at Mark Bammer. Raised an eyebrow.

"I'll light a fire under the investigators. And let me see if I can rework that interest rate."

"Okay. In the meantime, let's get Ella set up with a new account so they can't keep stealing her money."

Mark nodded. A few minutes later, she was signing for a new account. "And the loan."

"It needs to go to underwriting. It'll be a week, for sure, maybe ten days"

Ramen noodles it was. "Fine."

Adrian stood. "Ella, I'll walk you out. I'll be back in a minute for my appointment, Mark."

They walked in silence for a beat. Adrian paused outside the bank door. "Are we still on for the sauna?"

"I'm hot enough, maybe."

He smiled.

"Yes. Fine. And thanks, by the way."

"Of course. Why have a big money-grubbing company if you can't put it to good use?"

Ella laughed. "How do you know Mark anyway?" She stepped off the curb and walked toward her car.

"I met him briefly when I came through on a scouting mission for the Westerman project."

She stiffened at the reminder.

He walked next to her, his arm brushing hers. A warmth ran up her shoulder, crossed her chest, and settled somewhere near her traitorous heart. Adrian Vassos was turning out to be someone very different than she expected.

Stopping at her pink VW, Ella looked fully at Adrian. The wind ruffled his already unruly hair. He hadn't grabbed his jacket on the way out and now stood in a navy Henley, shoulders hunched against the breeze.

"I won't keep you. I'll see you back at Evergreen."

He raised his hand in farewell as she slipped into the car. This time the VW roared to life on the first try. If only everything in her life would be that easy.

Adrian watched Ella pull away from the curb then walked back into the bank. After seeing the limited resources of the bank, he was unsure if he still wanted to do business here, but he was left with little choice. Better to bank in the small town where they did business.

He ran a hand through his still-damp hair. Showering off the grime from the morning work had been invigorating. He'd managed to get most of the dirt off his shoes too. Tomorrow he would definitely need to take Darek up on the offer of work boots. His thoughts drifted back to Ella. The look of gratitude in her eyes, her blonde hair lifting in the breeze. *Focus, man.*

"Are you ready, Mr. Vassos?" Mark Bammer's voice boomed through the lobby.

"Let's get to it, Mr. Bammer." Adrian took his chair, moving his jacket over to the one Ella had sat in.

"Oh, please. Call me Mark. I think we're going to have a good working relationship. I'm always more comfortable with first names. I understand you hope to use our bank for the construction loans you will need for the Westerman project." Mark laced his hands together and leaned back in his chair.

"Yes, I'd like to use as many local companies as possible, including your bank. I want this project to benefit the whole town." Adrian crossed his legs and leaned back as well, mirroring the banker.

"I assume you have the required permits and what not?"

"I'm working on it. I have a meeting scheduled with the planning commission next week."

"I'm sure a company like yours will have no problem getting the necessary paperwork to get started. Basically it's just a money game at this point. Pay for the permits, get the work done." Mark brushed the air with one hand as though waving a magic wand.

Adrian straightened. "Yes. I'm hopeful the town will see the wisdom of what we're trying to do. We hope to not only provide a place where families can have a good time but also provide Deep Haven with a new income stream."

"You don't have to convince me. I'm already sold on the deal. Anything that makes money will be good for Deep Haven."

Adrian didn't know if he would put it that way exactly...but Mark was still talking.

"Let me know if you need any arm twisting on getting the

permits from that planning commission. They can be stubborn sometimes about new things. They worry too much, if you ask me."

Adrian had zero intention of asking him, but it didn't really seem to matter as the banker continued.

"As for me, I like to see new things in town. New things mean more opportunities. Communities that aren't embracing progress tend to stagnate and die."

Adrian found himself defending a town he didn't even live in. "I think Deep Haven is charming. That's part of what drew me here. I'd hate to see that uniqueness destroyed."

"Oh sure, it's charming. It's just also stuck in the past. Something new and exciting like your water park is just what this town needs to shake it up." Mark suddenly stopped his tirade and began tapping at his computer. "Now, I understand you've had some trouble with the local law enforcement. I'm sure that will be no problem. Nothing a little money here and there can't smooth over."

The abrupt change in topic caught Adrian off guard. Sheesh, news did travel fast in this town. Also... "I'm actually doing community service." The hours spent picking up trash shone nobler than before.

"Sure. Sure." Mark didn't look up from the computer screen. "Like I said, it shouldn't be a problem. Getting into an altercation with an officer should have no bearing on your loan approval."

"I wasn't... It wasn't..." But, never mind. No one was ever going to believe him. *I believe you. I know something about being misunderstood.* Ella's voice in his head again.

Mark's printer spat out a few papers. He pulled them off, glanced over them, and handed them to Adrian. "I'll need you to fill these out. Pretty standard stuff. Viability of the company, that sort of thing. We'll look at any major losses in the last five years. I'm sure it's no big deal."

Adrian's heart rate ratcheted up a notch. Major losses. He hoped total failures didn't count. "Okay. I'll take care of these immediately."

Maybe it would take more than Bear Creek's reputation to convince Deep Haven of the value of his project. Adrian would need to show them he was worth it.

He made his way to his cabin, found the place warm, and was working off his shoes when his phone buzzed. He'd missed a call and had a voicemail waiting for him. It must have been the spotty reception along the highway. He clicked into the voicemail and his father's voice came out of the speaker.

"Adrian, I'd like a status report. How are you getting on up there? Need me to grease a few wheels? Let me know how it's going. Call me back."

Adrian debated calling him back right then just to get it over with, but a pretty girl was waiting in the sauna. Or so he hoped.

He threw on a pair of athletic shorts and a T-shirt, deciding against wearing a jacket for the short jog. Grabbing a towel, Adrian headed out to the path toward the sauna. He left his phone, and thoughts of his dad, in the cabin.

The sauna was a ten-man building located at the end of a tiny trail behind the resort. Smoke spiraled from the chimney. He loved going to the sauna after workouts and sometimes utilized his father's home sauna. It was a good way to work out the stress of the day.

Stress and snakes and hopefully whatever was eating at Ella.

As he drew nearer, he heard pounding. He searched for Darek, but the man was nowhere in sight.

"Help!"

The voice came from inside the building. He picked up his pace.

A log from the pile near the sauna had fallen in front of the door, effectively blocking it closed. He'd nearly reached the door when suddenly it heaved open.

Steam billowed out as Ella stumbled into the cool night. She stood in the open air, wearing shorts and a blue T-shirt, gulping in breaths, covered in sweat.

"Are you okay?"

She stared at him, her eyes wide, then turned away, covering her face. Sweat soaked the back of her shirt, ran down her neck, her legs reddened from the heat.

"You could have died."

And that wasn't helping, clearly, because she started sobbing.

"Hey…" He stood there, not sure what to do. "Um…" Adrian was reaching out for her—sort of on instinct—when she looked at him.

He dropped his hand.

"Sorry. I know I'm over-reacting. It's just been a terrible week and…" She exhaled hard. "All I could think of when I was trapped in there was that I was going to die."

"It's okay. I get it."

She shivered then, the T-shirt and athletic shorts no match for the March air.

"Maybe this is the wrong thing to say, but it's cold out here. Should we move inside the sauna? I'll prop the door open."

She looked dubious.

He stuck the offending log into the doorway, making sure the door of the sauna didn't shut tightly. "C'mon. No one dies on my watch."

She eyed the door, but followed him inside. "It *is* warm in here."

He offered her his towel to wipe her face and she slid in beside him on the bench.

After a moment… "Remember how I told you about my mother dying?"

"The chlorine spill, right?"

"Yes. She was trapped in a tiny room and couldn't breathe. When I tried the door and it was stuck, I realized that was probably how my mom felt. Terrified in a small space and finding it harder to draw a deep breath."

Her closeness, and her story, stirred a desire in him. *No, no, Adrian.* She needed a friend, not a guy trying to wheedle his way into her heart.

"Well, you managed to get yourself out of that mess, but I wouldn't have let you turn into a smoked fish."

"That's gross."

He laughed.

"But yes, that would have been the third time you've had to save me today. I'm not normally this helpless, I assure you."

He nudged her shoulder with his. "I think you mean the fourth time."

"What?"

"I've saved you three times today already. This would have been a fourth."

She frowned. "The snake, the bank. That's two."

"Don't forget my white-knight act when your car didn't start and I gave you a ride to the courthouse. That makes three." Oh, she was fun to tease. The way her face lit up at the challenge did something funny to his heart.

"I had that situation perfectly under control, thank you very much." Good. The trauma of being stuck in the sauna was already wearing off.

"I don't know, your car was pretty dead out there."

"Be kind to Ariel. She's gotten me out of many scrapes."

He laughed. "Ariel?"

"Don't laugh. I had a *Little Mermaid* phase in high school. I named my car after Ariel because she's the same color as Ariel's dress in the movie."

And he had nothing for that. Except, "You must really love that car."

"I do. My dad bought her for me when I turned sixteen. We had driven past a used car dealership and I saw it on the lot. I begged him to get it for me and he bought it on the spot. That might be the only thing he ever bought me that he actually paid for. He must have had a run of luck at the casino the night before." She nudged his shoulder this time. "Your car's not so bad either. I've always loved the Porsche 911."

Sure, they could talk about cars. It was a safe topic. Because right now, sitting in a sauna with a pretty girl, he needed to concentrate on something pragmatic. Maybe they could move on to baseball next. Go Twins.

"Yeah, she's a beauty all right. Graduation gift. Of course, Alex thought he deserved the car, but he didn't need one. Dad had already given him a BMW. To this day he hasn't stopped needling me about it. I think he's mostly jealous that I got the fun car and he has the sensible one."

"Why doesn't he just sell it and get something he wants?" Ella draped the towel around her neck. Leaned back against the caramel-colored wood lining the walls.

"Maybe he thinks Dad wouldn't approve."

They grew silent, soaking in the warmth. A wisp of cool air tempered the heat, however.

Ella sat forward, turned toward him. "Okay, I have to know. Why does your car smell like a fish died in it every time you turn on the heat?"

"Oh, sure, go for the jugular."

"I'm just wondering if that article in the tabloids was right about you driving drunk into the lake."

What—? Ouch. Did she really believe that about him?

"Well, the lake part is true. But I swear I wasn't drunk."

She shot him a skeptical look. "You just drove into the lake for fun? In the middle of November? C'mon—any good

Minnesotan knows the ice isn't ready until January. Even for a Porsche."

He rubbed a hand along the back of his neck. "I can't decide if the story is more embarrassing than that, or less."

"Why don't you let me decide, Andretti?"

"The truth is, I had a big fight with my dad about whether I could take on the Westerman project. I wasn't really paying attention to where I was going, kind of driving aimlessly, you know?"

She nodded and he continued. "I turned down one road that ended strangely. It was basically in the lake. It wasn't marked, but I think it must have been a boat launch. You couldn't tell the road ended in the water in the dark. By the time I realized what was happening, it was too late. The front end of my car was submerged."

And now, if he wasn't already red-faced from the sauna...

"You obviously didn't drown, so what happened?"

"A friend of mine from Kellogg, Boone Buckam, happened to drive past and spotted my taillights sticking up out of the water. He pulled me out with his pickup."

"Your friend had good timing."

"Yeah, God's timing, I think." And he didn't know why that slipped out, more of a reflex than actual thought. But, maybe... Huh.

They fell silent.

"I can nearly hear you thinking something," he said.

She gave a tiny amused laugh, and it spiraled straight to his bones. But it reminded him of their time in the elevator. Even as Roger, that anonymous hour or so was the most real he'd been in a long time. Maybe ever.

He'd never wanted to leave.

"Adrian, why are you even here, in Deep Haven? Couldn't you get the paperwork for the water park done over the phone?"

"I wanted to meet the people, get a feel for Deep Haven."

"There must be more to it than that. You'd already picked your spot, the Westerman Hotel."

"I really want to see this project through. To show my dad I can do it on my own."

She shifted the towel. Crossed her long, slim legs in front of her. "So, you wanted to get the lay of the land, and you wanted to prove yourself. I still don't see why you needed to come up here."

"Truthfully?" Was it getting warmer in here? He should have propped the door all the way open.

"Yes, of course, I want the truth."

He was afraid of that. Hopefully he wouldn't scare her off. "I'm not sure I realized it at first, but it was partly because I was hoping to run into you."

She sat up straight. "Me? Why would you care anything about me?"

"I felt bad about what happened. You never got to pitch your idea to my dad, and...well, I really wanted to hear it."

"Really?"

"Yes, really. My entire life I've been seen as the poster boy for our company. But my father doesn't take me seriously. I'm not the dealmaker. And definitely not the guy in charge of new projects. In the elevator, I was just Roger. Just a guy going to a party. You took me seriously." He sighed. "I'm sorry again, by the way."

She leaned forward, bracing her hands on the bench, her eyes down. "I forgive you. I mean, who knew you'd be such a likable guy?" She turned her eyes to his again and smiled. Not a half smile either. A full hundred-watt smile that lit her eyes like bright sunshine.

Whoa. He was in trouble.

"Hey, do you know if the Christiansens have a laundry facility up here?" she asked. "There isn't a washer in my unit."

Laundry. Yes, they should talk about laundry while he figured out how to breathe. "Not that I've spotted. Why?"

"I only have these clothes and the clothes I wore earlier today. I need to get them washed. They smell like roadkill."

"Don't you have other clothes?"

"I was lucky to even have these in a bag in my trunk. I wasn't allowed back into my house after being arrested, and they won't let me in to get my things until I pay last month's rent. So I'm kinda stuck for now."

"What do you mean, they wouldn't let you in?"

"My landlord claimed my rent check bounced and changed the lock. When I broke in, he had me arrested. My lawyer said I have to pay the fines before I can get any of my things."

Adrian could admit to a crazy urge to track the guy down and—

"Anyway, I could really use a laundromat. I could also really use some soap supplies, but that's not happening anytime soon."

"Why not? Can't you just pick up some more? If you're short on cash, maybe I could pick them up for you."

"That's sweet of you to offer. But I couldn't accept it. Besides, they don't have the right kind of organic oil here in town. I usually special order it. I'll just have to stretch what I have somehow. And find a laundromat."

"I have a better idea. Why don't we get some of your own clothes back?" A plan started coalescing in his mind.

"What are you talking about?"

"I'm talking about a little nighttime justice."

She gave him a look. "Nighttime justice? Overdramatic much?"

"That's the pot calling the kettle black, but okay. Just taking back a few things that are rightfully yours. How are you at picking locks?"

He grinned at the understanding dawning in her eyes. "Better than you'd think."

Probably not. Because he had a feeling he'd underestimated his cohort in crime.

"If we're going to get in trouble, let's earn it." He held up his fist.

She bumped it.

Yes, this day could have been much, much worse.

CHAPTER 8

*T*his was crazy.

The entire thing was just…off the hook, and Ella was headed for big trouble—she knew it in her bones.

And it all started when Adrian held her after her embarrassing outburst about being momentarily trapped in the sauna.

She'd practically had a meltdown, just like she had in the elevator, and…

And he had simply caught her. Taken her in his arms, just like in the elevator.

Prince Charming to the rescue, again, and she had to stop thinking that way. Right now.

Because right now, Mr. Charming was also Adrian the Cat Burglar, and she was his accomplice.

Ella wondered how much community service she might do for the misdemeanor of rescuing her clothing and cleaning supplies.

Yes, it must have been those crazy vibes that made her agree to his crazy scheme. Which was why she now found herself, once again, picking the lock at her old house.

Behind her, Adrian claimed to be standing as a lookout. Clad in black jeans, his black wool jacket, and a black beanie, he certainly looked like someone out of *The Mod Squad*, the old TV show from the seventies.

Don't look at him.

Because every time she did, she wanted to laugh. And laughing would lead to getting caught.

Or worse, him smiling back at her, and then her foolish heart would start thinking of him again as Mr. Charming, and no, no, *no…*

Despite his coming to her aid at the bank and time spent talking in the sauna, they were still two very different people who wanted very different things in life and Deep Haven. She'd better remember that. She needed to keep things casual.

Just a fellow bandit.

"It won't be breaking, just entering, if you're any good with a lock pick." Misplaced logic perhaps, but Adrian's challenge lit an inferno under her.

Because it was *her stuff*. She wasn't actually *stealing*.

After asking her old neighbor, she'd found out Mr. Hansen hadn't actually rented out her apartment yet. Didn't surprise her he'd lied about having multiple renters lined up. What exactly had his little stunt gained him except an empty apartment?

Oh well. That just made it easier to get her stuff back.

Okay, maybe not *easy…*

Click. The doorknob gave under her hand and she swung the door open.

"C'mon, we're in." Her hissed words plumed out in a fog in the cold night air.

The tiny house was already beginning to smell musty from being shut up for the past couple of days. She didn't dare turn on any lights, so she used the flashlight on her cell phone to look around.

"We should take only the bare minimum. Wouldn't want anyone to suspect we've been here," she whispered.

"Just point me in the right direction." A light flashed on as Adrian turned on his own cell phone.

Ella retrieved a canvas grocery bag from the kitchenette and handed it to him. "Fill this with half the supplies in that box over there. I'll grab a few extra changes of clothes from the bedroom."

In the elevator, I was just Roger. Just a guy going to a party. You took me seriously. She'd liked Roger. Too much.

Too bad Adrian had shown up. Adrian and his plans to poison Deep Haven.

Overdramatic much? Her own words filtered back to her as she sifted through her clothes, choosing things at random, trying to make the piles look the same as before.

Maybe, but she should remember that the entire time she was flirting with Roger in the elevator, *Adrian* was lying to her. Truth was, it was hard to reconcile the Adrian Vassos she'd spent time with and the Adrian Vassos who featured heavily in the gossip sections of the paper.

Okay, if life with her dad had taught her anything, it was that someone's public persona could be very different than their private one, and in Adrian's case much of what was reported about him could conceivably be misconstrued. Just look at what happened to her. She was hardly a criminal...

Fine. If she had to do the time, she may as well do the crime.

Best to look at the situation based on cold hard facts. The facts added up to Adrian being a good guy. His apology was sincerely delivered, and he'd proven on the highway to be a good worker who didn't shy away from hard, dirty work. His broad shoulders and green eyes didn't hurt either. She shrugged off that last thought. Better to remain impartial while she figured out if she could really trust him or not.

She added extra socks and another pair of jeans to the duffel bag of clothing and walked back to the other room.

Just as she reached the kitchenette, Adrian appeared in the

dark and pulled her down behind the breakfast bar. What in the world?

"Shhh. Turn off your light." He crouched beside her, his breath light on her neck. "There's someone outside."

"Who do you think is out there?"

"Hopefully not your landlord, or worse, Sheriff Hoover."

"I think you mean Sheriff Hueston."

"Him either."

She bit back a laugh. *Oh, Ella, you're in such trouble!*

Adrian shifted until they were face-to-face. "Ella."

She leaned in to see him and hear his quiet words.

"This was a dumb idea. I don't want to get you arrested again."

"You don't need to apologize for anything. I decided to come here of my own free will. Besides, you were right. I need more of my own things and I can't afford to buy them right now."

A clatter on the porch startled her. She lost her crouched balance and fell into him.

"Now this feels familiar."

His voice rumbled right through her. Yes, it did. Oh, it did.

"Do you think someone is coming in?" They both held their breath for a heartbeat. Two.

"I think it was a cat."

Ella put her hands on his chest and looked up at him. His magnetic green eyes met hers.

And then, his gaze dropped down to her mouth.

"Ella?"

"Yes?"

"I'd really like to kiss you."

"Yes." What? No! But her mouth clearly didn't listen to her brain and frankly, the rest of her didn't either because she tipped her face toward his.

Adrian cupped his hands along Ella's jawline and leaned in. Pressed his lips to hers. Sweetly, softly. Very prince-like.

Yeah, well, she was no princess. Her hands gripped the front of his shirt and she deepened her kiss.

He caught on, and suddenly his arms were around her, his kiss turning serious. From flirty to something more.

Something that felt dangerously real.

Yes, she was in trouble.

The sound of "Walking on Sunshine" broke through the quiet in the cottage. Ella gasped and pulled away, scrambling to silence her phone. The light from her screen bit through the darkness, and she saw Colleen's name flashing back at her.

"Hey, Colleen," she answered with a whisper. "Sorry, I can't talk right now."

"But—"

Ella barely heard her friend's protest as she swiped off the call.

Adrian leaned in close, and Ella's thundering heart picked up speed. "I'm going to go check outside. Make sure no one is out there." He left and came back in a moment, his cheeks flushed from the cold. "Everything's clear. Just a cat."

"Good. I'm going to call Colleen back really quick—she'll probably worry if I don't. Then let's get out of here. I can't believe I let you talk me into this."

Adrian grinned and pretended to tip his beanie at her.

She hit the speed dial for Colleen, who answered on the first ring. "Sorry about that, Colleen."

"No, I'm sorry for the late call, but I just got off my shift. I hadn't heard from you since the other night, and I wanted to make sure everything was okay. That phone call ended a little weirdly."

Ella laughed, a short bark with no humor. "Well, I'm not sure about the 'okay.' 'Weirdly' kind of sums up everything about my life right now." She sat with her back to the kitchen counter and briefly filled Colleen in on the past few days. "So, now I'm living at the Evergreen Resort and trying to put my life back together."

"Oh, Ella. You really can't catch a break, can you?"

She stared at Adrian waiting patiently for her to finish her call. Huh. Maybe, finally, she had.

"What about Mr. Water Park Vassos?" Colleen asked. "Have you seen the prodigal son around town? Wasn't he supposed to come up there and do some stuff for the town's approval process?"

"Adrian?" Goodness, did her voice just squeak? Across from her, Adrian raised an eyebrow. "Um, yeah, I guess he's been around."

He grinned, something slow and languid and dangerous, and her entire body heated.

"I hope you can avoid him. I know how upset he made you. If you do see him, tell him he's a no good, tabloid happy, lying dirtbag from me."

Oh. Uh, "I...I don't think he's that bad. I think maybe he's just...misunderstood."

Across from her, he raised both his eyebrows. Then he winked. Oh boy.

The man was committing all sorts of crimes here. Thievery of her heart. Kidnapping of her common sense, and maybe even first-degree murder of her righteous anger.

"Okay, maybe I'm wrong about the tabloid happy part," Colleen said. "So, you're just going to drop the whole anti-water park thing? That doesn't sound like the passionate Ella Bradley that I know and love."

"No, I'm definitely still opposed to that. I'm just trying to figure out how best to work on that problem." She turned her back to Adrian. "I'll call you in a couple of days when things settle down."

"Okay. Be well, Ella."

Ella hung up the phone. Glanced at Adrian. He stood against the other side of the breakfast bar, arms folded.

"Misunderstood?"

"Colleen sure has some perfect timing." Ella's face heated.

"Not that bad, eh? I must be getting to you." Adrian waggled his eyebrows again.

"Would you stop doing that?" The heat in her cheeks traveled down her neck. "You look ridiculous." That wasn't the only word for how he looked. Standing there in the black jacket that showed off his broad shoulders, he also looked...dangerous. Dangerous to her heart anyway.

"What is this problem you mentioned?" He pushed off the countertop and picked up the bag of cleaning supplies. "Maybe I can help you figure it out. I'm actually good at business stuff. Contrary to popular belief and the ravings of online tabloids, I'm not just a pretty face."

"Haha!"

They made their way out of the cottage, and Ella carefully checked to make sure the lock held.

What if he were willing to hear her out? Invest in her company. But that might mean abandoning his proposal for his water park. And that didn't sound likely at all. "I just need to figure some things out on my own."

The clouds from earlier had cleared, leaving the night clear and cold. A million diamond stars winked at them from the sky.

"You can't get this view in the city, that's for sure." Adrian paused on the sidewalk a few steps from the car and gazed upward. "I don't think I've ever seen so many stars."

"Yeah, they're pretty amazing."

Adrian casually draped an arm around Ella and pulled her closer.

A light flashed at them. Held.

"Hey guys, what's going on?" Out of the blackness of the street corner came someone carrying a heavy-duty flashlight. Adrian grabbed a bottle of cleaner and held it in front of himself. What was he going to do? Protect her with vinegar and essential oils? Ella stifled a groan and stepped away from Adrian and toward the figure.

Besides, she recognized the voice. Sheriff Hueston. He was out of uniform, and it occurred to her that he might live nearby. He held some sort of shopping bag.

"Hello, Kyle."

Behind her Adrian took in a breath.

"Hello, Ella." He looked at the house, back at her. "Everything okay?"

Aw, he was probably doing the math. Breaking and entering her own residence, twice. Nice.

Kyle shined his light on the ground, enough to illuminate their faces. "I see you've met Adrian."

Adrian stepped forward. Lowered the cleaning bottle. "We're just out for a walk."

"Huh. Doing some cleaning as you stroll Deep Haven?" Kyle raised an eyebrow.

Oh, he was so onto them. And the crazy image of Adrian and Kyle suddenly throwing down right here on the sidewalk made her step up to Kyle. "I broke into my old place," she confessed.

"*We* broke in," Adrian said.

"Fine, *we* broke in. My bank account was drained by whoever stole my information, and I can't buy any clothes or cleaning supplies until that gets cleared up. Mr. Hansen is holding my possessions hostage because he thinks I won't pay him what I owe."

"Ella. So you thought, what, that you would just break the law *again?*"

Thankfully, she heard a twinge of sympathy.

"I'm sorry, I really am. I hoped it wouldn't be a big deal. I just wanted to grab a few things so I could fulfill my commitments to my clients." How was she supposed to pay back her debts if she couldn't work? Her clients hired her because of her own products, not just because they needed somebody to clean their places. They could get replacements in a hot minute if she couldn't do what she'd been hired to do.

"It's my fault—" Adrian started, but Ella waved him off.

"No, I'm the one who did the lock picking. I'm the one who made the decision to go through with the idea."

Adrian turned to her. "But we wouldn't have come here if I hadn't egged you on."

"I'm not a fourth grader. I know better."

"Guys, there's no need to fight about who is more guilty," Kyle broke in. "The way I see it, you are both culpable."

Perfect. Jail time would be the end of any respectability she had earned in this town.

She was cataloging the list of clients who would fire her and barely heard Kyle's next words.

"However, I didn't see you breaking and entering. I didn't actually *catch* you doing anything wrong. Since I'm not on duty, I'm inclined to give you a pass. It's your lucky night. I promised Emma I'd be right back with this medicine and 7Up. I'm not breaking a promise to my sick wife just to take you down to the station."

Did he just say... "Wait, what are you saying?"

"I'm saying so long as Ed Hansen doesn't complain about vandalism or anything amiss, there's no need to add to your community service hours."

"Seriously?"

But Adrian had stuck out his hand to Kyle. "You've done a good thing here, Hueston."

Kyle smiled, shook Adrian's hand. "Just Kyle." He turned to Ella. "By the way, my wife loves that smelly soap you made for her." The sheriff turned back the way he had come, jogged up a nearby front walk, and went inside.

Ella met Adrian's gaze. His eyes sparkled in the starlight.

"Did we just..."

"Yep. We just got caught...and freed. Like a couple of fish."

Ella started laughing and next to her, Adrian grinned.

"I thought we were in big trouble," he admitted.

"Me too. I thought you were going to fight him."

He lifted a shoulder, something sweet in his eyes. "Anything for you, Ella."

Oh, no, no...

But standing there, looking up at Adrian in the cold night, Ella knew the truth. She was in trouble.

Big trouble.

If these donuts did the trick, Adrian owed Lucy Brewster down at World's Best Donuts a bouquet of flowers. He whistled as he strode into the municipal building, his arms loaded with baked goods and his laptop bag across his chest. He'd picked up enough pastries for the group he was meeting with this afternoon. At least he hoped he'd bought enough. Lucy had said there were usually four to seven people at the meeting. He figured a dozen of their finest glazed raised donuts should be plenty.

Along the hall hung a photo gallery of the town's officials. His gaze snagged on a picture of Sheriff Hueston, and for a moment he was right back outside Ella's old house last night, under the moonlight. He grinned as he thought about their evening. Getting in trouble had never been so much fun. He hoped Ella had gotten enough of her stuff.

Adrian dropped a donut off with the administrative assistant who, blushing, pointed him in the direction of the conference room. He entered the room she'd indicated and stopped short. The bland, off-white room held an oval table, several rolling chairs, and a small group of people deep in discussion.

"I guess I'm a little late." He checked his watch. "Is this the planning commission?"

A hulking man wearing a blue Deep Haven Fire Department shirt rose from the head of the table. Long brown hair with a dark beard, and he looked like he could snap a tree in half with his bare hands. "Not late at all. Come on in. We just had some other business to attend to, so we decided to meet early. I'm Peter Dahlquist. You must be Adrian?"

"Hi. Yes. Nice to meet you." Adrian set the donuts on the table and shook hands with the remaining members of the board. "I brought donuts."

An older woman who had introduced herself as Ingrid Christiansen reached for one. "I never pass up a donut."

"If we can't have your cookies, Ingrid, we'll have to settle for World's Best, I suppose." Nathan Decker helped himself.

"Ingrid Christiansen? Any relation to Darek up at Evergreen?"

"You might say so. He's my oldest son." Her eyes gentled. "My husband and I used to run the resort, but now Darek handles most of the business."

Adrian winked at her. "As a fellow resort owner, I can tell you he's doing a fine job. The property is well maintained, and my cabin is very comfortable."

"Thank you. It means a lot to me to hear that."

Peter spoke up. "Now, Adrian, why don't you tell us about these plans of yours."

Adrian set his computer up on the end of the table. "Let me show you my vision for the Westerman property." He took them through the PowerPoint presentation. "In this last graph you can see our projected numbers for revenue, including projected figures for income generated in taxes for Deep Haven. This project will be a boon to your community."

Peter sat back in his chair. Tented his fingers. "This all looks good on first review. What are you doing about labor and construction companies?"

"My plan is to use as much local labor as is feasible. Of

course, there are some specialty systems that need to be installed by an expert, but much of the construction can be done by companies in the area. My goal would be to use seventy-five percent, more if we can, of local companies."

Around the table, the others nodded.

"I think your plan is ambitious. I do like the idea of tearing down that old Westerman Hotel." Ingrid tapped her finger on the table. "That place is getting ready to fall down on its own. But how will this impact the environment?"

"If I get the go-ahead from you this afternoon, I'll be putting in a request for an environmental study. I can promise you that we won't move forward until we are sure that the beauty of the North Shore is preserved."

More nodding. He forged ahead. "I'm asking for your permission to begin the process of obtaining the necessary studies and permits. I will be submitting my full plans at your official meeting in a few weeks."

Nathan cleared his throat. "I don't know, Adrian. This all sounds good, but we like to keep things by the book."

"I can guarantee that's what I want too."

Nathan glanced at the others. "You have our permission to get that environmental study, but any further permissions will have to wait until our full meeting. It's only fair to warn you that they can move slowly on decisions like this."

Okay. This wasn't the end of the world. He just needed to get that environmental study. Work a few hours of community service. Oh, and convince the members of the town council that this water park was a great idea for Deep Haven.

Moving slowly meant more time to spend with Ella. And he didn't hate that idea. Not at all.

Soapmaking was part chemistry and part magic.

"I hope Evergreen doesn't mind me using their slow cooker to make this batch of soap." Ella had found the pot in the cupboard of her cabin. A good thing too, because bars of soap often took six weeks or more to cure. Cooking the soap this way sped that process up to overnight. She glanced over at Adrian studiously measuring out ingredients, an errant bit of hair falling into his eye.

They'd had separate community service assignments today, so she hadn't seen Adrian since their little B&E escapade the night before. She'd gotten home from the morning's assignments, had lunch, and then started pulling out some soap recipes and supplies. She'd been pleasantly surprised to hear Adrian's knock on the door.

"I thought I'd check in on my fellow cat burglar," he'd said as he leaned against the doorframe. The midafternoon sun glinted in his hair. He was back in his professional clothes. Looking like he'd just walked off the cover of GQ with his wool jacket, white button-down, and a pair of charcoal-colored dress slacks. Ella glanced down at her own torn jeans and Blue Ox long-sleeved T-shirt. There was a glob of coconut oil stuck near the hem of her shirt.

"You've caught me messing with our spoils." She gestured toward the kitchen. "I'm making a few batches of soap. I'll need them in the next few days for my jobs." If no one else canceled, that is.

"Oh. Good. I'll leave you to it then." He turned to go.

She had hesitated and then, "Wait." Her traitorous mouth had seemed to speak on its own. "You could stay and help, if you'd like." Why would he ever want to do that?

But his lips had turned up a fraction. "I'd like that."

Now, he had rolled up his sleeves and was hard at the task as though it was the most natural thing in the world to be doing.

She moved to his side. Gave the soap a stir. "We have to check it every half an hour until it's the right consistency."

"How do we know when that is?"

"We should be able to see the change."

"You might be able to see the change, but this just looks like oily soup to me."

"That's why I'm the cleaning lady and you're not." She went around him to the sink, accidentally brushing against his arm. "Oh. Sorry. This kitchen is pretty small for this project."

"I didn't mind." His cheeky look almost undid her.

"So, where did they have you for community service today?" A safe topic.

"I worked down at the Art Colony. They had a tree come down a while back and needed help getting it cleared away."

She stared at him.

"What?"

"You hauled away a tree?"

"Yes. Well, myself and some others. Carol was there. Too bad you missed out. Why are you still staring at me?"

"I'm just trying to picture you chopping up a tree in your Italian leather shoes."

"Oh, that. Darek loaned me some of his work boots. Some work pants too, actually. His brother Casper, down at Wild Harbor Trading Post, said he could hook me up with some that were my own size when I'm ready. You're still staring."

"Sorry, it's just that I think you know more people in this town after a few short days than I know after having lived here for six months."

"It's no big deal. I like meeting people." A beat passed. "What I don't like is speaking in front of large crowds of them. You know, if you keep staring like that, your face will freeze. That's what my grandma used to say anyway."

She couldn't help but laugh. "I can't believe there's something that Adrian Vassos isn't confident about. You seemed to have done just fine at the shareholders meeting the other night."

"All an act, believe me. I was terrified the whole time."

"Somehow that makes you just that much more human. You know what the secret to speaking in front of people is, right?"

"Picture them in their underwear?"

She felt her face flaming. "No. It's to share your heart with them. Talk about what you are passionate about and they won't seem so scary anymore."

"Thanks, that helps actually. I'll be sure to remember that when I'm in front of the town council in a few weeks."

"Unless I talk you out of the crazy water park scheme before then." She pointed her spoon at him.

He held up his hands in front of his chest in a surrender position. "That's not likely, but you're welcome to try."

She gave the contents of the slow cooker a stir. "This soap looks ready. I'll pour it into the molds. Then we can mix up some vinegar-based cleaning spray."

The soap flowed into the molds in thick ribbons. She took a spatula and smoothed the surface of each gloopy mess, tapping it a few times to release any bubbles. Now if only her financial woes could be smoothed over as easily.

CHAPTER 9

*T*hings were finally going his direction.

In the three days since the sauna, the break-in, and the kiss, Adrian could barely keep his mind on the tasks he needed to do for the water park approval process. He owed Athena an update. Waiting here in the car for Ella to come out of the donut shop with breakfast and coffee before their appointed community service seemed as good a time as any.

Before the phone call connected, he spotted Ella walking out of the store clutching a bag and two cups of coffee. Athena could wait.

He slid his phone in his shirt pocket then hopped out of the car to open Ella's door. The brown jacket they'd rescued from her house accented her blonde hair, and the wind wisped it around her pink-and-yellow-striped beanie.

"Thanks." She handed him his coffee. "Black, as ordered."

"Just what I'll need to face another morning of garbage duty." In the car the scent of coffee and sugary donuts warmed the air.

"Oh, come on. It's not that bad. At least you'll get to use the garbage grabber thingy again."

He waggled his eyebrows at her. "That's right! Think of all the things I can—"

"Just drive, Romeo."

A few minutes later, they pulled up in front of the courthouse. Weird. The van used by the highway cleanup crew wasn't anywhere in sight. Maybe they were later than he thought.

"We've got the two of you scheduled for trail cleanup today," the clerk informed them after checking her list. "Carol canceled." The clerk handed them a map with a trail circled in red. "We'll send you out to the Pincushion Trail. You can start at the trailhead and just clear away any small debris that has fallen. Pick up any trash. If there are big trees down, make a note of how far along the trail and we'll send someone out to take care of those. Come back here when you're finished and we'll record your hours."

"We can handle that." Picking up sticks was a job he could definitely do. Much better than trash duty. He glanced at Ella. "You know where this trail is, right?"

"Yep. You're in for a treat." Ella smiled up at him.

A day with Ella out in the woods, with the fresh air and sunshine? Yes, he was totally in.

Sheesh, he was turning into a regular Ranger Rick.

"Do you need some gloves? We could stop at the store on our way," she asked as they left the building.

"I've got some in my trunk, how about you?"

"I have some in my bag."

Of course she did. Still, he watched, dumbstruck, as she unearthed a worn pair of gardening gloves from the depths of her purse.

"All right, let's get going then."

Between the morning sunshine, the smell of coffee in his car, and the sweet taste of donuts lingering on his lips, he was a walking "Life is Good" T-shirt.

He drove into the small lot at the trailhead. Ella wasn't

kidding about the beauty of this area. Even the bare branches of the trees embracing the sky were beautiful. Getting out of the car, Adrian stretched as he looked around. Down below them he could make out glimpses of Deep Haven and Lake Superior beyond. The water shone, reflecting the cerulean sky. The air was heavy with the scent of pine and the breath of spring.

Ella came and stood next to him. "I love coming up here. This pristine wilderness reminds me why I got into science in the first place. It reminds me why I wish people were more careful with the products they use."

"It's hard to believe people wouldn't care about that after being in a place like this."

"I guess people just start taking things for granted."

"What's with the name? Pincushion?"

"This trail is named after the Pincushion Mountain. Most people don't think Minnesota when they think of mountains, but the peak elevation here is over 1,100 feet, so the area counts as a mountain." She stopped abruptly and put her hand over her mouth. "Sorry, I tend to spew useless trivia."

"I don't mind. I bet you even know the stats on how likely it is to get lost up here." He walked up to a sign that denoted the various trails that circled the so-called mountain.

"I don't know the exact number, but I do know that around two thousand people get lost on trails just like this each year."

Adrian tugged his gloves into place. "I don't know if that seems high or low."

"I know, right? There's been a lot of talk around Deep Haven lately about starting a Crisis Response Team for lost hikers and other emergencies. I guess they would really love to purchase a helicopter and everything, but no one has that kind of money around here."

They headed out on the longer trail, and he picked up a couple big branches and tossed them off the path. The snow was nearly melted away, leaving the rich, loamy earth exposed.

"Tell me more about your cleaning products."

"One of the first chemistry classes I had in college included a lab on making soap. It was such a fascinating process to me." Ella cleared a few sticks away from the center of the trail. "You take two very different things, lye and oil, and when mixed they completely change into something new. It's almost like magic. I started tinkering around with different formulas, using essential oils and other natural and sustainable ingredients until I found some that worked really well."

"Magic, eh?" Kind of like this walk in the woods. Oh, right, they were supposed to be working. He stooped down and hefted a small log into the underbrush lining the trail. "And that's what you've been using to clean houses? Your own blend of soaps?"

"Yep. My customers appreciate the natural ingredients. They're willing to pay a little extra."

"Did you always want to be a natural soap guru?"

"You don't have to flatter me. I know what I am—just a glorified cleaning lady." She walked ahead of him a few paces.

"Don't sell yourself short. You're much more than 'just a' anything. Besides, I think you dodged my question."

She sighed then met his eyes. "I've always wanted to use science to make the world a better place. I think we can save lives through better use of resources. I know it sounds nerdy, but there it is. I figured it would be good to stick to what I know, and I know cleaning. That seemed like a good place to start."

"I don't think that's nerdy at all. In fact, I think it's admirable." Suddenly his dream didn't seem so shiny or important. "Could that soap stuff work on a larger scale?"

"That's what I wanted to talk to your father about. I would love to see my formulas used all over the world, starting in the hotel industry."

"Wouldn't it be harder to control your product quality as you scale up though?"

"Actually, larger could potentially be easier. A bigger order can mean lower prices, especially on the specialty ingredients. As demand for those things becomes greater, more people will start making their products without toxic ingredients." She turned to him, met his gaze. "Just imagine—one company truly could change the world."

He loved her passion for her product. He couldn't remember the last time he felt that passionate about anything. Even his water park project. It felt like a means to a dream that didn't seem quite so important.

They worked in silence for another moment before she spoke again. "What about you, Adrian Vassos? Why water parks?"

"I used to think it was cool—the family business helping families have fun together. But really, it's just about money, and every woman I date looks past what we do to my bank account."

"That's harsh."

"Or maybe I've just been dating the wrong women." He looked up at her and she too had stilled, holding a branch.

The breeze whispered through the trees.

"Well, stop doing that, then." She smiled.

He smiled back.

She tossed the branch into the woods and turned back to the trail. "Why this park, Adrian? Why here? Why now?"

She was just so easy to talk to. "I really need a win with this one. My last project flopped so badly, I thought I was going to be written out of Dad's will."

"C'mon, it couldn't have been so bad he'd kick you out of the family."

"Well, out of the company anyway, which amounts to the same thing." His dad's words from that disaster tasted bitter. *If you can't get something this easy done right, maybe you don't belong with Bear Creek.*

"Do you want to talk about it?"

No, definitely not. But, something about the sunshine. Okay, yeah. "Two years ago, I spearheaded the development of a hotel resort in Iowa. We were building from the ground up and had included a fifteen hundred square foot indoor water park." He picked up a stick, tossed it away. "I thought everything was in order—I'd done an environmental study, gotten city planning approval. The financial backing was solid. The project should have been a slam dunk."

Ella grabbed one end of a fallen log and tried to shift it off the path. "Uh oh. It sounds like there's a 'but' coming."

He joined her and together they moved the dead tree aside. "Yeah. Even though I was the one who had made the connections with the local people, promising them I'd oversee the project personally, midway through the build my dad called me home. He sent Alex down to complete the project."

"Your brother, right?"

"You got it."

"Why would he do that?"

"I've always been pretty good at getting people to agree with me. My dad needed me to talk to some investors, and then I got involved in things back in Minneapolis. Meanwhile, Alex ignored the recommendations for the water reclamation system and put in a shoddy replacement. The system broke down and soon the park was losing thousands of gallons of water a day."

They worked in silence for a beat. Two.

"Okay, I'm no water park expert, but that doesn't sound good." Ella's voice broke into his thoughts.

Adrian rubbed his forehead. "It gets worse. I'd promised to use local workers, but Alex thought it would be better to save some cash, so he brought in outside contractors. We lost a lot of goodwill with that move. And then, before we were able to replace the water system, a drought hit that area."

"Oh no!"

"We tried trucking in water for a while but that solution became too expensive. We were forced to shut the whole thing down, and now the place is just a five-million-dollar eyesore not far off of Interstate 35."

Ella walked over to him, put her hand on his arm. "That is terrible. I'm sorry. But I don't know why you're beating yourself up about all that. It sounds more like Alex is the one to blame."

"Alex isn't the one who made promises he didn't keep. The truth is, I welcomed my dad's call back to Minneapolis. I'd started to feel overwhelmed and that maybe I'd overpromised. But I should've seen it through instead of letting my father dictate my decisions. I should've kept my promises." He looked at Ella's hand still on his arm. She let go and started gathering sticks again.

"It still seems to me that you're not giving yourself enough credit."

"I just want to get it right this time. I intend to stay until I see this project through. The company can't afford another multi-million-dollar flop."

"I had no idea you have so much riding on this deal." Ella paused, a handful of sticks in her hand.

He tried to laugh it off. "Only my whole future." Except, it emerged flat, and just a little desperate.

But he was desperate, frankly. The success of the water park was his whole future.

She walked up to him. "I went to a few water parks when I was a kid. They're fun. I just can't help thinking there must be a better way to keep them clean. I know not everyone will end up like my mother, but some will. And don't we have to try to make things better for those people too?"

She had a point. Maybe he could look at less toxic systems.

Surely there could be a compromise somewhere. "Maybe I will have to look into figuring out better business practices. Also, I've been researching ways to reduce water use. Make my mark on the resort industry."

He would have thought he'd promised to catch her the sun the way her eyes lit up at his suggestion.

"Adrian," she said softly. "Those other girls are idiots."

He paused, his gaze roaming her face. The sun shone in her hair, her beautiful blue eyes.

"I mean," she continued, "why should they care about your bank account when what they should be caring about is your sweet ride."

Oh. But the laugh burst out of him. "And here I thought you were being nice to me." He growled and made a lunge at her. She laughed and spun away out of his reach.

"Let's face it," she teased from a safe distance. "Your brilliant architectural mind, your obvious business smarts, your snake handling skills, they all pale in comparison to a *Porsche*. Any girl would fall for you in a heartbeat if she saw you drive up in that."

He didn't hear her finish her teasing sentence, his mind snagged on the word *brilliant*. Except, it wasn't really true, was it? He'd failed before, big time.

Only now, as he stood in the path, watching her walk into the forest, he didn't have to wonder if coming to Deep Haven wasn't indeed the most brilliant idea he'd ever had.

His cell phone buzzed and Athena's name popped up on the caller ID.

"Go ahead and take it." Ella walked on ahead. "I'll keep working."

"Thanks, it'll just take a minute." He swiped open his phone.

"Adrian! I thought maybe you got lost in the wilderness up there. I haven't heard from you for a week." Athena's rushed greeting made him smile.

"I'm not lost up here, I've just had a lot going on."

"Uh oh, that's your 'I'm in trouble and I don't want my favorite cousin to know about it' voice."

"I suppose it is. I was calling to update you on the Westerman project, but I guess I should bring you up to speed on the other things going on."

He summed up his brush with the law and the subsequent community service sentencing, glossing over the night in jail. No need for her to know about that part. He also didn't tell her about working with Ella. That relationship was much too precious and potentially fragile.

Time to move on to why he had called in the first place.

"I finally got the environmental impact study scheduled. The planning commission put it on the calendar for next week."

"That's good. Are the locals still interested?"

He sure hoped so, although he knew one local who was definitely not interested. Changing Ella's mind would be a challenge but one he was willing to undertake. He needed this project to succeed. Surely she would understand that.

"I will need to talk to the mayor. See what it'll take to get approval. Although at this rate, I may need to buy a helicopter to get the deal done."

"What? A helicopter? You mean for commuting back and forth?"

"No, a medical helicopter for their Crisis Response Team. Forget it. I'm just spitballing."

He heard silverware scraping a plate. "A medical helicopter. Wow. Would your dad go for something like that?"

"I think he'd be on board. Forget I said anything. It might not go anywhere."

"Sounds like a boring week. Up in the middle of nowhere with nothing to do."

"It's not as boring as I thought it might be." He glanced at Ella farther up the trail remembered their break-in a few nights before. The night they shared that kiss.

Not boring at all.

"Well, lonely then."

Not lonely either. But before he could open his mouth to say as much, Athena forged on. "By the way, I'm having brunch with Alex right now. He wants to say hi."

"Hey, Golden Boy!" Alex's distant voice echoed through the phone line. "Don't get distracted and screw up that business deal."

Nice, bro. Adrian ignored the urge to engage. "I hope you're making Alex pay for the brunch, Cuz."

"I always do."

He checked his watch. "Listen, I better get going. Lots to do yet today."

"What is there even to do on the back end of nowhere?"

"Kayaking, hiking, birdwatching."

Athena must have been drinking one of her designer coffees because he heard her spitting something out. "Birdwatching? Seriously?"

Ella had nearly rounded the bend up ahead.

"Listen, Athena, I'll call you later. Right now I've got to go."

His phone pinged with a text. Alex's number popped up. *Any sight of your sexy, hard-headed elevator girlfriend?*

Adrian thumbed in a reply. *Have some respect. Also, not my girlfriend.*

Another ping. *Whatever you say. I'd better let you go. I'm sure you have important business.*

Yes, right now he had to go and enjoy a beautiful hike with a beautiful girl. Did working community service count as a date?

This wasn't a date.

And she was not going to fall for Adrian Vassos.

They were here to pick up trash, for Pete's sake, and sure, he was charming, and yes, they'd shared a kiss, but...well, she and Adrian were two *very different* people. One look at his fancy wool jacket screamed that truth.

He came from a family of real money and power.

She came from lies.

Sure, he was a great kisser, but she needed to hold onto her heart. She could only rely on herself, and no broad-shouldered, dark-haired, intense-eyed Greek man was going to change her mind.

No matter how much she wanted to kiss him again.

Maybe I will have to look into figuring out better business practices. Could he really mean that he would sacrifice his proposal? Still, she wasn't going to fall for him, no matter how many business practices he reevaluated.

They were different people, with different kinds of lives, despite their shared criminal past.

She paused on the trail to let Adrian catch up. The sun blazed overhead in a rare show of March warmth and the sky winked a blue topaz. Ella breathed in the scent of pine and wet leaves. Other people might turn their noses up at the mud and grime of the spring season, but Ella loved the promise of new beginnings it always brought.

As she and Adrian hefted another large fallen branch out of the path, she spotted a tree with tiny pine cones on it that had fallen over just beyond the cleared path.

"Those little pine cones would look so cute tied on my pine-scented soap." She pushed aside an aspen branch to look closer.

"I don't think you should be leaving the path." Adrian's warning was ridiculous. It wasn't like she was going deep into the woods.

"Nonsense, I'll be right over there. I'm just going to take those pine cones and pine sprigs. They'll be removing this tree anyway, so it's not like I'm harming anything."

"It's not the tree or the woods I'm worried about, it's you."

She paused. He cared about *her*? Things had been a little awkward between them since the kiss. She wasn't sure how to bring *that* up, but she supposed they needed to talk about it.

"Thanks, but I'll be fine."

He started to climb over the trees after her, but she held up her hand. "Stay there. I'll be out in just a minute." She reached down and snapped the sprigs off the dead tree. With a twist of twine, these would be the perfect ornament for her soap packaging. She generally wrapped the bars in wax paper and stamped them with her logo, but this added touch would take the product to the next level. She'd have to keep her eyes open for more.

She glanced at Adrian. A shaft of light filtered through the trees and landed on his shoulders. In his designer jacket and jeans, and hiking boots, he looked at home in the woods. Well, maybe a little overdressed for this neck of the woods. She was sure his jacket cost more than her car, but at least he'd traded his Italian shoes for something a little more practical.

Yes, she was right when she said he'd dated the wrong women. He needed a woman who would see past his money to the man who wanted to do something significant with his life. *I've been researching ways to reduce water use.* Maybe their goals weren't so different after all.

There. A dozen pine sprigs now rested in her pocket. She made her way back over the downed trees and out onto the trail.

"Get what you needed?" Adrian stood waiting for her.

"Yep. All set." Ella checked her phone for the time. "We have another hour and a half before we're done out here. Let's try to make it to the overlook before we finish."

"You know, I think I've spent more time outside with you these past few days than I've spent outside the previous ten years combined."

"You must have spent time outside as a kid. I don't know any boys who didn't grow up pretending sticks were guns and trees were bad guys." She moved past Adrian, aiming for a piece of garbage. She stuck the shiny wrapper in her pocket.

"Yeah, when I was young we lived in a house with a backyard and a swing set. I'd spend hours out there, picking up sticks and building things with them."

"No stick guns for you?"

"I was a lover, not a fighter."

She glanced over her shoulder, and he was grinning.

Oh boy. She looked away.

"Actually, it was those stick houses that made me interested in architecture. It's why I got my degree in that field." He caught up to her.

"When I was a kid I used to find the smallest twigs I could and then weave them into nests for birds," she said.

"You know that birds would never use those, right?"

"Of course, I know that now. But my mother used to put them in the crook of a tree. She said that doing things to improve the life of someone else would make the world a better place to live in for everyone." She picked up a few twigs and twisted them into a knot. Handed it to Adrian.

He turned it over in his hands. "Your mother sounds wise."

"I know it sounds cheesy, but my mom's words are why I want to improve the lives of others and make the world a better place."

"Not cheesy. Noble." He hung her twist on a branch. "Let's leave this here for the birds to enjoy."

"Why did *you* stop building things out of sticks?"

"After my dad grew more successful with his hotels, he moved our family into the penthouse of his newest acquisition, the oldest, grandest hotel in downtown Kellogg. After that, we didn't have a yard or sticks."

"Wow. I've seen movies where people live in penthouses, but I didn't think anyone did that in real life." See? Different people.

She and her dad were basically squatters. Adrian's family lived in a penthouse.

"I don't think it was a real life. I missed the simple home and the neighborhood. My family was never the same after we moved. Mom and Dad fought constantly, and that's when Alex started acting like he was better than everyone else. I missed having my family from before."

Huh. Maybe they weren't so different after all.

On the trail ahead, Ella spotted a clump of fur. "Hey, what's that?"

"It looks like a rabbit."

"This little guy must have had a run-in with a fox." Her eyes pricked. Was she crying over a rabbit? These last weeks must be taking a bigger toll than she realized.

"Let's move it off the trail." Adrian bent down and moved the dead rabbit a few feet from the path. He covered it with leaves then held his hand over his heart. "Here lies Peter Rabbit. He fought the good fight, but his race ended far too soon. May he rest in peace."

Ella giggled. Oh great. First crying and now giggling? This guy was really getting to her. "Thanks for that eulogy. Let's head to the overlook."

A few feet farther and around the bend, Ella's breath caught. She hadn't been up here in a long while. Dropping away in front of them, the valley unfurled. A blanket of trees draped the landscape. Even the barren, silvery aspens awaiting their spring buds were breathtaking. In the distance, Lake Superior stretched away into the horizon. She stopped well back from the edge of the slope.

Adrian passed by her and stood looking across the valley. "Come over here." He held out a hand to her.

"I'm good, thanks." Her stomach quivered. "Maybe you should come back over here."

"Oh. Right. The heights thing." Adrian backed up a step. "It's perfectly safe right here, I promise."

She couldn't do it. Except. She looked at Adrian's outstretched hand. Maybe she could trust him. Her feet crunched over the nearly melted snow as she edged closer to him. Adrian continued backing up and joined her, meeting her halfway.

"Beautiful," he said.

"Yes, this is a great place."

But he wasn't looking at the view...he was looking at her. "Ella."

Her heart beat double time. "Yes?" She stepped toward him. Her gaze landed on his lips.

She was going to kiss him. Yes. She could almost hear Colleen, the romantic in her head. So what if they were different? They had a lot of similarities, a lot of—

"Careful!"

But her foot slid on a patch of wet grass, and before she could catch herself, her feet went out from under her. She landed hard, flat on her back, the wind knocked out of her, and lay there like a fish, gulping for air.

"Ella?" Adrian knelt beside her. "Are you okay?"

She gasped, the air suddenly whooshing in. "Oh—oh..."

"Just take it easy." He held out his hand, and it occurred to her that he seemed to always be there when she was in trouble.

She sat up, still catching her breath.

"Sorry, I was trying to warn you. That spot is really slippery."

Ella grasped his hand and he pulled her up. She wobbled a step and he reached for her.

And just like that, he slipped on the wet grass and ended up on the ground.

"Adrian!"

"I'm fine."

"I'm sorry, what was that you were saying about it being slippery?" She couldn't help but laugh.

"Ha ha, funny girl. Come over here and help me up."

Ella offered her hand and he grabbed it, but with a swift pull, he tugged her down. Ella shrieked and landed half on top of him and half on the ground. They slid a few inches down the incline, and he rolled over to stop them.

He grinned at her, his face just inches away. "There, that's better."

"Lying in the mud is better?"

"Anywhere is better when you share it with someone. Even the muddy, cold side of a hill." His gaze dropped to her lips.

"Adrian—" She was half tucked under him and suddenly very aware of his presence over her, trapping her, or maybe saving her from sliding down the embankment.

"Yes?"

"You have mud on your face."

He reached up to wipe it off, but only succeeded in spreading the smudge around.

"Here, let me." Ella used the handkerchief in her jacket pocket to wipe the spot away. "There, much better." But Adrian grabbed her wrist and held her hand next to his face.

"Better for sure." He wormed his other arm under her shoulders until she was clasped against his chest. She could feel the mud oozing into her jeans but somehow that didn't matter.

Just the sense that, despite the chilly mud, she was safe.

With Adrian Vassos, of all people. The irresponsible playboy.

His gaze flicked to her lips and she held her breath.

Then he bent down and brushed his mouth against hers. She tasted the sweetness of the sugared donut on his lips and smiled against him.

"What's the smile for?"

"I knew kissing you would be sweet, but I didn't expect the sugar."

Adrian smiled, something of heat in his eyes, and kissed her again.

And then his touch wasn't so much sweet as something to savor. He took his time, deepening their kiss, probably aware that there was nothing to rush them out here under the sky and wind. He made a little sound, deep inside, as if in pleasure, and she agreed. Everything went tingly and she felt herself unwinding, the tight coil that was always inside her loosening.

As if with Adrian she could relax.

One of Adrian's hands tangled in the hair at the nape of her neck, and she found her own playing with his long dark hair.

He finally leaned away from her, something dark, even possessive in his eyes. "Good thing Carol isn't here. We'd get written up."

She laughed. "Totally worth it."

He grinned, and no wonder he made the papers with that smile. "You have mud in your hair."

"You're pretty muddy yourself."

They were both completely soaked. There wasn't any way either of them was going to get clean without a shower and a laundromat. "I hope you don't mind that fancy car of yours getting a little dirty."

"I can always drive it into another lake to wash it off."

She opened her mouth. "Was that a joke, Andretti?"

He gave her another peck on the lips, heaved himself upright, then pulled her up. "Careful now, we don't want to slip farther down this hill."

No, no, not at all... "Hey, do you hear that?" From somewhere nearby, there came a faint squeaking sound. Gingerly, Ella picked her way across the hill toward the sound, Adrian following close behind. Under an overhanging rock, in a pocket of dirt, Ella spotted a layer of fluffy grass and something squirming. She took a step closer and caught her breath.

A den of bunnies wriggled in a hole under the shelter of the rock. "I think we were wrong about that rabbit on the trail. Must have been a Flopsy or Mopsy, not a Peter. This must be her nest. These babies are all alone."

Adrian shucked his jacket off and crept closer to the den. "We've got to rescue these little guys." He picked the bunnies up one at a time and nestled them into the cashmere folds. "There are seven of them. Look." Cradling his jacket as if it contained live dynamite instead of rabbits, he handed it over to her.

They nestled between the arms of Adrian's jacket, piled on top of each other, appearing quite content to have shifted to a new home.

Safe.

Adrian pointed up to the overlook. "Let's finish up on the trail and then get these guys to the wild animal sanctuary."

Rich. Handsome. A good kisser. And he rescued bunnies.

Oh, who was she kidding? So much for not falling for the man.

CHAPTER 10

*S*he should have stolen back a better shirt. Sitting in Grace Christiansen Sharpe's kitchen talking about her cleaning supplies would have been so much easier if Ella had grabbed that floral blouse out of her closet when she'd raided her own belongings with Adrian.

After the morning on the Pincushion, then a stop at the wild animal shelter, Ella had some clients to take care of. She had been cleaning for Grace and Max when Grace stopped her—no, ambushed her—and asked if she would be interested in doing a video.

"I'm making a vlog to document our lives with Huntington's disease," Grace had said an hour ago. "If we can help another family make it through…" Grace put her hand over her mouth. Ella put an arm around her shoulder, and Grace took a deep breath. "Anyway. Your natural cleaning products have helped a ton. Not using aerosol sprays and heavy toxins makes Max feel much better."

"It makes me happy to hear that." Ella pulled back from Grace and picked up her spray bottle again.

"Wait, I have the best idea. Why don't I interview you about your products, and you can explain how they're different from other things out there? You have a website, right, where people can buy soap from you?"

"Yes, I do." In theory, anyway. She'd had the website for a year now, and every month something like two orders trickled in.

"Perfect. We can plug your website and help people."

Ella had been caught up in Grace's enthusiasm. "Okay. I'll do it. When should we schedule it?"

Now, an hour later, sitting at Grace's table, her favorite soft, purple work T-shirt didn't quite seem the right thing for a video. "Shouldn't we wait until I've had time to change out of my work clothes? Or prepare a statement or something?"

"Nonsense. You look great. That T-shirt, with your hair pulled back under that lavender handkerchief, makes you look approachable. Very down to earth." Grace fiddled with her cell phone, setting it up on some kind of stand attached to a light. "I'd rather do this off the cuff—you'll seem more relaxed."

Ella wasn't sure about that. Her heart rate had increased, and there was a bead of sweat currently making its way down between her shoulder blades. She concentrated on the table. A rich, golden wood, its surface was polished to a high sheen but scarred with nicks and bumps. And yet, despite its flaws, the table was beautiful.

She touched one of the nicks. Had she really kissed Adrian? Again? One of these days she would need to convince her brain that they still didn't see eye to eye.

"Got it." Grace sat down in the chair to the right of Ella. "We're already recording, but I'll edit this part out. This isn't a live vlog, so don't worry too much. If you stumble or can't think of something to answer, we'll just move past it and cut that part. Or, if you want to go back to something, I can splice it in."

Ella nodded. Why had she said yes, again? Oh. Right. Her website needed exposure, her bank account needed to be fed, and most importantly, Grace was her friend. At least, she really, really hoped Grace was her friend.

Grace spoke into the cell phone camera. "Hello, Team Max family. I'm here with my friend Ella Bradley. Ella is a whiz at making natural and organic cleaning products. She uses them at my house here in Deep Haven, and I'd love for you to hear more about her and Essentially Ella, her soap company. Ella, why are organic cleaning products so important to you?"

Ella paused. Swallowed. "It all started when my mother died." Was she really going to tell a million strangers about her mother? If she wanted her soap business to grow, she needed to talk about it. She concentrated on looking Grace in the eye. Her friend's pale eyes held encouragement. "My mother had asthma…" The story became easier in the retelling. Grace punctuated the interview with questions and insightful comments. Soon, Ella didn't even notice the camera was on.

"Thank you for sharing this with me," Grace said as she turned off the cell phone camera. "I didn't know much about you before. You're usually so quiet when you're around."

"I don't talk much about my past."

"I can understand why, but anytime you feel like having a chat, I'm here for you. Max and I plan to stay here as often as we can." Grace wound up the cord attached to the lighting rig. "While you're here, why don't I take a look at your website? I can add a link to my vlog if you'd like."

"That would be great. I'd love that."

Grace set up a laptop on the table, and Ella opened the editing page on her website.

"Essentially Ella. I like that." Grace clicked a few buttons and then typed in her own web address. "There, now you're linked to me. We can share traffic." She smiled at Ella. "Mind if I look around a little more?"

"Not at all. I knew enough to get myself set up, and I've read a ton of material on building websites, but I'm still a newbie. If you can offer advice, I'd love to hear it."

"Uh oh, I think we have a problem." Grace continued navigating around the site.

"What is it?" Ella leaned toward the screen.

Grace moved the cursor and highlighted a section. "See right here? Your website isn't secure. Anyone could just come in here and access your information. How are you set up for payments?"

"I have them directly linked with the bank."

"Ivy told me about your trouble with the bank. I think it's possible this is how they accessed your money. Don't worry though. I can close this loop without any trouble." She tapped a few more keys. "Done." She saved her work and shut the computer down. "Now, how about a cup of coffee while we have a chat off camera? Max won't be home for an hour, and I could use some girl talk."

"I can do girl talk."

A few minutes later, they sat in Grace's living room, hands wrapped around steaming cups of coffee.

"Rumor has it that you've been seen around town with a very handsome, eligible bachelor." Grace waggled her eyebrows at Ella.

Ella felt her face heating. She gave a small laugh. "Seen doing community service, you mean."

"Is that what the kids are calling it these days?" Grace winked. Ella couldn't help the laugh that burst from her. And, wow, laughing with a friend was the perfect cap to this day.

"Thank you again for not canceling our contract when you heard about the jail time, by the way." The sip of coffee she took warmed her through the middle.

Grace waved off the comment. "Of course I wouldn't cancel over something as silly as that. Ivy told me that it was pretty much a misunderstanding anyway."

"Well, I appreciate it all the same. Not everyone in Deep Haven felt the same way." She still cringed as she remembered the calls from several others who abruptly canceled their appointments because who knew what she would "steal" from them.

"Not everyone in Deep Haven is as smart as me." Grace grinned. "They don't know what they're missing."

She leaned forward. "Now, tell me seriously, is there anything between you and Adrian? Because if not, I might have someone to set him up with."

Ella looked quickly at her friend.

Grace's eyes twinkled. "Ha! I knew it. You *do* like him."

The morning on the trail—and in the mud—flashed through Ella's mind, and she smiled a slow smile. "Yeah, I do like him."

The words drew her up.

She liked him…a lot. But that didn't get her bills paid or help her grow her business. Adrian wasn't small-town. More, she disagreed with everything he was doing.

Clearly, she'd lost her mind.

But, oh boy, if she didn't look forward to seeing him again.

He shouldn't be here.

"'Tis so sweet to trust in Jesus…" The congregation around Adrian joined their voices in song, but Adrian's mind wasn't on the hymn. Or Pastor Dan's message.

Sure, he remembered a few tidbits. Like the reference— Isaiah 25—and especially when Pastor Dan had wrapped both hands around the edges of the pulpit and leaned forward and spoken almost directly to Adrian. "Friends, we can fully trust God. Even when believers are unfaithful, God still shows up. He is always there for us. Even in the darkest night, His faithfulness surrounds us."

Sure, sure it did. Surrounded others, maybe, but not him. And he couldn't exactly blame God for that.

Because all Adrian could think about—in the middle of church, no less—was Ella sitting a few rows in front of him. Her yellow dress kept drawing his eye and, along with it, the way she'd felt in his arms when he'd kissed her.

And boy, had he kissed her. Had sort of forgotten that they were out in the open on a clear, sunny day. But she made him feel, well, wanted. Normal. Just a guy named Roger kissing the pretty girl he was falling for.

And see? This is why he was the biggest of sinners. Because he was in church, and now the song was ending and Darek, next to him, was turning to introduce him to a few faces.

Darek had been home after they'd gotten back from the animal shelter, and Adrian had told him about his project. To his surprise, Darek had mentioned a resort owners group in town and invited him to sit in on one of their meetings. *The more tourists we can get interested in spending time on the North Shore, the more it benefits all of us.*

Adrian hadn't expected that sort of camaraderie. So, of course, he'd agreed to attend church and meet a few of the local owners.

The pastor dismissed them, and the elderly lady he had squeezed in next to laid her hand on his arm. "I haven't seen you in town before. Are you just visiting?" Her eyes were more piercing than her age implied.

"Yes and no. I'm here pursuing a business deal." Darek was sliding out of the pew the other direction.

"Oh, very mysterious. I'm Edith Draper."

"Adrian Vassos." He shook her hand.

"It's always nice to sit next to a handsome man in church. What kind of business deal?"

This lady reminded him of his grandma. Grandma Vassos always wanted to know everyone's affairs too. "I'm actually looking to get permission to tear down the Westerman property to put up a new hotel and water park."

"Oh, very fancy. I don't go for water parks much myself, but you might be able to convince some of the younger members of the council."

"When it is built, I'll take you on a personal tour." Adrian patted her hand.

"I'm sure a handsome man like you will have better things to do." She followed his line of sight, straight to where Ella stood chatting with Grace Christiansen Sharpe and a few others.

Adrian smiled down at the old woman. "I don't know what you mean."

"Nonsense. I see the way you're looking at Ella Bradley. These eyes might be old, but they're not blind. She's a sweet girl. I hired her to help me do some spring cleaning. That girl is a whiz at what she does."

"I'll be a gentleman, I promise."

"If you don't, you'll have me to answer to. Now, I'd better go see what those ladies are discussing. I hope it's Cole and Megan's wedding." Edith took his hand in both of hers. "It was nice to meet you. Good luck with your hotel."

Adrian watched her join Ella and the other women in their conversation.

He'd lost Darek. Maybe he'd wait for Ella by the door. Walking out of the sanctuary, Adrian caught sight of Darek, who looked up and motioned him over. He was talking with a bigger man, black haired, solidly built.

"Adrian. This is our mayor, Seb Brewster."

Adrian shook his hand. "Mayor."

"Adrian is hoping to get a permit to renovate the Westerman place," Darek said.

Recognition entered Seb's expression. "I have the permit on my desk. Sorry I missed the meeting the other day. You're taking it before the town council in a couple weeks, right?"

Adrian nodded. "Do you have a few minutes for us to talk?"

The mayor glanced at his watch. "My wife has lunch plans, but we can always set up an appointment this week."

Darek had gone to glad-hand someone else, so Adrian put on his best PR smile and gestured to the door. "I don't think it will take long. Let me walk you out to your car." They dodged a kid who was scampering after his friends. "I just wanted to know how you think people are feeling about my water park proposal."

"I'll be honest with you, Adrian. People are pretty skeptical. It's hard for them to see something like that being a benefit to our town."

They stopped for a moment to greet Pastor Dan at the door. Adrian thanked him for his message.

"I'll be thinking about that one for a while to come. I appreciated your insights."

Dan put his hand on Adrian's shoulder. "If I can remind people every Sunday how much God loves them and how He is faithful, I feel I've done my job."

"I'd say you earned your living this week," Adrian said, and yep, he was a sinner. If he was looking for God's approval, maybe he shouldn't daydream about blondes in church.

He and Seb made their way out the church door. But once outside, Adrian came to a halt and faced Seb. "What will it take to make this happen? I've already got the environmental study under way as requested. What do I need to say to the council to get them on board?"

Seb frowned at him. "I'm sorry, am I hearing you right? Are you suggesting a bribe? Because that's not the way we do business around here."

Adrian held up a hand. "Nope. Not a bribe. Just...I need people to see that we want to help the community. Be a part of things here. Any ideas?"

Seb rubbed his chin. "Okay. Right now the council is pretty

distracted by the need for a Crisis Response Team. We're trying to figure out how to continue to build and fund the team." He started walking again.

Adrian fell into step beside him. "Yeah, Ella mentioned something about that team. Maybe I could create some goodwill and attention to my project by donating something. Supplies, a vehicle."

Seb laughed. "How about a helicopter?"

Adrian stopped. "A helicopter."

"I was kidding." He held up a hand. "Really. That's way out of bounds."

"I have connections. And we're fully committed to this town. We could find something second hand, in good shape. Or, you get something new and we give a sizable donation and help with fundraising."

Seb stared at him as if to assess his words. "And no strings attached? Really?"

"Really."

Seb grinned. "Wow. Huh." He pulled out his keys. "Adrian, if you bought us a helicopter, the town would be so happy, they might let you build *three* water parks."

"I'll have to see what I can do about that then." Adrian shook Seb's hand again.

Seb tightened his grip momentarily. "You do know that the permit itself will cost you a pretty penny, right? We've had others in town look into it, and it was too expensive for them."

"Yes, sir. I'm aware that permits cost a fair amount."

"You're trying to build in a prime location, and it's right on the water, so it's not that the town of Deep Haven is just trying to scalp you out of your money. There are other issues at play." Seb let go of his hand and looked him over. "We care about our town and the environment around us. It's part of who we are."

"Me too," Adrian said, and realized that he was telling the truth. "Let me see what I can do."

Seb gave a quick nod as he slid into his car. "Just so we're on the same page. No quid pro quo."

"Absolutely. Just a donation from a concerned citizen."

"Well, all right then."

"I'll be in touch." Adrian stepped back as Seb pulled his car out of its spot. He glanced around, hoping to spot Ella. Shoot, it looked like she had already left. He'd wanted to make arrangements for them to grab lunch together. Maybe he could still find her and convince her to go for fish and chips at the Loon Cafe.

He pulled out his cell phone and dialed her number. "Hi, Sunshine. Want to grab some lunch?"

A beat, then, "I'm sorry, Adrian, I really can't. I'm already in the middle of work."

He walked toward his Porsche. "C'mon. You need to eat."

"I grabbed a sandwich in my cabin. Duty calls. I have several cleaning jobs that need to be done this afternoon. I've already lost too many clients over the whole jail fiasco and can't afford to lose more." Her voice dropped low. "I'd like to see you though."

"Okay. I understand. Stop by later. I want to see you again. Maybe we can get dinner."

"It's a date."

They hung up, and Adrian decided to head downtown since he'd been wanting to try the food at the Loon Cafe. He swung in and got an order of fish and chips to go. Balancing the food on the seat next to him, he drove to the Westerman Hotel property and parked in the lot. Here and there, weeds grew up in the cracks of the pavement. A board was nailed over the spot where the front door of the hotel should be. The roof sank in the middle.

Adrian imagined the artist rendering of the finished hotel and water park. He could see where each of the waterslides would jut out from the building. He picked up his to-go container. Got out of the car. Avoiding the biggest potholes, he headed to the back of the property where it bordered the water.

A picnic table, weatherworn and graying, clung to its place on the rocky beach. Watching carefully for slivers, Adrian sat down and opened his lunch. A cool breeze blew in from the lake, rustling his napkins. He scooped up a rock from the ground to hold them in place.

In his pocket, his phone rang.

"Hello, Athena."

On the phone, Athena's voice raced.

"Slow down, Cuz. I can barely hear you."

"I said, I have a surprise for you. Actually, *two* surprises. First, I'm in town! I came up here to rescue you from the drudgery of this backwater town. After our phone call at brunch the other day, Alex suggested I come and check on you."

"You didn't need to do that. I'm fine up here. I've actually been enjoying myself." More than enjoying himself, but she didn't have to know that.

"Yeah, right. As I recall, you've been *birdwatching*." This, as though it were the seventh circle of hell. "You needed an intervention and needed it quickly."

"I will be glad to see you, that's for sure."

"That's because I'm your favorite." Athena's voice held a smile at their old joke.

"True. You're like the sister I never had—nor wanted."

"Oh, stop."

But he loved Athena. And, she was always on his side. "Do you want to meet for lunch? Where are you?"

"Where are *you*? I thought you'd be in your cabin."

"I came in for church." Sorta. Oh, he had some serious repenting to do.

"What? First birdwatching and now church? What's with you?"

"I don't know, Athena. There's just something about being

here that feels...freeing, maybe." Pastor Dan's words ran through his head again. *God loves you just as you are.* "Anyway, lunch? I just got fish and chips, but I could go back and get another order for you. I'm sitting and staring at the Westerman Hotel. Getting a little inspiration."

"Actually, you should finish up your lunch and head back to your cabin. I left the second surprise there for you."

"Is this surprise also one of Alex's suggestions?" Because if so, Adrian would need to watch his back.

"Don't think I'm capable of surprising you on my own?" she teased.

"That's not it."

"Kidding. Anyway, if you still want to get together after you see it, give me a call. I booked a cabin at Evergreen too."

"Fine. Talk to you later." Adrian hung up.

He bit into a french fry. The salty, greasy fry was perfectly cooked.

Right now, life was pretty perfect. So what if he had added to his rap sheet? So what if he'd maybe promised to spend money on a helicopter without getting his father's approval? So what if he was living in a cabin the size of his closet in Minneapolis?

In fact, he might be on the way to a small-town life he never knew he wanted. He would get this project done and make his dad respect him and gain a great life.

Especially if he could figure out how to convince a certain blue-eyed blonde that he wasn't the bad guy. They could both have a happy ending. He'd just have to figure out how.

CHAPTER 11

The sweet refrain from church that morning set the mood for Ella's afternoon. "'Tis so sweet to trust in Jesus..." The song danced around in her brain as she swept her cloth over an end table in Cabin 3 at Evergreen Resort. A new peace was settling in her heart as she reflected on the words Pastor Dan had spoken.

You have done wonderful things. She wanted to trust that scripture—really. In fact, she could almost even admit that God was doing wonderful things in her life. Her job here at Evergreen was proof of that.

Even her friends at church. She hadn't expected Ivy, of all people, to pull her into the group of women planning Megan's wedding shower, but there she was, in the group, like she belonged. She'd attended church sporadically over the past six months but never really felt like she fit in anywhere. But today was different. Everyone had just...included her, like she had been part of the conversation all along.

Maybe that's what having sisters was really supposed to be like. Sophie had been an enemy from the moment her mother married Ella's father, lying about her, stealing her belongings, and making Ella out to be the antagonist.

It still galled Ella, just a little, that Sophie had been Adrian's date. But it didn't matter.

After all, he had kissed *her*. Twice.

The process of cleaning up the cabins and getting them ready for the summer season had been going pretty smoothly despite the time she had to take off to tend to her other jobs, not to mention the time she spent at community service. With Adrian.

She gave the wood-paneled cabin a final look before she packed up to move to the next cabin. Each of the seven Evergreen cabins followed a similar building structure. One main room housed the small kitchenette, a tiny living room, and a nook for a dining table. Off the main room was a minuscule hallway leading into a full bathroom and two small bedrooms. Darek had written a list of what things to take care of in each cabin. She made a note of the small tear in the screen on the front window and then checked Cabin 4 off her list. Time for a break.

She glanced at her phone, hoping for a text from Adrian. Nope. Nothing. He must not be home yet. She remembered her promise to check in with Colleen so she dialed her friend and made her way back to her own cabin.

Colleen answered as Ella's door swung shut behind her. "Hi, Ella! How's Deep Haven these days? Are you settled in at Evergreen?"

Ella brought her friend up to speed on her activities, carefully editing Adrian out of the retelling. But she couldn't stop thinking about him. She got some water from the tap. Too bad her budget didn't stretch to iced coffee.

"You got quiet just now." Colleen's voice broke through her thoughts. "Is everything okay?"

"I'm fine. I was just thinking about my community service projects." That wasn't lying.

"Anything interesting happening with those?"

Ella told her about the baby bunnies she and Adrian had rescued. "So, then we brought them to the wild animal rescue place in town. I think they'll be okay."

"Wait, 'we'? Who's we?"

Busted. "Um, Adrian and me." Gulp.

"Adrian Vassos? 'My mortal enemy for all time because he lied to me and is building a germ-infested cesspool in my back-yard'—that Adrian?"

She winced. "I never said all that. He's not so bad."

"Not so bad? Really. Have you seen the articles about him? Hello? Do you not remember the dunk in the lake?"

"He is very different in person than he is in the tabloids. They just make stuff up."

"Yeah, I *bet* he's different. Probably much hotter. Am I right?"

A blush worked its way across Ella's face. "I wish you'd stop saying that about him. That's not his only good quality."

"Ella! What aren't you telling me? When you left my house, he was persona non grata, now he's not so bad? What changed?"

"I saw another side of him. He's actually sweet and kind and funny." She'd laughed more in the past few days with him than she had in the three months before. Somehow, despite her recent losses, she felt richer.

She blamed that on Adrian.

"He was so gentle with those rabbit kits. He wrapped them up in his jacket like he wasn't ruining a four-thousand-dollar coat just to save some bunnies. It was like money didn't even matter to him."

"It probably doesn't. But I think you're falling for him."

"I don't know, Colleen. Maybe. Am I crazy to trust him?" She rolled her nearly empty water cup back and forth in her hands.

"What if it's just me I can't trust? I've been on my own for so long, I don't know how to share my life with someone."

"I think it's time for you to learn that you can rely on other people too."

Ella walked over to the window. The snow up here hung on, sparkling under the sapphire sky, the lake padding softly against the shore. "He's not what I expected."

"C'mon, spill."

She took a drink of water. Fine. "We kissed."

"I *knew* it!"

"Stop. People can hear you cheering from here."

"Because I'm thrilled. Ella, girl, grab on to that man and don't let go. He's got it all—money, looks, a fancy sports car, kindness, and did I mention looks?"

"Can you be any more shallow?"

"Nope. And it's about time you had a boyfriend."

"He's not…" Except, the way he'd kissed her on the trail, she was certain he felt something for her.

"Fine, I will stop saying how hot your non-boyfriend is if you promise to keep me updated on everything that happens."

Ella laughed. "Fine. But I probably won't tell you *everything*. A girl deserves to have some secrets after all."

She hung up, but Colleen was right.

She should hold on to Adrian.

Trust him.

She checked her phone again. He still hadn't called. Which meant he probably wasn't back from town yet.

The perfect time to give his cabin a general cleaning too.

And if he just happened to be there…

She was grinning as she knocked on his door. No answer.

Fine. It was on Darek's list, so he expected her to clean it. She'd cleaned plenty of hotel rooms, cottages, and homes filled with other people's things.

Using her master key, she opened the door.

The aroma of oregano and tomatoes filled the small room.

And on the table in the dining nook were two place settings and a candle. She set her cleaning bucket on one of the chairs to better admire the setup.

That sneak. He'd come back and was making dinner for them. She briefly debated slinking back out so as not to ruin his surprise.

The door to the bedroom was ajar, however, and she spotted a suitcase near the bed. Maybe he needed to go home for a few days. Perhaps he wanted to spend the evening together before he left in the morning.

That's when she heard the shower running. He must be rinsing off before calling her to come for supper. Her whole body heated. Best not to think of him in the shower.

The shower turned off. "Adrian?" She didn't want him to be startled to find her there. When he didn't answer, she decided he hadn't heard her. No need to spoil the surprise—she'd just go to her cabin and wait for his call.

She took the two steps to the front door, put her hand on the doorknob to go, but remembered she'd set her cleaning supplies down on the chair. She hurried over the few steps and snatched up the bucket.

And that's when the bathroom door opened.

For a moment, Ella simply froze.

It wasn't Adrian. Instead, a shapely woman stepped out of the steamy room, wrapped only in a towel—dark hair flowing down her back, long lean legs, and an expression of surprise and not a little annoyance on her face.

"Sophie?"

"Ella?" Sophie adjusted her grip on the edge of the towel. "I thought you were Adrian."

Ella couldn't move.

"Are you here to clean?" She gestured to the bucket Ella held in her hand.

Numbly, and probably on reflex, Ella nodded.

"Now's not a good time. But, could you stir that sauce on the stove for me? I have the heat off, but I don't want it to burn."

She acted like she belonged here. Like she'd been *invited*.

Never mind that she was coming from the *shower*.

That *liar*.

She isn't my type. I don't plan to be seeing her again.

Right. And after Ella had kissed him. Twice.

Oh, she was stupid. She blinked back tears. This is what she got when she trusted someone.

Sophie disappeared into Adrian's bedroom, and Ella turned, her eyes blurry, then yanked the door open and rushed out.

She plowed straight into a man standing on the stoop.

Adrian.

"Whoa there, Sunshine." He grabbed her upper arms to steady her.

"Don't. *Touch. Me!*" She jerked her arms from his hands. Her cleaning supplies threatened to tumble from the bucket.

He stepped back. "Ella? What's wrong?"

"I'm an idiot, that's what's wrong."

She pushed past him.

He stood in the doorway, looked in. "Do I smell pasta sauce? Are you making us dinner? Have I spoiled a surprise?"

Really? She whirled at the bottom of the steps. "Why don't you ask your girlfriend? *Sophie.*"

Adrian looked inside, and his mouth opened.

Yep, that Sophie. The one who probably stood in the hallway in all her toweled glory.

"Oh." Adrian's voice fell flat.

"Yeah. Oh. You didn't think I would find out that you were two-timing me? Or is it that you're two-timing her? Doesn't matter, because whatever this was"—Ella gestured wildly between them—"it's over. Serves me right for trusting you. *Again.*"

"Ella, wait! I can explain." Adrian headed down the stairs after her.

She didn't look at him, kept stalking away. "Please leave me alone. Go back to Sophie. It's fine. Really." She should have known better anyway.

"Ella, I promise you, it's not what it looks like."

He touched her arm, and she rounded on him. "Don't touch me. Ever. Again."

He held up his hands in surrender. "Listen, I'm going to figure out what's going on and then I'm going to come to your cabin and sort this out. Please believe me. I didn't know she was going to be here."

"Right. Whatever. Have a fun time with my sister."

She turned, and this time he didn't follow her.

What just happened? And why was Sophie in his cabin?

Adrian's head spun.

This was definitely not how he had pictured his afternoon going. When Adrian had pulled into the parking lot at Evergreen, he was pleased to see Ella's car parked in its usual spot. They would be able to grab some time together tonight after all. Maybe even find a place to watch the sunset.

One glance inside his cabin and all his dreams for the evening had crashed and burned.

Sophie. In a towel. *Only* in a towel, her hair wet, smiling in a way that left nothing to the imagination.

He couldn't go in there.

He *had* to go in there.

Adrian took a breath and pushed the door to his cabin open. Sophie stood at the stove stirring whatever was in the pot.

In her towel.

"What are you doing here?" he ground out.

She turned to him, spatula held aloft. "Athena brought me. She said you were lonely. I decided to help you not be lonely anymore."

This was Athena's surprise?

Yep, he certainly was surprised.

"Sophie, please go put some clothes on." He pushed a hand through his hair. He was going to kill Athena.

"Okay, Adri. Be right back," Sophie practically purred and headed to his bedroom.

Of course.

When the coast was clear, Adrian stepped into his cabin and shut the door. Shrugging out of his jacket, he tossed it onto the loveseat, then walked over and snuffed out the candle flickering on the table. He sank into one of the chairs and pulled out his cell phone.

Athena picked up before the phone had rung twice.

"How did you like my surprise?"

"Seriously, Athena?" He took a deep breath to steady himself. "She's in a *towel*."

"What? Oh my—Adrian, you have to know I didn't suggest *that*. I thought you two could have dinner or something. I'm so sorry. At brunch the other day, Alex said he thought you were into her."

So he'd been right earlier. Alex had orchestrated sending Adrian a little *distraction* so he'd fail in his mission while here in Deep Haven. But the joke was on him, because Adrian didn't play the role of ladies' man anymore.

"She told me you even kissed her."

"*She* kissed *me*." Adrian put his face in his hand. "I was never attracted to her." Especially not after meeting Ella.

"Oh boy. I'm sorry. But I know she likes you. Maybe it's a chance for you two to get to know each other better."

"No. Absolutely *not*." The word *playboy* echoed in his head. Not anymore. Not for a long time.

"I meant with her clothes *on*."

"No. Not even a little. Which cabin are you in? I'll send her to you."

"Fine. I'm in Cabin 2. I really was trying to help. I thought you might be lonely."

"Next time you think I'm lonely, send me a book." He hung up.

Sophie picked that moment to saunter out of the bedroom in a slinky dress that hugged every curve. The neckline dipped dangerously low, and the skirt wasn't much more than a scrap of fabric. Adrian nearly groaned. This wasn't any better than the towel.

"Sophie, what are you doing here, really?" He looked her straight in the eye, afraid to look anywhere else.

She boldly stared back. "I'm making you supper. Or I was. I think the sauce might be burnt. I hope you like Ragu."

"You thought you'd make me supper, and...?" He wasn't sure he really wanted to know the answer.

"I think you can figure out the rest." She gave him a smile.

"Sophie, I...no. I'm not interested." Maybe once upon a time, but...well, something had changed inside him.

"Maybe I can change your mind." Sophie came over to him and ran her finger along his chest before resting her hand on his shoulder. "C'mon. Give us a chance."

He caught her wrist and moved her hand away from him. "It's not happening. I'm sorry you came all this way, but...no."

"I thought you liked me." She crossed her arms. "I thought we had something going at the gala."

He drew in a breath, not wanting to hurt her. "You seem like a nice girl, and we had some good moments at the party, but there wasn't a spark for me."

Her voice softened. "I can help you with the spark."

"No. Sophie. I don't want that. I don't want..." *You.* "I'm up here to work. And..."

"What? There's nothing to do in this backwater town except stare at the water or go hiking. There isn't even any good shopping."

"Hiking can be fun." Especially if you ended up in the mud with someone you love. Wait. Love? Did he really love Ella?

Maybe, because the word settled inside. "And not everything needs to be about shopping and manufactured fun." Listen to him, arguing Ella's case. She did have a point—there was plenty of fun to be had in the real world. He didn't have to build a water park to find fun.

Sophie's eyes narrowed. "I suppose you've been having all this fun with my stepsister. I bet you wouldn't refuse *her* company for a night."

His mouth opened, and he stood. "Please leave."

"Adrian, I came up here to spend time with you. What am I supposed to do up here for three more days?"

"I'm sorry Athena made promises on my behalf, but you need to leave."

"I'm not leaving! *You* leave!" A vein in Sophie's neck stood out.

"This is my cabin. You can share with Athena, or you can go home. Either way, go."

Sophie stood for a moment, then marched to the bedroom and slammed the door. Adrian heard the distinct click of the lock being turned.

This was a disaster.

But maybe not one he couldn't fix. He grabbed his jacket and made his way through the darkening twilight to Ella's cabin. The warmth of the afternoon was lingering into a rare balmy night.

He knocked on Ella's door. "Ella, are you in there? Let me explain." Nothing. "Ella, I swear to you that I didn't know Athena invited Sophie up here. There is nothing going on between us. I don't know why she thought it would be okay to hang out in my cabin." He knocked again. "Are you in there? Please answer the door."

Great. Just great. Athena and Sophie had probably ruined his chance to prove to Ella that he wasn't the guy in the tabloids.

He went back to his own cabin and found Sophie was still locked in the bedroom. Through the door, he heard muffled crying. Good grief.

Athena created this problem, and Athena could get him out of it. A few minutes later, he rapped on the door to Cabin 2. "Athena, come out." No answer. "Athena, are you in there?"

Overhead the stars were starting to appear. He shoved his hands in his pockets. What now?

Movement up the path caught his eye. Darek Christiansen was carrying a load of wood toward the fire pit.

"Hey, Darek. Need a hand?" Adrian intercepted Darek and grabbed a log slipping off the stack.

"Thanks." Darek gestured with his chin toward where the logs should be stacked. "How'd it go with Seb today?"

"Good. I'm going to present to the council. He thinks I might have a chance."

"That's good to hear. Everything okay in your cabin?"

Adrian barked out a laugh. "That depends. Are you asking about the accommodations or the fact that I have an unwanted visitor?"

"I hope you don't mean a raccoon got inside."

"Oh no. Nothing like that. My problems are of the two-legged variety."

Darek raised an eyebrow. "Want to talk about it?"

Adrian considered him. He looked like the kind of guy who'd never had a woman problem in his life.

At Adrian's hesitation, Darek added, "Sorry, I don't mean to be in your business. I have a lot of brothers and brothers-in-law, so it's easy for me to slip into big-brother mode. Sometimes it can be helpful to talk it out."

Maybe. "Need help moving some more of that wood?"

Darek nodded.

It was easier to talk in the dark, working, and Adrian found himself telling Darek everything about the past days. "Even when it's not my fault, things get screwed up, and I'm tired of it. Now I don't know if Ella will even speak to me again."

"You must really care about her."

He didn't want to tell Darek how much. "It's just that we're at cross purposes, you know? And then when I thought we were coming to some sort of understanding, this thing with Sophie happens."

"Ella has a good head on her shoulders. I'm sure she can see that Sophie is trying to manipulate the situation."

"It didn't look that way earlier today." He tossed a log onto the pile. It landed with a satisfying thump.

"Give her a little time to cool down. I'm sure she'll hear you out. Ivy and I have been very impressed with how she's handled herself around here and even in town. Everyone sings her praises. She's making a home here."

Adrian resisted the urge to sigh. "Maybe. Truth is, we have a bigger problem." He told him about the hotel and Ella's fight at the shareholder's meeting. "Let's say she forgives me—she has before. But the water park will always be between us."

Darek considered him, the glow from the garage light turning his face into hard, dark planes. Finally, "When I first met Ivy, she had to remove my son from my custody. That was a hard decision for her, but ultimately it was the right one. It took some doing, but eventually I saw that she was right and I came around. Maybe you need to make some hard decisions yourself and trust that Ella will come around."

He had his doubts.

"It comes down to doing what you think is right. Is it the right thing to pursue this water park, maybe even at the risk of losing Ella? Or is it right to pursue Ella even if it means giving up the hotel project? And at the risk of sounding like my father, ask yourself, who are you trying to please—God, or someone else?"

Huh. Adrian hadn't thought about that.

His father? Himself?

He didn't even consider God in the big equation. Should it matter? This conversation echoed his mother's words. *He loves you for yourself, not for what you can do for Him.*

They fell silent as they lifted the last few logs. The rough bark bit into Adrian's hands, but he ignored it and added another piece to the stack, the physical labor a cleansing of sorts.

Darek spoke again. "I'm sorry for getting preachy. Big brother kicking in again."

"It's no problem. I appreciate you being straight with me." They stacked the last logs next to the fire pit. A cool breeze blew across the lake, ruffling its surface, turning the water to silver. Nearby an owl hooted its melancholy song.

"Thanks for your help. I'd better get back to the house. I promised Ivy I'd be there to help get the kids into bed."

Adrian sat in one of the Adirondack chairs next to the fire pit. *Who are you trying to please?* Had he gotten so caught up in seeking the respect of his father that he'd try to earn that respect at any cost? How much was too much to pay? He'd spent these last few months running from his failure the year before. He'd put his entire focus into making the Westerman project something he could be proud of. He couldn't quit now.

Ella would see that this was important, that it didn't have to be a—what did she call it?—toxic cesspool.

The words landed in his heart with no less impact than when she had said them the night of the gala. Restless, he got up out of his chair and made his way along the trail to his cabin.

Night arched overhead, any hint of light gone. He needed to

get Sophie out of his cabin. A shower would help him think, calm some of his racing thoughts.

He knocked before entering, but getting no answer, he went inside. Sophie's things were still strewn around the small space. He carefully cracked open his bedroom door, letting his breath out in a rush when he saw the lump in the bed. Sophie had fallen asleep nestled deep under his covers.

Perfect.

He couldn't stay here, especially if he wanted to redeem his reputation.

He snagged a throw pillow and blanket from the couch in the tiny living room and headed out to his car.

CHAPTER 12

*D*on't *look at Cabin 5.*

Ella almost audibly spoke the words on the way to her car.

The early morning air was crisp and clean. A fog lay over the lake and rippled a short way up the beach.

Don't look at the cabin and don't imagine what might be happening in there. Like Sophie cooking eggs for Adrian's breakfast.

Ella tightened her jaw, refusing to cry, hating the burn in her throat.

She rubbed her gritty eyes. After leaving Adrian behind the night before, she had taken her supplies and attacked Cabins 6 and 7. Somewhere around 2:00 a.m., she'd realized her cleaning fury wasn't helping and went to bed. Now, too early, it was morning and time for another round of community service.

She had just enough time to deliver this package of soap to the post office. Her online business had gotten a little more traffic since the vlog with Grace had gone live.

She got to her car and stopped.

Adrian's Porsche was parked next to her pink VW, but a rumpled blanket and some clothes lay in the driver's seat.

She peered inside. No, wait. *Adrian* lay in the driver's seat, curled in a ball, his arms folded, wrapped around his stick shift.

Huh.

Probably they'd had a fight. Whatever had happened between him and Sophie, he probably deserved to be sleeping out here in the cold.

Aw, except, he looked wrung out and rough, and her stupid heart went out to him a little.

Against her better judgment, she tapped on the window.

He slowly sat up and then arched his back to stretch. Then he spotted her and drew in a breath. Set his mouth to a grim line and, flipping the key in the ignition, rolled down his window. "Good morning." His hair stood up on one side and was matted to his head on the other.

"You look pretty terrible, Romeo." Although, admittedly, still a good look on him.

Who was she kidding? The man would look amazing in a burlap bag. But being good looking didn't excuse his behavior.

"Thanks, I think." His voice was gravely with sleep. "What time is it?"

"It's 7:30. Have you been out here all night?"

"Yep."

"Why didn't you sleep in your cabin?"

He ran a hand through his hair, as if trying to tame it. "I asked Sophie to leave the cabin but she refused. I wasn't going to stay there with her, so this was my only option."

Oh.

She had no words for that. "I don't understand. I thought you two were dating."

"No! I told you we weren't together. I don't have feelings for Sophie and never did. I had no idea she was even coming." He opened his door and got out. She stepped back to give him

175

room. He shivered in the cool morning air. "I knocked on your door last night. We left things in a bad place."

"You can say that again. I spent last night wondering if what happened between us on the trail meant *anything* to you." She held her breath, didn't look him in the eye. What if he didn't feel the same way?

"Ella." His voice cut low, still containing the husk of the morning. "I enjoyed every minute of our time on the trail. Especially the part in the mud."

She looked up at him. He gave her a small smile, and shoot, but it worked its way into her heart, past her determination to stay mad.

"I suppose if I'd have stuck around to hear your explanation last night, I would have slept better."

"There's that."

Silence shifted between them. "I'm on my way to community service. Want a ride?" She stopped herself from brushing a lock of his hair down from its upright position. He deserved to be a little less put together for once.

His smile grew. "A chance to ride in Ariel? Who could say no?"

Adrian opened the passenger door on the VW. It wasn't fair how good looking he was after sleeping in his clothes. "Um, there's a box in my seat."

"Oh, that. Just toss it in the back. No, wait! Set it gently in the back. No tossing."

Adrian popped the back of the seat forward and moved the box as ordered. "This thing is pretty beat up. What is it?" He got in.

She pulled out of the small parking area. "It's a box my dad packed up a long time ago. I never had the nerve to open it."

"What's in it?"

"That's the thing. I don't know."

He stilled. "What? Why?"

She sighed, slowing as they got to the highway. "One time when we were being evicted for squatting, we didn't have time to pack up our stuff to move. My dad ran around the house throwing things into that box and taped it up before the police could escort us out. As a kid, I never wanted to unpack it because...I don't know. It's a bad memory."

"So, you, what—just drive around with it in your car?"

"When you say it like that, it makes me sound crazy." Truth was, she felt a little crazy. But not crazy enough to open the box.

She didn't know why, but knowing what was so important for her dad to keep felt like peeking into a part of him she didn't know.

Maybe she didn't want to know.

"Do you think you'll open it?" Adrian said.

"Honestly? I don't really know. I always imagined opening it up with my dad after he bought us a house with a white picket fence and a tree with a swing hanging on it. I imagined him saying, 'Now we'll never have to move again,' and how he would give me a key to the front door."

She flipped on her blinker to make a left turn. Overhead the brilliant sun played tag with the fluffy clouds racing through the sky as she momentarily waited at the stop sign.

"I'm sorry your dad never gave you that," Adrian said as she turned onto the main road through Deep Haven.

"Yeah, well, the only thing he gave me was a box full of his junk." She motioned to the box in the back seat.

He looked at it. Then, "Ella. Have you considered that not opening the box is your way of staying angry at him?"

She looked at him, frowned. "No. I've forgiven him."

"Have you? Because your hurt is pretty deep, and maybe you don't want to see anything else but his mistakes. Open the box. See what's inside..."

Ella considered him. Maybe he was right. She *was* still angry at her father. And frankly, she didn't want to know what was inside the box. Not if it meant opening new wounds. "I'll think about it." She looked over and smiled at him.

He took her fingers and settled their hands on the stick shift.

"Maybe after we finish for the day we can swing by the hotel. I'd love to show you what I have planned."

Something about the suggestion rankled. "Adrian, you won't convince me that this project is good for Deep Haven."

"Just give it a chance."

Ella sighed. "Okay, I'll listen to what you have to say and take a look at the spot, but no promises beyond that."

"I wouldn't ask you to change your convictions, you know. I admire them. I just think there's wiggle room." Adrian squeezed her hand. "I'm just asking for a chance to try to figure it out."

Okay, she could give him that. In fact, looking at him sitting in the front seat of her pink car, all rumpled from sleeping like a pretzel, she wanted to give him a whole lot more.

But he was right. She couldn't change her convictions.

"By the way," Ella said, "I called ahead this time. We're on cleanup duty again, this time downtown. I need to stop at the post office first." After their quick stop mailing her product, she swung into the lot at Bear Tree Park. Across the park a table was set up, and the usual crowd milled around gathering supplies. "The sun's up—maybe we'll even get a tan today."

"Actually, in a weird way, being outdoors reminds me of one of my favorite memories of my parents."

They got out, and she fell into step beside him.

"Back when my dad was first starting out—he had maybe two hotels at the time—we were all home on a Friday night, which was rare even back then. And Athena, who is more like a sister than a cousin, was visiting. We had our whole night planned—video games, movies, junk food. Typical middle schooler stuff. My dad was locked in his study, doing computer work, and my brother was up in his room watching TV. Just after the popcorn was popped, the power went out. There we were in the dark. My mom found a bunch of candles, and my dad lit a fire in the fireplace. Even Alex came down. We ended up cooking our supper over that fire and playing board games for hours."

"Sounds magical."

"I felt like we were camping indoors."

They stepped up to the group. Adrian signed in on the clipboard that Carol held out, then handed Ella the board and pen. "That was probably the last time my family ever had fun together like that."

His confession made her heart hurt. "I'm sorry."

He shrugged. "That's why I love building water park hotels so much."

"I don't understand. What do board games in the living room have to do with water parks?"

"It's a great place for families to have fun together. Seeing the looks on the kids' faces as their parents take time to play with them is worth every penny."

It was a sweet idea. She handed the clipboard back. "You know, there are plenty of things people can do to have fun together that don't include waterslides and chlorine. Especially up here."

"I haven't seen it. Not in my family at least. That one night of unplugging and not being so caught up in our electronics was what helped us reconnect. You can't bring a cell phone on a waterslide."

"Well, that's certainly true." She grabbed their stack of cleaning supplies from the table, holding the grabber away from Adrian. "I don't think you can be trusted with this thing."

He grinned, and she gave up her last attempts to hold a grudge.

Carol directed them down to a section of beach to start cleaning.

"One of my happiest memories was when my parents took

me camping. Like, real, actual camping. You know, outdoors," Ella teased.

"What's that?" He winked at her before starting down the rocky beach with his bag, picking up a Dairy Queen cup.

She laughed, then sighed. "For those two nights, sleeping outside and really connecting with my parents is something I'll never forget. I was pretty young but that experience has stuck with me. And then when my mom died, those memories became even sweeter." She chased down a napkin.

Maybe she should forgive her father a little for the life he'd made her lead. They both had lost something significant when her mother died.

Adrian held open the bag. "This outdoor camping you speak of sounds a little extreme. I mean, what did you do when you ran into snakes and didn't have a valiant prince to rescue you? It must have been scary."

"Oh, please." She stuck out her tongue, holding back a grin. "That was the one and only time I've reacted like that in the presence of a snake. It just surprised me, is all. I think *you* were the scared one."

"I wasn't the one who screamed." He nudged her. "As for me? Scared? Never. I can face down any wild animal the wilderness throws at me. I'll just bring my deluxe trash grabber." He took it from her and held it aloft like a sword.

"I dare you to go camping. See if you can live in the outdoors overnight."

"I'll go camping when you do something without preparing for every last detail. You might have to leave your Mary Poppins bag home."

"Never."

"See?"

"Okay, fine."

"Fine? Good. We'll go camping tomorrow night." He grinned, the sunlight shining in his eyes. Frankly, he looked a little like he'd been camping, with the layer of whiskers, his rumpled dress pants, and wool jacket. The poor man was definitely out of his element.

"Wait, what? No, we can't do that," Ella said, grabbing a donut wrapper.

"Why not?"

"People don't go camping on a whim in the middle of the week. I can't go camping on a random Tuesday night."

"Is there some rule against camping on Tuesdays that I don't know about?"

"Of course not. I just have responsibilities. Plus, we don't have any gear."

"It's just overnight. Today is my last day of community service. I'll talk to Carol and see if you can get the day off. I'll bet Darek has gear we can rent or borrow, and the rest I'll just buy in town. C'mon. It'll be fun."

He'd talk to Carol? Only, Ella would lay bets the woman said yes. And he'd just *buy* their equipment? Sheesh.

"I have responsibilities! Some of us can't just take off, buy what they want. I have three houses scheduled plus another cabin at Evergreen."

"I'll help you with your jobs. Together we can get it done in half the time. I'm pretty handy with a dust rag, and you know I can heft garbage bags. Tomorrow night, or your dare's off."

Ella considered him standing on the shore, the shimmer of the water behind him. She let out a breath. Honestly. The man would look good climbing out of a dumpster.

And, the way he smiled at her, with so much dare in his eyes, she couldn't help it. "Fine, but we need to get an early start. We have to canoe out to the camping area, so we need to be in the water by noon."

"I can do early. I'll meet you by 5:00 a.m. with my cleaning supplies. What? Why are you smiling?"

"I'm imagining you strapping a canoe to the top of your Porsche."

He grinned at her. "Guess I should add renting a truck to the list."

"Definitely."

Now all she needed to do was remember to pack her sanity.

Hearing Ella's laugh was the best way to start the day.

When Adrian had gotten home yesterday after community service, Sophie had not been in his cabin, and he hadn't seen Athena's car in the lot. He'd put the two of them out of his mind as he'd gotten in his car to drive back into town. During his stop at the outfitters last night to pick up supplies for the camping trip, he noticed a few other items he could use this morning.

He'd turned up at Ella's door sporting a ruffled apron and holding a pink and purple feather duster.

"Hello—housekeeping," he said in his best falsetto as she opened the door. He flourished the feather duster and struck a pose.

"Oh brother," Ella said, but her laugh sprinkled over him in a baptism of joy.

"Give me a minute, and we can get started." Ella disappeared back into her cabin. A moment later, she came back out carrying a clipboard and a bucket filled with cleaning supplies. "Here's the list for today. I've got one cabin across Evergreen Lake, and then two here at Evergreen. I thought we could start over there."

"Great. I'll drive."

"I won't argue with that."

As they made their way around the lake, Adrian told Ella about the plans he'd made for the night.

"I talked to Darek, and he can rent us the equipment we need

—tents and canoes and sleeping bags. He said we should start at Rose Lake."

"He's right about that. Rose is a good beginner spot. That's what I was thinking too. I've been there once with Colleen and her family." Ella reached for the dash and flipped on the heat. "It's a few hours' paddle and then a short portage to a great camping site. There's a hill that overlooks the lake. Great views of the sunset."

"Sounds perfect."

They pulled into the driveway Ella indicated. An A-frame style cabin rested on the shore of Evergreen Lake. Its wood timbers glowed golden in the morning light. "We only have to scrub down the kitchen and bathroom here." Ella opened her door. "The homeowners take care of the rest."

Adrian grabbed the cleaning supplies from his tiny trunk. "Lead the way, Princess." Ella keyed a code into the pad by the door. He followed her into the vaulted entryway of the house. Next to him, Ella toed off her pink Chucks, so he did the same, dropping his shoes onto a mat by the door.

He gave a low whistle as he followed her into the great room.

"This place is something else." The massive room was anchored on one end by a stone fireplace that arched two stories. Arranged around the fireplace were couches that looked deep enough to sink into and drown. The other end of the great room was a kitchen tucked under a loft. He spotted gleaming stainless steel appliances and granite cabinet tops.

"It can't be any more luxurious than what you grew up with." Ella's comment, tossed over her shoulder, hit its mark.

"Ha! True. My mother always insisted our house have the best of everything. I'm just loving the north woods vibe this home is giving off."

Ella set her bucket of supplies on the floor near the sink.

"Sure, it's cozy, and probably expensive. But I don't think it's much of a home."

"What makes you say that?"

"Simple. To have a home you need love." Her cheeks pinked. "I've never seen the couple who owns this place be in the same room at the same time." She motioned toward the fireplace. "The only thing that heats up around here is that."

"That's the saddest thing I've ever heard."

"I know. Every time I come in here, I'm reminded that I don't need much, but I do want my home to be filled with love."

"That is one thing we can agree on."

Cleaning the A-frame went quickly, with Ella cleaning the bathrooms and wiping down countertops, and Adrian vacuuming and sweeping the wood floors in the kitchen.

Soon they were back at Evergreen, crossing the cabins off their list one by one.

He could hear Ella humming in the other room of a tiny cabin as she scrubbed the sink in the bathroom. Midway through the first job, Adrian had realized that the soap Ella used was the scent he'd caught on her in that elevator.

Ella walked into the main room as he was spritzing the table with cleaner.

"What do you put in this stuff?"

"Oh, this one's my favorite. I use a lemon extract along with rosemary and mint. It makes everything smell so fresh and clean."

"I would never have imagined rosemary would smell so good in a cleaner. Don't they use that in cooking?" He rubbed a wooden chair, giving it a high shine with his damp rag.

"Yeah, I read about it in an artisan soap book when I first started playing around. The lemon balances out the earthy rosemary notes. And then I like to add the mint for a bit more brightness." She scrubbed at a spot.

"Missed that, sorry."

She shrugged. "I'm the pro."

Yes, she was. She had shortcuts and techniques that he'd never realized. Cleaning was actually a learned skill. A science, even.

"Your soaps and cleaners could easily be sold at any high-end store. They're amazing."

No, *she* was amazing. It was taking all his willpower not to pull her into his arms right on the spot.

"When I get the rest of my stuff back from my apartment, I'll give you a bar of my other popular scent, lavender and cedarwood. It is slightly more masculine." She stood back and admired her work, hands on her hips. Her passion for her work made her beautiful, her hair down around her face in wisps. "That's one of the fun things about this business—you can customize your scents to your customers' preferences."

He could see how this could work in a commercial setting. In fact, each hotel could have a signature scent. With the growing organic and green movement, featuring an all-natural, toxic-free cleaning scent might actually be a marketing edge.

If Ella was willing, he should be able to draw up some solid business ideas for her. His experience in the hotel field could shape that proposal into a winner. They could present them to his father together. Then he would take advantage of his other hotel and resort contacts to expand beyond Bear Creek Resorts. There would be no stopping them. This was a good idea—he knew it.

He opened his mouth to tell Ella his plan just as the door to the cabin opened, and Athena and Sophie stepped over the threshold.

"Oh, sorry, we're almost done here," Ella said.

"That's okay. We don't mind. Keep cleaning." Athena dropped her purse on the tiny loveseat in the living area of the cabin. It appeared she had embraced the whole Deep Haven vibe. Her normal designer clothing had been replaced by an outfit that could have come straight off the cover of L.L. Bean.

Sophie glanced at Ella, then cast a look at Adrian, clearly confused.

Athena too, because, "Adrian, what are you doing here?" His cousin looked between him and Ella. "Are you *cleaning*?" She frowned. "Is this part of your community service?"

He sighed. "Ella, this is my cousin, Athena."

Athena looked at Ella, then a slow smile creased her face. "Birdwatching, huh?"

"I don't understand," Sophie said. She wore a white rabbit-trimmed jacket and a pair of over-the-knee black boots, and set her purse on the chair he'd just polished. "What community service?"

Not that it was any of their business, but... "I'm helping Ella get her work done early. We're going camping as soon as we're finished."

"Camping?" Athena put her hands on her hips. Her eyes opened wide. "On a Tuesday?"

"What does everyone have against camping on a Tuesday?"

"I just always thought it was a weekend thing." Athena gestured vaguely. "It seems weird to go camping on a random Tuesday just because the whim took you."

"That's what I said!" Ella agreed. Okay, it might not have been the best idea to introduce her to his cousin after all. "But Adrian convinced me it was just as valid to go on a Tuesday, and I mean, he's not wrong."

Oh. He could get used to hearing Ella defend him.

"I'd love to try camping. Maybe we should come with you." Athena was never shy—the last few days proved that—but this was taking it to a new level. "I came up here to hang out with you, Adrian. And I'm sure Sophie would love to spend some extra time with her sister, right?"

Sophie looked a little green around the gills, but she nodded.

Didn't Athena see the awkward situation she was creating? Not everyone had the ability to be friendly with their exes like she did—not that Adrian would call Sophie his ex. Also, there was clearly some tension between Ella and Sophie. Couldn't his cousin sense it?

"Please, Adrian? There's nothing interesting to do in town."

Guess not.

Enough was enough. "Athena…" Adrian shot Ella a look of apology. Then he turned back to his cousin. "You'd hate it. You'd have to get different shoes."

She glared at him.

"Seriously, Athena, it's not going to be a walk in the park." He pushed a hand through his hair. "We're paddling out to the campsite in a canoe. You can only bring what you can carry." *Please don't come.* He tried to send her the message with his eyes, but she ignored him.

"What do you know about it? It's not like you're an avid canoe-person. What would you call that? A canoe-er? Canoephile? Canoeist?" Athena waved her hand in the air. "Whatever. I'm sure if you can do it, we can do it too. What do you think, Ella? We'd really love to spend some time with you both. We can handle it, right?"

Ella was standing, holding her wet cloth, a stripped look on her face. "You probably can handle it. The lake we have to cross is usually pretty calm, and the portage to the campsite is short. It's entry-level Boundary Waters stuff."

"That settles it then. Adrian, you go arrange for an extra tent and canoe, and we will join you on this adventure."

It was no use arguing with the hurricane that was Athena. Apparently this camping trip for two was now a trip for four. He hoped Darek had the supplies.

Adrian made his way over to the door, but Sophie grabbed his arm. "Adrian, can I talk to you for a minute?" Under her makeup, Sophie's eyes were swollen. He'd been right to leave the cabin the other night, but he still felt like a heel for making a woman cry.

"Sure, what's up?"

Sophie tugged him outside, onto the stoop, and shut the door. "I just wanted to apologize for the other night." She kept her eyes focused on her toes. "Athena told me that you...well, it doesn't matter what Athena told me. She was obviously wrong, and I made a fool of myself."

"Hey, listen." Adrian reached out and tipped Sophie's chin up until she looked him in the eye. "First of all, Athena is a force of nature. She sees something she wants, and she charges after it. Once she had us in her crosshairs, we didn't have much of a chance."

A tear gathered in the corner of Sophie's eye. She reached up and brushed it away. "I wanted her to be right. You are so handsome and kind and funny. I wanted you to like me."

He said nothing, not wanting to encourage her.

"I'll stay out of your way, I promise."

He smiled.

She leaned over and pressed a kiss on his cheek. Stepped back. "I can't wait to go camping."

She let herself inside.

He blew out a breath. Oh yes, this should be fun.

CHAPTER 13

*M*aybe a little spontaneity was just what she needed, right?

It's too bad Adrian didn't give her any time to plan this trip, as Ella could have provided each of them with a packing list. But that was supposed to be part of the fun, right? A spontaneous trip.

Ella let out a low chuckle, remembering their first twenty minutes after they'd divided themselves between the canoes. They'd needed a strong paddler in each, and she definitely wasn't going to have Adrian pair up with Sophie. She and Sophie took one canoe and directed Adrian and Athena into the other. They all went round and round in circles until each boat figured out how to work together to steer in a straight line.

A short while into their paddle across the lake, Ella felt her shoulders unknot. In the other canoe, Adrian and Athena tossed teasing insults back and forth like tennis players at Wimbledon.

Sophie turned slightly in her seat. "I think we're getting the hang of this paddling thing."

"You're doing great."

Something sparkled in Sophie's eye. "Are you thinking what

I am thinking?" She nodded toward the other two and lifted her dripping paddle. She held up her fingers—one, two, three—and the two of them dug into the water, splashing a spray over Adrian and Athena.

Athena shrieked in laughter, rocking her boat so it threatened to capsize. She and Adrian wobbled around until finally straightening out.

"Oh, it's on now." Athena finally caught her breath. "C'mon Adrian. It's their turn to get wet."

The two groups traded splashes, canoes rocking, until Adrian cried out, "Truce! Truce! Friends don't let friends capsize."

Ella, warmed by the sun and the companionship, thought about his statement. Could she count Athena and Sophie as friends? Maybe not yet. But...someday? The possibility ignited a flicker of hope.

She'd had her doubts about taking a bunch of city slickers out into the wilderness, but it wasn't that long ago she had been a city slicker herself. Statistically, this trip was the safest they could take.

Everything was going to be fine.

Probably.

They had reached the portage with a minimum of splashing. There was a bit of jockeying over who was carrying what pack, and then they hoisted the canoes and worked their way toward camp. At one point, Athena screamed and said something under her breath in Greek. "Something bit me!" She slapped repeatedly at her arm.

"It seems a little early in the year for mosquitos." Ella put down her end of the canoe and took a look at Athena's arm. "I guess it could have been a bee. Are you allergic? I have Benadryl."

"No, I'm not allergic. It'll be fine." Athena's annoyed look was already disappearing, even as a red bump appeared on her arm. Ella reached into her backpack and retrieved a tiny vial.

"Here, this is lavender and chamomile. Let's put a little on, and you'll feel better."

The sun was kissing the tops of the pines as they set up camp.

Sophie had approached Ella tentatively and asked, "Would you like to share a tent? Athena doesn't like to share."

Kind of awkward, but what could she say? Especially if they were going to forge any kind of a bond. "Okay." They placed their tent twenty feet from Athena's and near the lake overlook. Adrian set his up on the other side of the fire pit.

All in all, there had been relatively few mishaps, and now they had a fire roaring in the center of their camp. The forest ringed around them, the night rich with the scent of pine. On one side of the campsite, just beyond Ella's tent, the view stretched away, over the lake.

It was early in the season to start camping, but the chilly air made for a clear sky, the stars winking down from the velvety darkness. Another campfire could barely be seen flickering far off through the trees.

Adrian poked at the fire, sending sparks to the heavens. "I think this bad boy is ready. Let's roast some hot dogs."

Using fallen branches they'd cleaned, the group propped their hot dogs over the fire. Soon the scent of spicy, salty beef filled the air, mingling with the scent of wet underbrush and melting snow.

Using their fingers, they ate the hot dogs straight from the fire. A round of "Hot! Hot!" chorused from each of them.

"You know," Athena said, "I never thought sitting outside, eating tube meat off a stick after paddling a canoe for half of forever would be so enjoyable. Next thing you know, I'm going to take up birdwatching." She shot a grin at Adrian. "You've really got something going here, Ella."

The praise warmed her. "I wish I could take credit, but I'm afraid God put this place together long before I arrived." She laced another hot dog onto her stick and held it over the hot coals. "Have you always lived in Minnesota, Athena? Sorry, it's just that you have an accent."

"No, you're right. I was born in Greece, near where my and Adrian's grandparents live. We moved to Minnesota when I was nine."

"Oh, wow. That must have been hard. Such a culture shock."

"When my family moved over here from Greece, I was so mad. I was convinced that I would never have any friends and that my life was ruined. My parents didn't really care what I thought, and sometimes I'm not sure if they ever will. They don't care what the other thinks either, come to think about it. It's better if they aren't in the same room...or even continent." Athena laughed and shifted on her log. Put her arm around Adrian. "That's why I spent so much time over at Adrian's. He's my brother now. I'm just a meddling older sister."

He smiled down at her. "Remember the time we invited all those people over to my father's new resort and then ordered room service for everyone just to show off? My parents almost banned you from coming over after that."

On her side of the fire, Sophie sighed deeply. "It must have been nice growing up with siblings. I always wanted a brother or sister, but my mom never stayed married long enough to want another child." She glanced at Ella, something tentative in her stare. "Until Mom married Ella's dad, she'd never been with anyone who had other kids."

"Having siblings isn't all it's cracked up to be," Adrian said. "My brother, Alex, can be a real piece of work. If it weren't for Athena, I'm not sure I wouldn't have killed him before we got to high school."

He jabbed a marshmallow onto his stick, held it over the embers. "He played a terrible trick on me once when one of our water parks was short staffed. We were filling in as lifeguards, and I saw a kid go under the water. He stayed under for what seemed like a really long time, and I dove in and pulled him out. It didn't seem like he was breathing, and all his friends were all yelling at me. I was just about to start mouth-to-mouth breathing when the boy opened his eyes and started laughing. And he wasn't the only one—Alex put him up to it. He just wanted to see me freak out." Adrian paused, took his marshmallow off the stick. He downed it in one bite. "It wasn't the first—or the last—time that Alex and I got in a fistfight in front of guests."

"I can vouch for that," Athena said. "Sometimes I think Alex eggs you on just because he likes to see you riled."

Ella looked at Adrian and tried to imagine him in a fight. Maybe he would have fought Kyle for her outside her house, after their little B&E. Heat went through her at the thought.

Athena stood up and stretched. "Okay, kiddos. I'm heading to bed. It's been fun, but I'm bushed." She headed to one of the three tents circling the campfire. Nearby, the canoes rested together, silvery drops of lake water still glistening in spots on their hulls.

Sophie covered her yawn. "I think Athena has the right idea. I'm heading in too. Ella, are you coming?"

"I'll let you get settled in and then I'll join you."

Behind her, Ella heard the zip of the tent flaps. Adrian got up from his log seat and moved to the one Sophie had vacated next to Ella.

"Thanks for today," he said. He reached for Ella's hand, and she laced her fingers with his.

"It's been a good day, hasn't it? I wondered if Athena and Sophie would survive."

"Yeah, thanks for putting up with those two."

"What can you do? They're family." Ella smiled.

Adrian pulled her to standing. "I've been waiting all day to do this." He wrapped an arm around her back and his eyes dropped to her lips. Her heartbeat quickened, and she tipped her face up. She caught a glimpse of the diamond sky before her eyelids dropped shut, and Adrian pressed a kiss to her lips. Ella moved a half step closer to him and wrapped her arms around his shoulders, her fingers playing with the ends of his hair. He tasted like marshmallow.

Here she was, kissing a man with the smoky scent of campfire lingering in the air. Under the stars dancing in their courses above. Yeah, she could get used to this. She made a sound at the back of her throat and deepened the kiss, burying her hands in Adrian's hair. All too soon he groaned and pulled away. He rested his forehead on hers.

"You'd better get to bed before I do something we both regret." His gaze smoldered hotter than the coals in the firepit.

Using the water bucket, Ella doused the fire, then spread the ashes out to make sure the fire wouldn't start up again. Adrian checked that their picnic supplies were put away, then came around to her side of the campsite. He took her hand and held it a moment then dropped a quick kiss on her lips.

"Good night, Ella."

"Good night, Adrian." She pulled away from his gaze and climbed into the tent she was sharing with Sophie.

Inside the tent, Sophie had lit a tiny electric lantern. When Ella stepped in, Sophie sat up in her sleeping bag. She wore her hair pulled back, a sleep mask pushed up on her forehead.

"Ella, I swear I didn't know you and Adrian were a thing. Athena told me he liked me, and I…well, he's just so handsome, and I thought…I really wanted him to like me. Nothing happened that night in his cabin, I promise. I read way too much into our blind date at the gala, and told myself that he just needed a little more, um, encouragement. I'm so embarrassed."

Ella unzipped her sleeping bag, her mouth tight. "I forgive

you. The whole thing was just a big misunderstanding." Okay, not really, but she didn't want to fight.

Sophie lay back, then turned on her side to face Ella. "Thank you." She grew quiet. "I know this will be hard to believe, but I meant what I said out there. I've always wanted a sibling. And when Athena called us sisters yesterday...well, it sounds dumb, but I realized that maybe I should have given you a chance."

Ella looked at her, nonplussed. "I've always wanted a sister too." Her heart twisted. "So why have you always treated me with so much contempt?"

Sophie sighed. "My mom never wanted another child. I think she barely wanted *me*. When she found out your dad had a daughter, she basically went ballistic. She warned me not to have anything to do with you. I really don't know why...maybe she thought you would take all of your dad's attention or something. Since you were headed to college, there wasn't much else I could do than go along with her ideas. When your dad died, she said you'd taken all our money and were trying to ruin our lives. I didn't know you, so I didn't know she was lying."

Ella plumped her pillow. "That's funny, because there isn't any money. Dad squandered it all away on gambling. I found out after he died that it was basically a miracle that his business survived all those years. Every time he'd get a big contract, he'd head to the racetrack at Canterbury and lose money he hadn't even earned yet. We moved around a lot, and I'm just now finding out that it's because he was trying to stay one step ahead of his debts."

"Huh. We have a lot in common. My mom is a gold digger. Don't laugh, she is—she would only marry a man who had tons of money. And then she'd leave him just as quickly as she married him. I never knew how long any of my stepdads would stay my stepdad."

"I don't know what she saw in my dad. Maybe she should have asked him for his bank statements before tying the knot."

"I remember the night when she met your dad. She came home from a party—actually, it was the Annual Bear Creek Resorts Shareholders meeting and gala—and all she could talk about was the man she'd met there. Mike Bradley, the King of Clean."

"Maybe she was swayed by his single share in the company. Or those horrible billboards."

They grinned at each other in the dim light of the tent, a tentative, desperate entente.

"I think she saw her own face up there. Jackie Kent-Bradley, the Queen of Clean. It would be the closest she could get to being royalty. She had gone there as someone else's plus-one, but by the end of the night she'd totally ditched him for your dad." Sophie rolled onto her back.

"Marrying him must have been a rude awakening when she found out that my dad really wasn't worth anything, all appearances to the contrary."

"That's probably why she resented you so much. Despite all your dad's faults, he really loved you. He kept raving about the great grades you were getting in college and how someday his little girl was going to change the world."

They lay there silently for a moment. Ella's heart ached with what-ifs.

"I wish he would have been a better father. The funny thing is, I think he saw himself as a *great* father. I think he didn't even notice what moving around all the time and wasting his money on gambling was doing to me. How it made my life so unstable. He always talked big and dreamed big, but he needed a stabilizing force like my mother had been to keep him on track. No offense, but I'd always wondered why he chose to marry your mom. There were always a lot of women trying to get his attention, but he never seemed interested until he met Jackie."

"For what it's worth, he seemed to love her. And he definitely loved you. Maybe with you going away to school, he felt he needed someone to come home to. He didn't realize who he was marrying until it was too late."

Maybe it was time to let old misunderstandings fall away. Ella held her hand out to Sophie across the darkness of the tent. "I guess we have more in common than we thought. Friends?"

Sophie put her hand into Ella's. "Nope. Sisters."

Adrian sank deeper into his sleeping bag. Flipped off the camping lantern.

Who knew that paddling a canoe for two or three hours could be so tiring? It was worth every sore muscle to see Ella's hair shining in the sun and the delight on her face as she threw her head back and laughed loud and long at something Athena had said.

Even the struggle to get the tents set up couldn't dampen his spirits.

These past few weeks working with Ella had been so satisfying. He remembered Pastor Dan's message from a couple days ago. *Friends, we can fully trust God. Even when believers are unfaithful, God still shows up.* Adrian let the thought of God not needing him to change in order to love him sink deep into his heart. He didn't have to be funny or driven or perfect—God loved him for who he was, the real Adrian Vassos.

The night settled around him, the deep sounds of the wind in the trees, the occasional hoot of an owl.

So maybe he liked camping—

A scream ripped through the night air, sharp and bright.

He sat bolt upright. A wild cat? A cougar—?

The scream rent the night again.

No—it was *female.*

One of the girls!

Adrian fumbled for the zipper pull to the tent, finally zipped it open, and tumbled out.

Across the campsite, Sophie was jumping around, still screaming. Ella scrambled out of their tent, her face pale in the moonlight.

Adrian strode across the rock and reached Sophie's side.

"Something crawled in there with me and bit me!"

From the corner of his eye, Adrian saw a small furry animal scurry out of the tent.

All this over a chipmunk?

"Sophie, you'll be okay. Let me take a look at the bite." He reached out his hand.

But the chipmunk chose that moment to reappear. It scampered across Sophie's bare feet then ran off into the woods. Sophie, in full panic mode, jumped back, tripped over a tent stake, and screamed again. She ran several steps away from the tent.

Then, in a blink, she disappeared.

Adrian took a few more steps forward and halted.

In the darkness, he hadn't even seen how close they were to the cliff. "Sophie!"

He looked down, into the black of the night, unable to see her.

Sophie had stopped screaming.

"Did she go over?"

He turned and caught Ella as she hurried around to where he stood.

Athena, too, was out of her tent.

Ella laced her hand into Adrian's and leaned out over the precipice. "Sophie! Sophie! Can you hear me? Are you okay?"

He too leaned over. "Sophie, call up to us if you're okay."

No answer.

"I'll go get my flashlight." Ella ran back into the tent.

"What's going on?" Athena asked, her voice high and tight.

"Sophie went over the cliff!"

Athena walked out closer to the cliff's edge just as Ella returned with her flashlight and backpack. She pointed the light down the dropoff. Sixty feet away, the lake glimmered in the pinprick of light.

He could be sick. Halfway down the cliff Sophie lay sprawled on a small ledge above the water. She was on her side, her leg bent in an unnatural position.

"We've got to get to her." Ella took two steps off to the right.

"I'll go. Stay here." The last thing he wanted her—or Athena —to do was trip and fall going down a steep path in the darkness.

"Do you have any first aid training?" Ella asked.

"Just CPR and basic lifeguard skills."

She blew out a breath, then looked down again. Swallowed.

Oh right. Her fear of heights. Still, she looked at him with determination. "It would be better if I go, then. I took some premed in college and keep my first aid certificate up-to-date."

Of course she did. "You're right. It makes sense, but are you sure?"

Ella nodded. Rolled her shoulders and nodded again. Brave girl.

"Right. Okay. See if that ledge can hold all of us and then we'll come down."

Ella shined her light around them. "I'm sure there's a path just beyond the canoes. I saw something when we came up."

He looked in the direction she indicated, saw a faint break in the brush lining that part of the campground before the land dropped away to the lake. He gave a tight nod. "We'll light the way as best we can from up here."

Adrian held his breath and rubbed the back of his neck as Ella made her way over to the path and down the almost sheer hill. A roll of horror threaded through him as she stumbled. He reached for her as though he could bridge the gap and keep her steady.

Then she picked her way across the rocks toward her step-sister. He could hear Ella talking to Sophie the whole way down, the sound traveling in the clear night air.

"I'm coming for you, don't worry. We're sisters now, and I'm not losing you. Don't go anywhere, Sophie, I'm coming."

She knelt by her sister and pulled a first aid kit from her backpack. Adrian could hear her talking to Sophie in a low voice as she shined the light over her injuries and probed the wounds.

"Guys?" she called up a few moments later. "It's not good down here. I think her leg is broken, and she has a nasty gash on her forehead. She's unconscious but her breathing is steady."

Athena covered her mouth with her hand.

"Steady there, Cuz. We don't need you to pass out too." Adrian put his arm around Athena, and she clung to him briefly. Soothing her unraveled some of his own dread. Below them Ella was still talking.

"Call for help. I don't want to move her in case her neck is injured. We're going to need a rescue team."

Adrian went back to his tent and collected his cell phone. No signal. He grabbed his sleeping bag and a towel, headed to the cliff edge, giving Ella a warning to be ready. "Incoming!" He tossed the bag and towel down to Ella and Sophie.

"Athena and I'll head for one of those campfires we saw earlier along the edge of the lake and see if anyone has a cell signal. Stay warm—we'll be back as soon as we can."

Athena leaned into her tent, rummaged around for her jacket. "Okay, let's go."

Making their way back to the portage, they found the other path and headed into the forest along the lake.

"I can't believe I wanted to come out here." Athena pushed a tree branch away from her face. It swung back with a swish.

He ducked out of the branch's way. "She's going to be okay."

"Now is not the time for happy-go-lucky Adrian."

"I wasn't… Fine. Let's just find help."

A green tent flickered into view through a stand of pines off the path. Adrian took a full breath for the first time since bolting out of bed.

"Hello the campsite," Adrian called out.

"'Hello the campsite?'" Athena shot him a look. "Did you hit *your* head too?"

Adrian ignored her, because it worked.

The tent opened, and a big man climbed out, a woman right behind him. They both wore thermal long johns and flannel shirts, clearly prepared for this weather.

"Can we help you?" The man shined a flashlight on them, and Adrian held up a hand to ward off the light.

"Our friend is injured and we need help. Do you have a cell phone we can use?"

"Sorry," the woman said. "No signal."

"Yeah, we didn't have a signal either." He glanced at Athena, then back at them. "We need help."

"What kind of injuries does your friend have?" The man pulled on a pair of hiking boots, began lacing them up.

"She fell over a cliff. We think she has a broken leg." The odd angle of her landing flashed through his mind. "Maybe even something worse."

"Is she conscious?" The wife joined her husband in putting on footwear. She'd added a headlamp to her attire.

"No."

The man nodded at his wife. "Okay. There's a ranger station the next lake over. We'll paddle over and see if we can get some help."

"Thank you," Athena said.

Adrian shook his hand.

"Listen, keep your friend warm, but don't move her. She might have internal injuries."

"I should go with you," Athena said. "To show the rescuers where we are."

Adrian looked at her, but yes, that was a good idea.

His chest tight, he headed back to the campsite and cut down along the shoreline, climbing over the rocks then making his way up the hillside to the ledge. Adrian let out a breath when he spotted Ella's light. The fear that kept curling through him this past hour lightened. They would face this together.

"Hey," he said.

"Hey, yourself." Ella's quiet response did not fill him with confidence.

"We found help—they're going to alert the rangers."

"Good." She grabbed his arm and stepped away from Sophie, who lay motionless on the ground, wrapped in the sleeping bag. "She's got a compound fracture. We need to stop the bleeding. I tried to get it to slow down, but the best way to do it is to try and splint the leg. Can you look around for some straight branches? We'll also need to put some pressure on her head wound."

"Yeah."

He turned to go, but her hand on his arm didn't loosen. He turned back to her, saw the haunted look in her eyes. "It'll be okay, Ella." He would do everything in his power to make that true.

She nodded, and he pressed a kiss to her forehead, then headed back to camp.

Hunting around the campsite, he found the downed tree they'd taken their hot dog sticks from. He broke four branches from the tree, then rooted around in his backpack for an extra T-shirt. Wrapping the shirt around the stick bundle, he added a few granola bars to his pile, grabbed another sleeping bag, and headed back down the cliff.

"She moaned a couple times," Ella said as he walked up. She sat on a rock, the moon lighting her face, but her expression sent a chill through him.

He handed her the branches and then tore his extra shirt into strips.

"We'll need to be careful as we set her leg. She might have internal injuries, even spinal injuries. Keep her head still."

He climbed over Sophie and put his hands on her head. Blood saturated the rock and slicked his hands, and Ella handed him a piece of gauze to stave the bleeding.

Then she moved Sophie's leg just enough to close the open wound. Adrian drew in a shuddering gulp of air. Seeing Sophie's wound like that rammed home the seriousness of their situation. Ella bound the leg to the stick, then also ran a cord around the upper leg to slow the bleeding.

She nodded once. Took a deep breath. Then gave him a look. "Are you staring at me?"

"Not staring. Admiring. I could never have done all of this. Are you sure you aren't an ER doc or something?"

She pushed a piece of hair off her forehead. "I just retain a lot of information. I took an emergency medicine class and they talked about how to stabilize injuries. And a wilderness survival class at the Art Colony." Ella climbed up next to him. "Let's get that sleeping bag back over her." She took over holding the gauze, already well saturated, and he shook out the bag.

"I think the bleeding is slowing." She replaced the gauze with another piece.

He tucked the bag around Sophie, then sat back. Silence stretched out between them.

Ella was shivering.

She looked up at him and then away. "This is all my fault. I should have never said yes to this crazy trip."

"Are you kidding? No. We wouldn't be here if I hadn't

goaded you into it. You were right, Tuesdays are not good days to go camping."

Ella cracked a smile at that one. "No, you're right. Some things you just can't plan for."

She shivered again and he couldn't stop himself from moving over to her, wrapping his arms around her. "I should get your coat."

"Stay here with me."

Oh. Right.

She closed her eyes, put her head on his shoulder. "I'm scared, Adrian. What if Sophie's not okay?"

He tightened his grip around her. "You've done a great job caring for her. We'll watch over her until help comes."

"And pray," she said.

Right. Yes.

He sat there, holding her, thinking about Dan's sermon. *Even when believers are unfaithful, God still shows up. He is always there for us. Even in the darkest night, His faithfulness surrounds us.*

He stared at the stars, hoping.

Gradually she relaxed against him until finally he felt the tension leave her body. He loosened his grip and dragged a sleeping bag toward them. They both still wore their jeans and sweatshirts, but the air was turning bitter as it crept toward dawn. He draped the extra bag over both of them, holding her tight.

Then he turned off her flashlight, and the night cast over them.

But his gaze stayed on the stars, high above, blinking.

CHAPTER 14

*U*nder different circumstances, this could be considered romantic.

If they weren't out in the cold.

If her stepsister wasn't hurt.

If their rescuers weren't so far away.

Ella checked Sophie again for the hundredth time. Despite her light moaning, Sophie's breathing remained steady. But the fact that she hadn't awoken after her fall told Ella that her sister was in big trouble.

She fixed Sophie's sleeping bag, then went over to climb back under the one Adrian had saved for them.

On her other side, Adrian rested his back against the cliff face, the sleeping bag pulled up to his shoulders.

Above them, the clear night sky offered up views of dancing constellations. Together the moon and stars provided just enough light to make out the edges of the ledge they perched on. She tried not to think about that edge. It seemed like she and Adrian were always stuck together on some precipice.

Adrian reached for her hand. Without hesitation, she laced her fingers through his.

"She's going to be okay," he whispered, his breath tickling her ear.

"You can't know that."

"What I know is that you've done a great job taking care of her."

That didn't mean Sophie was going to be okay, but his words helped her stay calm.

"If it helps, we could talk about something else." His thumb traced a lazy line along the back of her hand.

Yes, maybe a distracting conversation *would* help. There wasn't anything more she could do for Sophie right now. "Okay. What should we talk about?"

"Whatever you want."

She nodded, sighed. Considered. "This is not how I pictured my life going."

"What? Stuck on the side of a mountain with someone you hated not that long ago? That's pretty much every girl's dream, isn't it?"

"I never hated you," she said. "You were just wrong. And annoying."

"Ouch. That's not much better." His grin in the moonlight told her he wasn't seriously wounded.

"I think you'll get over it."

"Honestly though, I promise not to tease. How did you picture your life?"

"In my dreams?"

"Yep, give me your wildest."

"I would have pitched my cleaning products to your dad. He would love the concept and put in an order for millions. I'd be happily making soap and renovating a little house in Deep Haven. Then I'd put up a picket fence, marry a prince, and have 2.5 children."

"That sounds like quite a dream. Maybe I can help make it happen."

Which part? She didn't want to ask, the dream suddenly too real for her to bear. Instead, "I don't know how you think you can make my dreams come true."

"Yeah, I'm not sure either. But I do have an in with the Vassos family. I could put in a good word. Maybe even help you put together a business plan. Working together, we could probably come up with something amazing."

"Are you serious?"

"I'm more serious about this than my water park."

Adrian looked deep into her eyes. The moonlight gleamed in a crown around his long hair. Here, on the side of a cliff, in the clear, cold air, Ella believed him. But what was he saying, exactly? Could he really mean he'd give up the park?

Sophie groaned, and Ella scooted out of the bag to kneel near her side. "Sophie, can you hear me?"

Sophie's eyes opened. "I hurt."

"You fell over a cliff. Don't move. Your leg is broken." She tucked the sleeping bag tighter around Sophie. "I've stabilized it for now but it's better to not move. Just stay still—help is on the way." She grabbed a water bottle from her backpack and rummaged around for a Tylenol. Moving slowly, she lifted Sophie's head, helped her take a sip of the water, and gave her the medicine.

"My head is throbbing."

"I'm afraid you got a pretty nasty cut on your forehead too." Best not to mention the fact that it looked like half her face was going to need stitches. "I cleaned it up as best as I could but you shouldn't touch it. My first aid kit didn't have any wide gauze so I didn't have anything to keep it covered. I know it hurts, but try to keep your hands down."

A tear leaked out of Sophie's eye and traced a track down her uninjured cheek. "I wish…"

"Shhh, don't try to talk."

"I wish I was at a spa." Sophie drifted back to unconsciousness on the words, and despite her concern, Ella smiled.

Adrian was sitting up, and Ella sat next to him, pulling the sleeping bag over them.

"She's right, you know. This would never have happened at a spa. Or a water park for that matter," Ella said.

"Maybe not, but then you wouldn't have these stars." Adrian leaned back against the rock again. His shoulder brushed against her.

"I guess that's true."

"Earlier tonight, before all this happened, I realized that I'd never seen so many stars before. It's funny to think that the stars are always up there—we just can't always see them. I guess God is like that too. He's always there even when He's unseen." He reached out and took Ella's hand and held it between his. "In our dark times, God shows up. I think there's a psalm that says, *In perfect faithfulness you have done great things.*"

She could feel the rough outline of a callus. A slight smile formed. His work during community service was more physical than his old desk job.

"I'm starting to see that," she admitted. It had certainly been true this past week.

They sat in silence for a few beats, his thumb tracing patterns on her hand. She could easily get used to that feeling. The safety it implied.

In the distance, a voice echoed over the water.

Adrian stood and extricated himself from the sleeping bag wound around him. "Maybe that's our rescue."

"They made good time." Ella stood too.

"I suppose they know the area."

She stared out into the darkness. *In our dark times, God shows up.*

Yes, she'd been rattling those words around her head for a while too.

A light flicked on then, way down at the end of the lake, a pinprick of hope. The light drew closer, multiplied, then two canoes veered toward the flatter shoreline. Soon the lights flickered through the trees and up the hill to their camp.

"Ella? That you?" Kyle Hueston called down. Next to him, Cole Barrett, Seth Turnquist, and Jensen Atwood also peered over the edge. Ella glimpsed Athena hovering behind them.

"Yep, we're down here."

The men picked their way down the hill, hefting emergency kits on their backs. Jensen shined his flashlight into Sophie's eyes while Seth probed her leg wound. Sophie groggily came to as they worked on her.

"Nice work on the splint," Cole said.

"Thanks." But it was hard to be glad for the compliment when her sister lay groaning on the ground. "I learned it from Peter Dahlquist during first aid training at the community warming house. I was able to stop the bleeding from her head injury, but I didn't have a big enough bandage to cover it."

"Seriously, you did a great job in a bad situation." Jensen added his voice. "I'll cover it for now. She'll need stitches at the hospital."

"I don't think she has a serious spinal injury. We'll need to carry her out on a litter though." Cole picked up one of the sleeping bags and glanced at Ella. "Wouldn't happen to have any duct tape, would you?"

"Actually, I do." Ella pulled a roll from her backpack.

"Really? Nice. Glad you're prepared."

Between them, Kyle and Cole slipped long, sturdy branches into the sleeping bag, securing them with the duct tape.

The sun was creeping over the distant horizon as the emergency response team worked to strap Sophie onto the litter, leaving Ella's makeshift splint in place. Ella and Adrian stood back as Kyle and the others debated the best way to climb the hill with Sophie. Ella slipped her hand into Adrian's and he gave it a squeeze.

Kyle lifted one end of the litter as Seth took the other. Step by step, they hugged the cliffside as they inched up the faint trail. Still on the ledge, Cole gathered up their gear. Adrian gave Ella's hand another squeeze and turned to help Cole.

She stood with her back to the sheer rock and watched as the men worked. Briefly closing her eyes, she willed her shoulders to untighten.

The sun peeked through the trees to the east and, with it, a rush of hope that maybe God had shown up in her life after all.

Finally. Adrian had liked holding Ella in the cool night, but Sophie's moaning and the fact that she'd barely woken had scared him.

The sooner they were home and safe the better, despite the lure of the stars and the sunrise.

"I'm going up with Sophie." Ella's quiet voice broke into his thoughts.

He nodded and then watched as she picked her way up the hill behind the men hefting the litter. Bending down, Adrian stuffed the leftover granola bars into Ella's backpack. She would want them as the day grew longer. Across from him on the ledge, Cole was winding a sleeping bag into a tight roll.

"This would all be so much easier if we had a helicopter," Cole said. "And faster too."

"Seb said something about that to me the other day. He mentioned your Crisis Response Team."

"It's still in the early stages, but, yes, we're working on a dedicated team. Right now we waste valuable time figuring out who is going to respond. It's not about territory, but utilizing resources the best. And there's no command structure. It would be so much easier if we were organized into one group."

Adrian shrugged the backpack onto his shoulder. "I can see the need for that."

"The pieces are coming together. But I dream of the day we can get a dedicated helicopter." Cole set down the sleeping bag. "Money shouldn't be such an issue when it comes to keeping people safe, but it is."

What if—

And the thought was a little crazy, but what if Adrian *could* get them that helicopter? It hadn't seemed like a real idea when he'd batted it around with Seb, but this crazy, horrible night had changed his mind. Deep Haven needed a rescue chopper, and he might be the man to get it done for them.

Surely he could convince his dad that it was the right thing to do. And if his dad didn't see the light, Adrian would have to see what he could do on his own.

He followed Cole up the path, picking his way around the stones and shrubs dotting the faint trail. When he reached the top, he surveyed the campsite. In the early morning light, it looked a little like a crime scene. Sophie must have pulled out a tent stake or two as she flailed around last night, and Athena had left the contents of her tent strewn around in her haste to help her friend.

In the distance, he could see the rest of the rescue squad transporting Sophie to the more accessible boat launch where they had pulled up their canoes, Ella and Athena trailing behind.

"Want me to help you break camp?" Cole gestured at the collapsed tent. "They'll need my spot in the canoe for Sophie. You and I could paddle back in one of your canoes and return most of this stuff to Darek. Under the circumstances, I'm sure he'd be happy to send one of his guys out to collect the rest. Or, if you're up to it, we could tow the second canoe behind."

"If you don't mind paddling with a rookie, I'd sure appreciate the help." Adrian longed to head into town with Ella and Athena, make sure Sophie was all right. But he couldn't leave this mess to Cole. "Give me a second." He jogged over to catch up with Ella and the others, her backpack in tow.

He handed her the backpack. "I know how you hate to be separated from your 3x5 cards." He winked.

"Thanks, Adrian." She offered what looked like a forced smile.

"Sophie is going to be okay. She's in good hands and you did a great job with her last night."

"I hope so."

"Don't forget what we talked about. We make a good team. I'd love to explore that more."

"I'll remember."

He leaned down and gave her a kiss on the cheek. One corner of her mouth turned up in a smile.

"I'd better get going." She held her backpack to her chest.

"Stay safe."

Athena stood nearby, arms crossed. He went to her. "Good job today, Cuz."

She laid her head on his shoulder. "I'm never going camping again."

Adrian shot her a wry smile. "I don't think any of us are eager to repeat this experience."

At the canoes, Kyle told Ella and Athena to ride with him, leaving Jensen and Seth to paddle Sophie. Adrian watched for a moment as they got settled into the boats then headed back down the trail to the campsite. Cole had made short work of taking down the tents and was waiting for Adrian to help bundle them into the compact storage bags that fit in the canoe.

Adrian wanted, no, needed, to get his mind off Ella, and the others making their slow way back to Deep Haven. He took a moment to really look at his companion. Cole, in his fatigues and work boots, hair military short, looked the part of a rescuer. Adrian had a sudden urge to rub a little dirt into his shiny new Lowa boots Casper Christiansen had talked him into adding to the stack of gear he'd bought at the outfitter store.

Was that only two days ago? The past thirty-six hours dropped on his shoulders, and he almost staggered under the weight.

He had the sudden urge to lift his eyes to the now unseen stars and maybe offer a prayer. He let it pass, though, and started packing up the cookware. "How long have you been living up here?" he asked Cole.

"Just a few months, but it already feels like home."

"Yeah, I've noticed that the people here seem ready to accept others as family."

Cole nodded, not looking up from his task. "When they see someone on the outside of the circle, or hurting or whatever, something about their Minnesota nice kicks in and they're filled with a desire to feed and adopt you." He shot a glance at Adrian. "Has Ingrid Christiansen given you any of her cookies yet?"

"Not yet."

"Well, that's how you'll know you've really arrived. Many of life's problems can be easily solved with a fistful of Mrs. Christiansen's cookies."

He could get used to the idea of family being something created from the people God put in a person's life.

It was midway through the morning by the time they got the campsite broken down. Adrian vacillated between comforting himself that Sophie was in good hands and worrying that the girls were safely back to town. Cole must have sensed the direction his thoughts were going because as they loaded the gear into the canoes at the edge of the lake, he stopped and looked Adrian straight in the eye.

"They're going to be fine. This rescue team has seen much worse, believe me. I've heard about a time when they rescued a whole bunch of Boy Scouts from a summer storm. Your friend is in good hands."

"Thanks, man. My head knows she's fine. I just can't quite convince the rest of me."

They launched the canoes, Adrian in front, Cole steering in back. The second canoe was tethered behind and full of the overnight gear. The sun sparkled across the lake water, mocking the seriousness of the morning.

The strain of his already sore muscles cleared Adrian's head. "Tell me more about the Crisis Response Team."

His paddle partner was quiet for a moment before answering. "Living on the edge of the Boundary Waters Canoe Area makes rescue difficult. When an accident or other crisis happens on the edge of town or near the county line, precious time is lost figuring out who should respond. We're trying to form a team who would be first responders for any crisis. This team would then delegate to the appropriate agency as needed."

"What kind of helicopter would you be looking for?"

"It would need to be capable of being outfitted as a patient transport and large enough to carry a few key members of the team to where they need to go. The hours saved in getting to remote sites could mean the difference between life and death for people."

"Yeah, I can see that." Even with their camping supplies, spending a night on the side of a cliff wasn't pretty.

"Trouble is, a chopper like that could set us back a million bucks or more to buy outright. You could probably get a used one for half that. People around here are motivated to support the effort, but they're not wealthy."

When they finally paddled into the bay they had launched from the day before, the well-worn black Evergreen truck in the parking lot looked better than a thousand Porsches. Working quickly, they secured the canoes to the rack and climbed into the cab.

"I know you must be ready to get to the hospital. Why don't you let me take care of the truck and equipment, and you can take off?"

Cole's offer eased the anxiety in his chest. The hour-long drive back to the Evergreen Resort passed in silence while Adrian did some research on his phone. He whistled low. Cole was right. Helicopters weren't cheap. Not that he was surprised.

Still…it wasn't entirely out of reach.

Cole pulled up next to Adrian's Porsche in the lot. After a quiet "thank you" to Cole, he got into his car and headed toward town.

But Cole's words about the chopper hung in his mind. What if buying that helicopter was why Adrian was really here? What if God—the one he didn't see, but whom Pastor Dan said was always working—had brought him here for just that reason?

CHAPTER 15

The paper underneath Adrian crackled as he shifted into a better position on the exam table. This examination in the Deep Haven ER was completely unnecessary as far as he was concerned. When he'd arrived at the hospital and asked for Athena and Sophie, the staff insisted he be checked over.

Ella had already taken off in the ambulance with Sophie, who'd been transferred to Duluth.

Now he was trapped in this sterile hospital room waiting for the clean bill of health he was sure to receive.

"Breathe in." The stethoscope of the petite ER doc traced an icy path on his back, bare beneath the hospital gown. Thank goodness they'd let him keep his pants on. "Good, breathe out." Adrian complied. "Other than those cuts on your hand, I think everything looks fine." The doctor came around to the front of the small examination bed to face Adrian.

He spied her name tag—Dr. Renee. "Remember to keep yourself hydrated. That's the best way to recover from an adventure like yours."

Adrian ran a hand through his unruly hair and rolled his shoulders.

The doc tucked her stethoscope into her pocket. "It was good to meet you, Adrian. Be well."

Adrian tugged his shirt back over his head and then topped it with his new flannel jacket. His responsibilities piled themselves on his shoulders. First, call Ella to check on her and Sophie in Duluth. Next, figure out the water park deal with the town. It seemed he was the only one in a position to buy them a helicopter. What good was his job if he couldn't use it to benefit people?

Ella's voicemail picked up after the fourth ring. "Hey, Sunshine. It's me. I hope you got some rest in that ambulance. How is Sophie? I'm coming down there to be with you. See you soon."

He checked in on Athena in the adjacent room. She was wrapped in a blanket and giving a statement to Deputy Morgan. He waved to her and received a slight smile in return.

"Deputy Morgan wanted to clarify a few details with me." She pulled the blanket tighter. "They let me take a nap first."

"We'll be done here in a half hour or so," the deputy sheriff said.

Perfect. That would give him time for a short face-to-face with Mayor Seb to discuss the research he'd conducted over the last few hours during the never-ending wait.

Outside the hospital, he called Seb's office, but was informed by the secretary that Seb was out.

"You could try looking for him at the Java Cup," she added. "Sometimes he works there. He says it keeps his finger on the pulse of the town." She lowered her voice. "I think he just doesn't like to drink the sludge that passes for coffee over here."

Adrian gave the expected chuckle and hung up.

A few minutes later he walked into the coffee shop and was relieved to see Seb sitting at a table in the corner. Music poured from an overhead speaker—Elvis crooning "Heartbreak Hotel." He hoped it wasn't a sign.

Adrian grabbed a black coffee from the barista and sat across from Seb. "Let me cut to the chase. After last night, I can see the need for a dedicated helicopter. I found one from a rescue team out west that is upgrading—a Bell 420 rescue chopper. It's in great shape, and they're willing to give us a deal. Or we can keep looking around if that one doesn't suit your needs here. The point is, if my father agrees, I can have the funds available to purchase one in a week or so."

Seb leaned back in his chair. "Hi to you too, Adrian." He took a sip of his coffee. "Listen, I just need to remind you that this isn't a rubber stamp on your project. Yes, we desperately need a helicopter, but we're not going to push through the permit if it doesn't meet the needs of the town. Just so you know that."

Adrian took his own swallow. The black coffee washed bitter across his tongue. "Yep."

"All right then." Seb held out his hand, and Adrian shook it. "Thanks so much. The Crisis Response Team will be thrilled."

Adrian ordered a caramel, vanilla, non-fat latte with whip for Athena and headed back to the hospital to pick her up.

This could have ended so badly.

Ella sat next to Sophie in the sterile hospital room. The gray-green walls blurred in her vision as she focused on her sister's chest rising up and down with each breath.

She picked up Sophie's hand and held it between her own. Sophie had been sedated and wheeled into surgery immediately upon arrival. The doctor who performed the surgery said that Sophie's leg should heal well, but he thought her forehead would likely scar from the gash she'd received. Ella was just glad she was alive.

Sophie's purpling face looked younger without her customary makeup. Her eyes were smaller too, now that her false lashes had been wiped away. She looked innocent and vulnerable.

The door to the hospital room burst open, and Ella stilled as her stepmother stormed in.

"My baby!" Jackie came straight to the bed and pulled Sophie's hand from Ella's grasp. She moved between Ella and the bed, bending over Sophie. Ella took the hint and got up from her chair.

"She's going to be okay, Jackie. The doctor said Sophie's leg will heal nicely. If you want, the doctor will be back in an hour or so—"

"This is all your fault. You let this happen to her."

Ella opened her mouth, but had no words of argument.

"You know she's not cut out for *camping*."

"I think she did just fine." Ella wanted to tell Jackie about the way Sophie had learned to paddle and how she'd gamely helped with the tents even after breaking a nail and ruining her manicure.

"My baby spent one night in that forsaken wilderness and she comes back broken and scarred. I knew she shouldn't ever be allowed to spend time with you."

Ella had nothing.

"You're just like your father. Never thinking about other people."

Wait a minute. No, she wasn't. She was methodical, prepared—

"You always think your ideas are going to somehow pan out. You're a dreamer, and now my daughter got caught in the middle of it." She leaned close. "I'm going to sue you for all you're worth."

Now that was a laughable threat. "Feel free."

"Get out." Jackie turned away from her, back to Sophie. "Get out. Now."

Before Ella could react, a nurse in pink scrubs filled the doorway. "Is there a problem in here?"

"Call security. I want this person removed at once." Jackie spoke in the tone of someone who was used to getting what she wanted, and fast.

"Jackie, please, let me stay until Sophie wakes up. I want to talk to her for a few minutes."

"Nurse. Security. Now." Jackie rounded on Ella, eyes blazing, color high on her cheeks. She spoke through clenched teeth. "You are lucky she is alive. Otherwise I'd be pressing charges for manslaughter."

Manslaughter? Jackie was prone to overreacting, but—

"Don't come around Sophie ever again. Do you hear me? Never again. You're nothing but trouble. A disaster waiting to happen."

Ella left before promising anything. She had a sister now and didn't intend to lose her. Walking out the door, she nearly ran into a uniformed security officer.

"I'm sorry, miss, but I'll have to escort you downstairs." The officer grabbed her upper arm.

She jerked away. "Don't worry, I'm leaving."

"I'll have to escort you out anyway—hospital policy in these situations." The guard walked close by her side through the ward and into the elevator. People turned to look as they passed by.

Great. Still the convict.

Mercifully, the guard left her at the sliding glass doors of the hospital entrance. The doors slid open with a squeak, allowing a blast of March air to brush against her face, cooling her heated cheeks.

She sank onto a bench just outside the door. Perfect. Now what? At least she had her backpack. She pulled it to herself.

"Ella?" Athena was walking down the sidewalk. "Are you okay?"

Ella nodded. "I just...Jackie is up there."

Athena frowned.

"Sophie's mother."

Her mouth opened. "I see." She glanced at the hospital, back to Ella.

"Room 305," Ella said.

"Thank you." Athena started for the door, then, "Do you need a ride or something? Adrian is parking the car. He dropped me off. Maybe he can take you home."

Ella didn't know how to answer. Yes. No. Maybe...but really, maybe she should stop relying on anyone else, right? "I'm fine."

Athena nodded and left her.

Ella dug out her phone, but it was dead. She wasn't sure who she'd call, anyway. She couldn't exactly Uber back to Deep Haven.

Jackie's words burrowed inside. A dreamer. Just like her father.

She sat, frozen, the chill in the air finding her soul. She *was* a dreamer. Holding on to the idea if she could just find the right backer, she might make a go of her big dreams.

But here she sat, homeless, carless...she had nothing.

Yes, just like her father.

But it didn't mean she didn't have good intentions. Adrian's words found her. *Your hurt is pretty deep, and maybe you don't want to see anything else but his mistakes.*

Maybe she didn't.

But maybe there was more to her father than she realized.

Footsteps on the sidewalk made her look up. Still.

Was that Alex? What was Adrian's brother doing here? Though they'd only met briefly at the shareholders meeting, Ella recognized his bulldog look.

She rose from her spot on the bench. "Alex, right?"

He stopped and smiled. "And you're Ella. I'm so sorry to hear about your sister. Athena called me."

"You just missed her. She went up to check on Sophie." Ella rubbed her arms as the sun went behind a bank of clouds.

"I'd better get up there too. Athena sounded pretty shaken up." He started toward the door then paused. "Ella, actually, I was going to track you down this week. I found something that belongs to you." He slipped a hand into his pocket and pulled out a small object.

"My thumb drive! I thought I lost that at the party. Where did you find it?"

"On the floor at the shareholders meeting."

"Thank you for rescuing it." She reached for the device but he held it back.

"I hope you don't mind, but I looked at what's on it."

Kind of an invasion of privacy, but who was she to complain? She'd lost it, after all, and someone needed to look at it to see who it might belong to.

"I think your plan is brilliant. Making organic soaps and cleaners for the hotel industry could radically change how we do business." He tossed the thumb drive in the air and caught it.

Oh. "Thanks…"

"I'd like to buy into your business. I could front you the money for a stake in the company."

What? "I—"

"Don't say yes or no yet. I know you'll need to think about it. In the meantime, I wonder if you could help me with a favor."

"What is it?"

"I heard that Adrian is promising all sorts of things to your town to get them to sign off on the water park deal. He's even promised them a helicopter."

She blinked at him. Frowned. Then, "No. That's not true. He's rethinking the whole water park idea."

"Hardly. You don't know the truth. He promised them a helicopter. The problem is, our dad isn't going to support that idea. He isn't going to buy the helicopter. If Adrian keeps moving forward, he's going to fail." Alex put his hand on her arm. She stared at it for a moment. "I just don't want to see my brother embarrassed again."

"Adrian would never buy the votes like that. He isn't that kind of guy." She yanked her arm away.

"You don't know him like I do. Please, talk some sense into him."

Ella had no words.

Alex handed her the thumb drive. "I hope we have an understanding. I look forward to doing business with you." A minute later, she heard the hospital doors open and close.

Could she trust Alex? No. She barely knew Alex. No, she trusted *Adrian*. She turned back to the park bench when her gaze landed on a familiar set of shoulders.

Adrian.

She couldn't help the smile. He still wore the jeans he'd spent the night in and the heavy flannel he'd bought the day before last. His face had a five-o'clock shadow, and he looked deliciously scruffy. She had the strangest urge to cry.

Adrian always seemed to show up for her. Last night around the campfire, he'd seemed open to the idea of walking away from that ridiculous water park hotel. He'd even told her some ideas he had for her soap business.

She got up and walked toward Adrian. Yes, she would let him help her. Let him believe in her. Show him that she believed in him too.

An SUV pulled into the clergy parking spot and Pastor Dan got out. He spotted Adrian and greeted him. Gave him one of those handshake-backslaps men gave their friends.

She drew closer in time to hear Pastor Dan say, "I hear we're getting that helicopter thanks to you."

Adrian's face brightened. "You heard right."

Wait. What?

"I appreciate it. Deep Haven will be safer." Pastor Dan spotted her. "Hey, Ella. Seb called and said you were down here. I had another parishioner I needed to check on, but I'd hoped to see you too. How are you doing?"

She waved off his concern. "I'm fine." Physically anyway. "It's my stepsister Sophie who could use a word of comfort."

"Okay then, I'll get in there and see if she's up for a visitor." Pastor Dan waved at Ella and went into the building.

Which left her standing in front of Adrian. Exposed.

They looked at each other for a moment as the silence stretched between them.

"You're buying a helicopter?" Her stomach tightened.

Adrian ran a hand through his hair. Gave her a smile. "That's the plan."

"So, I guess we're getting a helicopter and a water park." Her numb lips could barely form the words.

"I guess so."

Ella's stomach plunged all the way to her toes. He had lied about giving up the water park idea, had played her for a fool. And she'd willingly walked into it.

Alex was right. Adrian Vassos didn't believe in Ella—in her dreams—after all. Worse, he didn't care about her the way she'd thought.

So much for his sentiments last night, their kiss under the stars. That must have just been the romance of the campfire talking.

He'd never meant any of it.

She was such a fool. People like him were always the same. Ella had known they had nothing in common, and yet she'd finally allowed herself to hope. To dream.

To trust.

Yes, *fool* just about summed it up.

Adrian reached out his hand to her. "It's for the good of the town. They need the helicopter."

As if he cared about that. He just needed the permit to go through. Too bad for him that it wasn't going to happen.

And yet, some small part of her almost felt sorry for him. "Don't you know that your father isn't going to support you on this one?" Ella's voice broke. "You're going to make a fool of yourself."

"What makes you say that?"

"Alex was just here. He told me." Ignoring the hand he still held out to her, she crossed her arms over her heart. "He also said he'd loan me the money to build my business."

He stared at her, as if trying to comprehend her words. Then, "What? You're taking money from Alex? You don't want to do that. He's just using you."

"Well, you're just giving the town a bribe so they'll agree to your toxic cesspool!" And, oh, she hadn't meant to yell, but didn't he see what he was doing to her heart?

Adrian dropped his hand. "You'd better be prepared, because Alex will turn on you."

"I'm not sure I can believe you." And she should never have allowed herself to start. Should have stepped off that elevator the second he'd stepped on. Should have never accepted a ride to the courthouse that first day of community service. Should have never kissed him.

And definitely should have never allowed herself to care for the man.

But all the should-haves in the world didn't change the fact that she was here, her heart aflame, aching.

Broken.

"Can I give you a ride home so we can talk about it?"

Seriously? Didn't he know when to give up? His lies had been exposed and she wasn't going to sit around listening to them anymore. Because what if Ella forgot herself again—

allowed herself to believe his made-up version of the truth again?

She'd been lied to enough in her life, thank you very much. No more.

"Are you kidding me? I don't want to go anywhere with you." She needed to stay here anyway. It would take years to pick up all the pieces of her heart lying shattered on the ground.

"You came here in the ambulance, so I know you don't have your own car. Let me give you a ride back."

"No. I don't ride with strangers."

Adrian opened his mouth. Shut it. Opened it again.

She held up her hand. "Don't. You won't make anything better with whatever words are going to come out of your mouth. Don't waste your breath, because I don't want to hear it. Whatever we had going just won't work. We're too different." Ella turned her back on him. Walked to a bench stationed on the edge of the parking lot.

Adrian gave her a long look then went past her into the hospital.

She wrapped her arms around herself, tucked her chin into her chest. The bench was cold and hard. Behind her she heard the hospital doors swish open and closed. A few moments later her right side warmed as someone sat down. Pastor Dan had joined her on the bench. His dark brown hair fluttered in the wind.

"Sophie was awake when I went in there." He casually leaned back and rested one elbow on the top of the bench. "She said you saved her life. You're a hero."

Is this what being a hero felt like? If so, then no thank you. "I'd hardly call my actions heroic. I brought three city slickers into the wilderness without a real plan. I chose the campsite right next to the cliff. I must have left the tent zipper open, which is how the chipmunk got inside. Jackie is right. This was all my fault."

"I don't see it that way." Pastor Dan's gray eyes warmed as he smiled. "The way I see it is you treated your friends to a day on the water. You chose a prime camping location. Accidents happen. They're not anyone's fault."

She looked sharply at him.

"I notice more than people realize." He arched a brow at her. "That Adrian is quite a guy."

"He's something all right."

"I think he's trying to do the best he can. He's been asked to do a job in Deep Haven, and he's helping our town get the helicopter we need."

"Yeah, at the risk of polluting the groundwater and poisoning vacationers." Although, honestly, could she say it was really about that anymore? Because these days it seemed more like it was at the risk of her heart.

"I guess that's what the environmental study is for." Pastor Dan put his hands on his knees. Rose to his feet. "Adrian told me you need a ride home. Care to ride back with me?"

"That would be great. Thanks."

She may be headed back to Deep Haven, but she wasn't sure she would still consider it home.

CHAPTER 16

$\mathcal{H}$e wanted to do the right thing, which was why he needed to leave Deep Haven.

Adrian walked out of his cabin at Evergreen with his duffel slung over his shoulder. He gave Ella's cabin a long look, then turned to the main house to check out of the resort.

After he and Ella had fought in the hospital parking lot, he had gone up to Sophie's room and found that she was sleeping. The room was stifling with Jackie, Athena, and Alex all crowded in. He had asked Athena if she wanted a ride back to Deep Haven, but Alex jumped in and offered to take her back to get her car and things. That plan was probably for the best.

Now he was ready to get back to Minneapolis and sort things out with his father. He didn't know if there was any truth to what Alex had said, but he needed to find out.

Darek stood behind the desk in the resort office. "Adrian! I heard you had a brutal night."

"Yeah. We were pretty scared there for a while. The doctors in Duluth think Sophie will be okay though. Some scarring on her forehead, but her leg should heal just fine." He set his duffel on the floor.

"From the sounds of it, Ella was quite the hero. Cole said she seemed to know just what she was doing."

His heart gave a funny little jump. "She was pretty amazing. If Deep Haven ever gets their Crisis Response Team, you should ask her to join it." He set his wallet on the counter. "I need to check out. I've got to get home and work on some things."

Darek tapped a few buttons on the computer. "It looks like we have your credit card on file, so you're set. Did you ever get the other night sorted out with Ella?" He handed Adrian a slip to sign for the expenses.

"She was actually pretty amazing about that too. You were right. When I gave her some time and then explained what had happened, she came around. She and Sophie even came to some sort of understanding." He gave the pen and signed slip back.

"I'm glad to hear it."

Adrian picked up his duffel. Debated. Then, "Unfortunately, I screwed up today. Big time."

"Want to talk about it?"

What did he have to lose?

"My brother, Alex, showed up at the hospital before I got there, and I'm not really sure what happened. I do know that I said some things to Ella that I regret."

"I'm sorry, man. That's rough."

"The worst of it is, I can't stop thinking about how I feel about her." He shifted his duffel to the other hand.

"And how is that?"

"I think I love her." The words hung in the air. Yes. He loved Ella. She was passionate and funny. A hard worker and a dreamer. He could spend his whole life with a woman like that.

Darek gave him a piercing look. "If she's worth it, fight for her."

He wasn't so sure that was what she wanted. And he was tired of trying to get his own way. "Thanks, man. See you at the council meeting a week from Tuesday?"

"I'll be there."

Adrian slung his duffel bag into the passenger seat of his Porsche. The four and a half hour drive home passed quickly as he thought through and discarded numerous ways to apologize to Ella. Reaching the outskirts of Minneapolis, he checked the time—9:00 p.m. Not too late to swing past his parents' house where they now lived on Lake Calhoun.

The rambling house stood in a neighborhood of sprawling homes, mature trees, and old money. He drove into the driveway, and of course, the lawn service must have recently been through. The shrubs lining the front of the house were trimmed, and the dead leaves left over the winter were cleared away.

In the driveway his cell phone pinged. He took in a breath. The environmental study had come back. He read it quickly, and then again to be sure—but there was no mistake. His heart sank. With the proximity to the lake, in order to protect the water supply as well as the underground springs, the hotel's water supply would have to be housed in a separate tank at least a hundred yards from the building.

His thoughts churned the information over in his mind. There was no way around the facts. They'd have to buy another expensive lot just to hold enough water for the park. Plus, the environmental study recommended using the much more expensive UV filtration method rather than the standard chlorine.

He was looking at triple the cost of his original projections. At least.

Adrian stepped out into the night air. Low clouds obscured the weak half moon. In the house, the light of the front room shone through the window, illuminating the muddy lawn.

His mother answered the door, dressed in a pantsuit and pearls. He knew she wouldn't be caught in anything less than full dress.

"Adrian! Let me take a look at you." She pulled him into the front hallway. "Are you feeling okay? Your father and I were so worried about you when we heard about your friend Sophie."

"I'm fine, Mom." He bent and kissed her cheek. "I'm a little tired, but really, it's Sophie you should be concerned about."

"I'll say a prayer for her."

He glanced around. "I appreciate it. Listen, is Dad around? There are a few things we need to talk about."

"He's up in the study. You know your father, always working. I thought it would get better when we moved out of the penthouse, but he still pushes himself too hard."

"He neglects you."

"I've made my peace with our relationship. But, honey, when you settle down with the right girl, make sure your priorities are straight."

The right girl... What if he'd already messed up any chance to be with her? Adrian sighed before jogging up the stairs to his dad's study. He paused at the door, which stood ajar.

"Is that you, Adrian?" his dad called. "Come on in. I'm just finishing a few things."

Costas Vassos made his mark on the world by wowing and intimidating people, and his office was designed to reflect that. Glossy mahogany paneling lined three walls, while the fourth wall was all window. His desk drew the eye with its intricate carvings and massive size. It resembled more of a pirate's office aboard a man-of-war than a space for work.

Adrian pushed the door closed. Plush carpeting deafened his footsteps as he walked to the desk and sat in the buttery leather chair across from his father.

"So, you're back from the boonies, eh?" Costas leaned back in his chair, tenting his fingers at his chest. "Give me good news, son. Have you secured the votes?"

"I've managed to broker some goodwill with the council by agreeing to help them purchase a helicopter for their new Crisis

Response Team." He briefly outlined the crisis team's goals for his father. "It's not a slam dunk, but I'd say there is an excellent chance our permit will be approved."

But instead of the pride he'd expected to feel, Adrian's insides were hollow. Deflated. Why though?

Maybe because, deep down, he now wondered if all of this was actually good news. Despite the traumatic end to their camping adventure, the rest of the day had been really fun.

What if Ella was right? Maybe Deep Haven didn't need a water park hotel—especially given the increased costs reflected in the environmental impact study.

A sick feeling twisted Adrian's gut.

"I don't know." Dad cocked his head. "A helicopter is a significant cost. However, I've paid bigger bribes than that to get smaller jobs done."

Whoa, whoa, whoa. "It's not a bribe, Dad. They need the helicopter and we need them to see us as having their best interests in mind." Which Adrian did. Now.

"Of course, of course." His dad waved a hand in the air, dismissing his son's protest. "Good job, Adrian. You were always good about getting your way. Like a good businessman."

Adrian felt like he needed a shower. But a good scrubbing, even with Ella's soap, couldn't wash away the words. Was that really what his father thought—that Adrian would say anything in order to get his own way? He thought back and cringed as he remembered times when he had done just that.

Well. No more. He didn't want to be that man.

"Dad, there's something else you need to know. I just got the numbers back from the environmental study. Building a water park on the shores of Lake Superior isn't as feasible as we'd hoped." He rolled his shoulders back, lifted his chin slightly. "Unfortunately, it's my opinion that this deal shouldn't go through."

Adrian outlined the high points of the study. Surely Dad

would agree with him that doing this the correct way wasn't a financially viable option.

Yet once again, Costas waved Adrian's words away. "We can get around this, son. Talk to the right people, get them to sign off."

"Get them to... Wait, you're not suggesting we lie to the town, are you? To go forward with the subpar system? Because I won't do that."

"C'mon. Stop making this into a big deal. This is how business is done. You're just like your mother, blowing things out of proportion. Alex wouldn't have a problem with it."

Which further cemented Adrian's resolution. He didn't want to do business like his dad, never able to have family time. And he didn't want to end up with a family like the one he'd grown up in. He wanted his family to be the most important part of his day. He wanted that white picket fence and a woman to share dreams with.

No, not just a woman—he wanted *Ella*. They could build a life, a home, a business together.

"I'll be giving the environmental study to the local council. They deserve to know the potential dangers. I won't be a party to deception." He stood and walked to the door.

Costas stood. "Son, wait."

Adrian turned with his hand on the doorknob. "Dad, I love you. I always have. And I've always longed for your approval, but not this way. I'm so sorry, but I quit."

And just like that, he felt free.

No, he felt like Roger, the man in the elevator. "If you want to find me, I'll be in the great north woods."

Maybe she should leave Deep Haven.

Ella sat at Grace's kitchen table, staring at the check in her hand. In the week or so since the hospital, she had sleepwalked through her days, going through the motions of her cleaning jobs and finishing her community service but not really connecting with anything. A small part of her hoped one day she would pull in to Evergreen and park her Volkswagen Bug next to a sleek black Porsche again.

But the parking lot remained stubbornly empty. Then today, Darek had told her she'd gotten some mail and handed over an envelope that contained this check.

From Alex.

It came with a note: *I'm glad we will be doing business together.* She had stuffed the check into her purse—and with it, her pride —and driven straight to Grace's house. *I'm sorry to barge in on you like this, but can we talk?*

Grace had welcomed her like a friend. No. Like family. And now, she was puttering around the kitchen preparing tea for them in glazed pottery cups. Finally, Grace set a creamy-orange mug in front of Ella.

"I love this cup," Ella said. One side sported a yellow sun etched into it. On the other was written "From the rising of the Son."

"Thanks, I do too. A local artist, Liza, made them. She puts a Bible verse on each one. I think you got Psalm 113." Grace closed her eyes. "'Let the name of the Lord be praised, both now and forevermore. From the rising of the sun to the place where it sets, the name of the Lord is to be praised.'"

"That's beautiful."

Grace sat across from her at the table. "I'm glad you came over. How have you been?"

"Not good. In fact, that's why I'm here. I need a sounding board." She studied the contents of her mug. The dark tea and cream swirled in a whirlpool. "I need to leave Deep Haven."

"What? Why?" Grace leaned forward.

"'Deep Haven is a great place for second chances,' or at least that's what Colleen Decker keeps telling me. I came looking for security. A little house with a white picket fence. The whole works. I thought if I would just move into the right house, pay off my debts, and live a quiet life, I would find security. But maybe my stepmother is right. I am my father's daughter and I always will be." She took a long drink of tea and gathered her thoughts.

"Colleen is right. Deep Haven is a great place for figuring out who you are. Maybe it can even be a place where you discover that no matter what your earthly father was like, or how he failed you, you are loved by your heavenly Father and He will never let you down."

"I do believe God loves me. I just have a hard time believing He's in the business of turning my life around. I've always had to take care of myself."

"I can understand that."

"I don't know. Then I received this check big enough that it should be a way for me to launch my business, but cashing it feels like the wrong thing to do." She picked up the check again. Looked at *Alex Vassos* scrawled illegibly on the signature line.

"Security and dreams can coexist, you know." Grace stirred a spoonful of sugar into her mug. "Look at Max and me. At any time his Huntington's could flare up and start taking over our lives, but that doesn't stop us from living. We found our solid ground in God's never-ending love for us."

Ella let those words in. Turned them around in her mind.

"Another thing I've discovered is that love is precious. You have to hold on to it for as long as you can. I should know, since we don't know how much longer Max and I will have together."

Both women fell silent.

Ella nodded at Grace's cup. "What does yours say?"

Grace held a mug covered in waves of indigo. She turned it around to read the inscription. "Mine is Many Waters from the Song of Solomon. 'Many waters cannot quench love, nor can rivers drown it. If a man tried to buy love with all his wealth, his offer would be utterly scorned.'"

Many waters cannot quench love...

Ella paused, the words knocking the breath from her. Because somewhere in the middle of community service, sparring about the water park, and being trapped on a cliff, she'd fallen in love with Adrian Vassos. Many waters had not quenched what she felt for him.

But she'd messed up. Had allowed her past hurts to drown out the truth—that he wasn't a stranger after all. Because the Adrian she knew—really knew—showed up for people. Always kept his promises. There had to be some reason he had agreed to purchase a helicopter. But she hadn't given him the time of day to explain it.

And she also couldn't discount what he'd said about wanting to work with her to reach her goals. Maybe the two of them could even figure out a plan together to decrease the riskiness of the water park.

Oh no. The water park. Ella put both of her hands on the sides of her mug, her heart aching. She'd told a few people that the town wasn't getting a helicopter after all. Why had she ever believed Alex over Adrian? And why had she ever even considered accepting the check from him? It was a betrayal to Adrian.

But she'd already lost Adrian. If she didn't accept this money, she might miss out on her dreams too. And then what would she have left?

We found our solid ground in God's never-ending love for us.

Oh. The truth rustled through her. Because money, dreams —even being loved by a man—none of those was the answer to finding security. Mike Bradley had tried to provide for his daughter using money as a shield, but he'd failed every time.

But her heavenly Father, on the other hand...he would never fail. Hadn't He already proved his ability to provide for her again and again these past weeks?

With trembling hands, Ella picked up the check Alex had sent her. "You're right, Grace. I need to find my security in God and not in earthly things." And with freedom blossoming in her chest, she tore the paper into pieces. "I don't want to partner with Alex under the terms he set. I'm not sure I want to partner with him at all."

Grace swept the pieces of the check off the table and dumped them in the garbage can. She dusted her hands together. "Good. I'm glad to hear it. Now, about leaving town. Can you dream big and live in a small town?"

"I suppose so. Why?"

"Maybe I'm overstepping by bringing this up, but I just don't want you to count yourself out yet." Grace sat back at the table. "I was chatting with Darek and Ivy just before you got here, and they mentioned wanting to put in a large order with you for Evergreen."

Ella set her mug down with a clunk. "Are you serious? That's great. I would be honored." Tears pricked her eyes.

"I'm sure Ivy will chat details with you soon, but we were thinking that the summer cleaning staff could use your products, and then we could commission signature soaps for the cabins. Maybe it's too on the nose, but I wondered about a soap with a pine scent."

"People would love that. The soaps could double as a souvenir of a place they loved to visit. I have lots of ideas for packaging too." The little pine sprigs she had collected with Adrian flashed into her mind. Her heart pinched, but she shoved that aside and focused on this new opportunity—which could very well be the start of her new beginning.

Except. Wait. She couldn't make that much soap in the kitchenette of her cabin. Even the small amount she'd made with Adrian almost maxed out her space. This deal was busted before it even began.

Ella met Grace's gaze for a moment, then lowered her eyes.

"I'd love to work with you guys. I really would. But it takes quite a bit of space and time to make new soaps." She thought quickly about alternatives. Found none. "I could probably have things ready by June, but as much as I love my little cabin up at Evergreen, I don't think it's big enough to make as much soap as you're talking about."

So much for that dream. Cleaning cabins was going to have to pay the bills for a while longer.

"Actually, I've got more good news for you. Have you ever been to Footsteps of Heaven?"

"Of course." Every Deep Haven resident knew of Mona Michaels' bookstore and coffee shop.

"The other storefront there is currently empty. I overheard Mona saying she's ready to rent it out again. I put out a little feeler, and I think she'd be willing to rent to you." Grace set her cup on the table and slipped a cell phone from the pocket of her jeans. "As a bonus, she also has an apartment above the store. Maybe she would give you a deal if you rent both out. There would be plenty of space to set up a workroom to make soap stuff."

"That sounds amazing." Unbelievable even. But even with the deal with Evergreen, how could she possibly afford it?

Still…maybe God had something up His sleeve. Provision, even if it didn't look the way she'd always envisioned it.

"Should I give her a call right now?"

"I guess so." Ella paused, nodded. "Yes. Please."

Grace swiped open her phone and within moments was outlining for Mona what she had just suggested to Ella. After a few short sentences, she hung up the phone. "She'd love to talk to you about the place. She asked if we could come over tonight, and I said yes. I hope that's okay."

Ella nodded, then tossed back the last of her tea. "Grace, you're a lifesaver."

Grace waved off the compliment. "That's what friends are

for." She sipped her drink. "What got you into soapmaking in the first place?"

"I made my first real batch of soap in college for a chemistry class. Since my dad ran a cleaning business I thought it would also make a good topic for an environmental study term paper. I found out that soap is really simple—mix an oil and some lye in the correct measurements, let it rest, and boom—soap. The whole process was almost magical. Two unlike substances coming together to be more powerful than one of them on their own."

"That sounds a lot like our relationship with God. When we allow Him to change us and to make us into something new, powerful things can happen. Like it says in 2 Corinthians 5:17, 'Therefore, if anyone is in Christ, he is a new creation. The old has passed away; behold, the new has come.'"

"I love that thought. 'Behold, the new has come.'" Ella couldn't help but throw her arms wide on the "Behold."

"It's a favorite verse of mine. I like to read it when I need a reminder that I'm not bound to who I used to be. I am a new person."

"It seems like this town is full of new creations. Maybe that should be Deep Haven's theme verse." The two women grinned at each other over the table.

Twenty minutes later, Ella was standing in the Footsteps of Heaven, Grace on her heels.

Mona stepped from behind the counter. "Oh, good. I hoped you'd be able to stop by tonight." The owner went to the door separating the bookstore from the empty space on the other side of the converted Victorian home and unlocked it. Pushed it wide. "Here it is."

After walking through the door, Ella turned a circle inside. The same golden wood shelves carried through into this storefront. Wood flooring was laid in an intricate pattern. A chandelier hung from the ceiling.

"This is beautiful." She could already begin to imagine the possibilities.

"There's a small washroom at the back. The public bathroom is on my side of the building, so you could partition off the back for a workroom. That's what Liza did when she worked here. I took down the temporary partition so prospective renters could see the whole area." Mona ran a hand along one of the shelves. "Of course, the whole place could use a new coat of paint. And a heavy hand with some cleaning supplies. I suppose you would know a thing or two about that, huh?"

Ella smiled. A genuine smile, despite the pinching still deep inside her. "I do know a thing or two, yes."

"Is the apartment upstairs still vacant? Ella needs a new place to live," Grace said from her place in the doorway. "Not that we don't love having her onsite at Evergreen. She just needs someplace more permanent. Someplace to call her own."

Oh. Those words wormed their way down. Settled in. A place of her own. Permanence. But she was learning that permanence didn't necessarily mean an address. Her security couldn't be found in where she lived. Her security had to be found in Jesus. He was the only one who never changed. He'd never let her down and He never would.

It was too bad Adrian couldn't have been part of her security too. She had to put that thought aside, however.

"Yep, that space is available too." Mona swung the keys around in her hand. "Should we go up and look at it?"

"No need. I already know I'll love it." She could really make a home here. "I'm almost afraid to ask, but what are you thinking for rent?"

Mona named a price far under what Ella expected.

"You can't mean it. I know you could get more than that for this storefront."

"I'm giving you a little discount because you'll be renting both spaces. Besides, I like you and it's been far too long since

I've had a reliable renter. This price is for a one-year lease. I suppose we could consider a month-to-month lease, but I'd have to charge you more."

A one-year lease. Did she dare make that leap? Was she ready to call Deep Haven her home, to really settle in? She did some quick mental math, and with the order from Evergreen, figured she could cover the rent, continue paying back her student loans, and even have enough left over to eat.

In perfect faithfulness you have done great things. The verse Adrian had quoted drifted through her mind before settling in her heart.

"Mona, you have a new renter."

Grace hugged Ella. Laughing, Ella turned and gave Mona a hug too.

"I think you and I will get along quite well. I've missed having something creative going on in here." Mona let her go. "I'll go get the papers to sign. How soon can you move in?"

"How about today?"

Ella's joke backfired when Mona shot back, "It's a deal."

"Ha! Okay, well, I can't really move in today. I'll sleep at Evergreen tonight and then move the rest of my stuff tomorrow. Anyone know where I can find a bed?"

"There might be an extra in the storeroom at Evergreen," Grace offered. "I'll have Darek check tonight. You can at least use that until you're able to find something you like."

God was showing up for her again. Being her security. Just as He had promised. It was appropriate that she was starting the do-over to her do-over at the Footsteps of Heaven.

CHAPTER 17

*H*e had to get this right.

Adrian had spent the past few days figuring out how he could fund the helicopter on his own without any Bear Creek money or strings attached. He'd finally ended up selling the majority of his shares in the company and now had the money ready to go for when the town picked out which chopper they wanted.

Standing outside Deep Haven City Hall, Adrian took a deep breath and checked his watch. Showtime.

Or not, because clearly he was late.

He slipped into the back. There were rows of chairs running through the long, narrow room holding over a hundred people. The town council sat lined up at a table behind the podium, where Seb stood.

"I may have jumped too quickly at this opportunity," the mayor said.

Wait, *what?*

"You know I love this town, and I do my best to make the right decisions. When Adrian Vassos came to me with this project, I saw the benefits. I also saw the drawbacks, but I felt that the economic boon would outweigh those." He sighed. "However, recently I became privy to some information about the Vassos's last project, and...I'm a bit concerned. Apparently, in a previous project, it seems that Adrian might have made a lot of promises to that town and then left behind a ruin of a resort."

What? Who ...?

Alex. It had to be him, after the way his brother had cozied up to Ella and tried to sway her to his side. Unbelievable. Except, maybe not.

"What about the helicopter he promised us?" Peter Dahlquist spoke from his place behind the table.

Seb cleared his throat. "I hate to say this, but I'm not certain if we can trust Adrian Vassos."

A murmuring sound rose through the room, and Adrian didn't know whether to run or defend himself. But he couldn't deny the truth in Seb's statements. Sure, there hadn't been malice behind his previous actions, but he *had* made a lot of promises that he hadn't been able to fulfill. His intentions had been good this time too, but maybe these townspeople wouldn't give him the time of day to explain himself.

And really, with his past, could he blame them?

So much for his new life in the north woods.

He was opting for a quick exit when a blonde at the end of a row near the front stood up.

Ella. She looked good, too, wearing a dress, her hair in a messy ponytail. Just seeing her made him ache.

Especially when he had no doubt she was going to add to his list of misdemeanors.

"Excuse me." She paused until the murmuring died down. "I just wanted to say that if Adrian promised you a helicopter, then you will be getting a helicopter. You can trust him."

What?

And then, he must have blinked, because Ella picked up her bag and slipped out the side door.

He wanted to go out the back and catch her, but at that moment Seb spotted him. "We'll let the man speak for himself. Adrian, why don't you come up here?"

Adrian passed down the center aisle and up to the podium. *Share your heart with them.* Ella's words gave him the courage to turn and face the town. In the crowd, he spotted many faces he knew. Casper and Darek, sitting with their mother. Kathy from the Java Cup. Mrs. Draper. Even Carol from his community service.

"Friends, thank you for giving me the opportunity to speak today." He gripped the sides of the podium. "I had planned to come here to pitch my idea for a water park resort on the site of the old Westerman property. It's a great location, and I fell in love with the idea of providing a place for families to enjoy spending time together. Many of you know I had hoped you would vote on giving me the permits tonight."

Around the room, heads nodded, but more than a few people crossed their arms.

"Instead of asking for your support, I want to ask for your forgiveness. It is true that I wanted to get this project done and even promised a helicopter in order to make that happen. Even though the mayor was clear that there would be no quid pro quo, I see now that my actions could have been construed as misleading or even as a bribe. I'm sorry for that." In the third row, Darek dipped his head in a silent salute.

"One more thing. I've recently received the results from the environmental study of the site, and after much consideration, I will be withdrawing my permit applications."

The room erupted.

Seb stepped to the microphone. "All right, everybody. Let's settle down. Adrian, please explain yourself."

He outlined the study's highlights. "Bottom line, there are ways to make it work. But none of them is feasible financially. And I won't recommend anything that will harm the lake. Deep

Haven's natural beauty deserves to be preserved. Bear Creek Resorts may try to still convince you to grant the permits, but I urge you to turn them down."

"What about the financial benefit to the town?" someone near the back called out. Adrian thought he saw Mark Bammer's bald head.

"Good question. I crunched the numbers, and if the water park systems fail, the cleanup would cost far more than the park's revenue. I don't think Deep Haven can afford to build this park."

"So your promises really were just empty words," someone else called out.

He hung his head a moment. "I spoke those things in good faith. I see now that I should have framed things differently from the start. One thing that I promised, however, will be acted on." Adrian took a breath. "I will buy that chopper for the Crisis Response Team. I will leave it to Deep Haven to decide what chopper to get. But it will happen. I promise. I hope you will believe me."

He walked out of the room, not acknowledging any of the questions shouted at his back.

In the hallway, Darek intercepted him. "Really? You're still getting the chopper?"

"Yes, well, someone once asked me why I was doing all this. I figured out the answer...because it's the right thing to do."

Casper came out the door, trailed by Edith Draper and Ingrid Christiansen. Casper slapped him on the shoulder. "Wow. Ella really went to bat for you tonight."

"I got here just as she was leaving."

"Well, what are you still here for?" Edith asked. "Go after her."

"Maybe it's too late for us."

Casper clapped his shoulder again. "You definitely don't want to let her get away."

"I have to agree with my little brother," Darek said. "Go after her, man. You know she's worth it, so fight for her."

"Oh, for crying in the sink." Ingrid this time. "Go get your happy ending."

He finally knew what he wanted. And it wasn't something money could buy. Hopefully he had one more chance to get this right.

It was funny how quickly a place could start to feel like home.

Ella stood in the center of her little soapmaking kingdom, taking stock. She had done as Mona suggested and partitioned off the front of the store for displaying her products and created a small room in the back for mixing and developing new soaps. As time went on, she planned to hold soapmaking classes.

Friday, after she signed the lease, Ivy had called and told Ella she could reclaim her things from Ed Hansen's place. Maybe her dream of going commercial had to be put on hold for now, but she was pleased with the way things looked.

Ella had come straight here after leaving the town council meeting. She'd surprised herself by standing up and saying those things about Adrian. But someone had to defend him. Especially since he wasn't there to defend himself.

The scents of lemon and mint were redolent in the air. Her first batch of her newest soap lay curing behind the partition, and the essential oils flavored the air. Those bars wouldn't be ready for six weeks, so in the meantime she would sell her current inventory. She ran a finger over the pine soap wrapped with twine and the pine sprigs she'd picked up on the trail.

I enjoyed every minute of our time on the trail. Oh, Adrian. Why couldn't she trust that he had meant those words? Too late now. She'd pushed him away. Again. He wouldn't be coming back this time.

She and Colleen had spent all of Saturday moving her things into the space.

Colleen had come in the front door, arms loaded down with a cardboard box, its bottom flaps straining to pop open. "I still can't believe how much soap you have. What were you planning to do with it all?"

Ella had grinned at her friend. It had been the right decision to invite her to help set up the store. "I was fiddling around to find the right recipe to pitch to Costas Vassos. Things may have gotten a little out of hand."

"A little. There's enough soap here to clean all of the North Shore."

"That's good because new inventory takes time to make and cure. I got behind during all the hullabaloo with community service. Not to mention, I didn't really have the space for more in my little cabin."

"Community service and being wooed by Adrian Vassos."

A pang shot through her. "Too bad nothing ever came of that."

Colleen popped a hand to her hip. "You're totally blushing. I think you still have feelings for him."

"Yeah, feelings I can do nothing about."

"Remember that verse I told you?"

Ella nodded. "God is a very present help in trouble, from Psalms. I remember."

"Good. I guess that this is a 'trouble,' too. He wants to help you in this chapter." Colleen set the box down and headed back out the door. "There's one last box in your car. I'll go grab it."

Huh. It was still strange to think that God might be interested in helping her. That He desired to be part of even the small details of her life. She thought she had to do it on her own, but just when she needed Him, God swooped in to save her. Just looking around at this place was proof of that.

The door jangled and Colleen came back in. Ella went to her

and hugged her, the package in Colleen's arms making the gesture awkward.

Ella pulled back. "You were right, you know."

"I usually am. What about this time?"

"Deep Haven is a place for second chances. I came looking for security, but I found that security isn't found in a picket fence or a steady income." She thought back to the sermon Pastor Dan had preached and the hymn they'd sung afterward —"'Tis So Sweet to Trust in Jesus." *I'm ready to start doing that, God. Help me rely on You.* "I'm finally seeing that I can't just rely on myself all the time."

She couldn't plan for everything all the time. Some things just had to happen on faith.

"Yes, Deep Haven is pretty great." Colleen's eyes sparkled. "Sometimes I really miss it here."

"If you ever decide to move home, you can always split the apartment with me. There's plenty of room, and you know I'd love it."

"No, no. For you, Deep Haven was a second chance. For me, moving home would smell an awful lot like defeat." She set the box in her hands down on the floor. "This was the last thing in your car. I'm off to grab supper at Mom and Dad's. See you later."

"Thanks for all your help."

Ella spent the next two days cleaning the shelves and making a new batch of soap.

Now, in the growing Tuesday evening twilight, Ella lined her soap boxes up against the wall. Her new display tables would be coming soon. Mona had asked her husband, Joe, to make some to match the shelves hanging on the wall and he had hoped to bring them sometime today.

Her foot kicked a dusty, battered box. Her dad's box.

This must be the last box from her car that Colleen had brought in.

She sat on the floor and hefted the box onto her lap. If she was going to trust God with her life, it was time to let go of old grudges. A memory of her father handing her the box whispered through her mind.

Hold on to this. We're going to want it later.

"Dad, I held on to it. I'm ready to forgive you. Maybe you were a better man than I believed." A tear glided down her cheek and she brushed it away with a dusty hand. "I'm ready to see what you thought was so important to save."

She slid her fingernail into the tape and sliced it through, lifted one flap then the other.

The box was full of framed photos. Huh. Of all the things her dad thought it was important to have with them, their family memories were at the top of his list.

She hadn't expected that.

On the top of the pile lay a photo of her mom and herself. They were in their tiny backyard in North Minneapolis, standing by the maple tree. Ella remembered the brilliant color of that tree in the fall. Her mom was cradling something in her hands, a five-year-old, pigtailed Ella smiling at her with a gap-toothed grin. She squinted and looked closer. Her mom was holding one of the bird nests Ella had worked so hard on.

She traced a finger over her mom's face. "Thanks for believing in making the world a better place, Mom." She stood and propped the picture next to her *All Things New* sign resting on one of the shelves lining the wall.

Returning to the box, she picked up the next picture. In the shot, her mom looked at her dad, love shining in her eyes. Her dad held a feather duster and a piece of paper. An official-looking stamp graced one corner of the paper. It must have been his article of incorporation from when he started his business.

You're just like your father.

Maybe she was.

Maybe he had harbored big dreams...and his frustrations had led him to big gambles.

The thought loosened something inside her.

Have you considered that not opening the box is your way of staying angry at him?

Not anymore.

Her throat filled. According to Sophie, he had really loved her. She'd lost sight of that. Without her mother to ground him, her dad had been doing the best he could. *Oh, Daddy. I'm sorry.*

Sophie's voice tiptoed into her head. *Despite all your dad's faults he really loved you. He kept raving about the great grades you were getting in college and how someday his little girl was going to change the world.*

I'm trying, Daddy. One clean house at a time.

The memory of Adrian holding a feather duster in that ridiculous apron blotted out the picture in front of her. She released a laugh—or was it a sob? Adrian. She wanted him to look at her the way her mom looked at her dad. No. She wanted to be the one looking so supportive. How could she have missed it all along? Adrian had encouraged her dreams and wanted to help her, but she'd pushed him away. She should have supported him. Yes. Even showed him that she loved him.

She loved *Adrian*. She didn't care about a hotel or his money. She didn't care about his car. Okay, maybe his car, at least a little... No. She loved the spontaneous, fun-loving, supportive man who always seemed to be there for her. Who loved all her little quirks.

And she needed to tell him. Like right now. On a Tuesday.

She didn't need a plan—she just needed Adrian.

She checked her phone for the time. If she left right now, she could be there before midnight. She'd try his office first. If he wasn't there, then she'd search all of Minneapolis.

~

Adrian paced outside the door to Footsteps of Heaven.

Freedom. That was the word Adrian would use to describe the past week. Leaving his dad and Bear Creek Resorts behind left him free to seek God's approval and not his dad's. He didn't have to try to make people like him because *God already did.*

Which left only one thing unfinished. The one dream he really cared about.

Last week, over the glowing embers of his dead hopes of being respected by his father, this had seemed like a good idea. Even a few days ago as he sold off his shares in Bear Creek Resorts, this plan had sounded solid. But now, standing in the doorway of Ella's shop, looking at her as she sat peacefully on the floor surrounded by the bits and bobs of her new business, he knew the truth.

This would be harder than any other proposal in his life.

In front of Adrian, Ella sat on the floor, cradling a worn box. Her jeans, pink Converse, and T-shirt looked better than the finest gown. More like the Ella he'd grown to love. The word settled in his chest. Yes. He loved Ella.

He stepped inside. Cleared his throat. Held up the blue shoe he'd rescued from the stairwell those weeks ago at the Shareholders' Gala.

"I found something that belongs to you."

Ella startled. Turned to him. It seemed to take her a moment to understand what he was holding, her expression unreadable. "You didn't have to come all this way to return my shoe."

"I didn't. I came because I want to invest in your business. I've considered your pitch, and I want to buy shares in your company."

She stared at him, nonplussed. Then, "What do you mean? I never pitched to you. I never pitched to anybody."

"Let's call it your elevator pitch then."

Ella stood, leaving the box on the floor. She brushed off her hands as she fully faced him. "I can make a much better pitch than that one. In fact, I've already gotten a head start on building a business."

"Whatever you're selling, I'll buy it."

"You can't buy my love—I will freely give it."

"Does this mean you've forgiven me?"

"I've had time to think about it." She moved a half step closer. "It's not in your character to do something harmful. You must really believe in this water park idea. I'd like to help you figure it out."

Oh. "That's too bad because I spiked the water park deal. The environmental studies weren't something I could live with, and my dad wasn't willing to change the plans to protect the area."

"What? But you can't. That was your dream."

"Proving myself to my dad was my dream. I've learned that proving myself to him isn't what's important. Being a man who seeks God's approval is." He took a chance and stepped toward her. She didn't back away.

"But what about the helicopter?"

"Oh, the town will still be getting the chopper. I sold my shares in Bear Creek Resorts to buy it."

She cocked her head at him. "So, basically you are saying you're broke?"

"I have a little set aside."

"I can offer you a half share in my company." And then she was in his arms. Fitting so close that it seemed they were never apart.

He pressed his forehead to hers. "Ella, I believe in your dreams. I came back to tell you that. Also, to tell you that I'd love to help you make your dreams come true. I want to hold the strings while you fly."

She rolled her eyes.

"Okay, that sounded more romantic in my head. What I mean is, I want to be your cheering section." He put his hand to her face, breathed in lemon and mint. "I promise to be a good man for you. You will be my priority. We will create a home together."

She put her hand on his, then turned her face to kiss his palm. "I've learned that God is the One I should rely on. But I'm going to need a partner. Someone to hold my hand while we trust in Him together."

He leaned down and tasted her lips. Soft and generous. She buried her fingers in the hair at the back of his neck and kissed him deeper. Suddenly, she pulled back. He almost groaned at the loss.

"I can't believe you're here!"

"Of course I'm here."

"Yeah, well, I was going to come down there."

"What? When?"

"Now. Today. On a Tuesday." She grinned at him. "I saw the picture of my mom and dad and knew that I had to find you. Be spontaneous. Just jump in Ariel and drive until I found you. But, you're here and now I don't have to wait."

"Wait for what?"

"Wait to tell you that I love you, Adrian Roger Vassos. I love the man from the elevator, but more importantly, I love who he turned out to be."

Adrian lowered his forehead to hers. "I love you too, Ella. I may not have a lot to give, but what I've got I'll give to you."

"I dearly hope that includes the Porsche."

He laughed. "Of course. Someday, I might even let you drive." Then he bent and kissed her again—just a penniless prince kissing his princess.

CONNECT WITH SUNRISE

Thank you so much for reading *Can't Buy Me Love*. We hope you enjoyed the story. If you did, would you be willing to do us a favor and leave a review? It doesn't have to be long—just a few words to help other readers know what they're getting. (But no spoilers! We don't want to wreck the fun!) Thank you again for reading!

We'd love to hear from you—not only about this story, but about any characters or stories you'd like to read in the future. Contact us at www.sunrisepublishing.com/contact.

We also have a monthly update that contains sneak peeks, reviews, upcoming releases, and fun stuff for our reader friends.

As a treat for signing up, we'll send you a free novella written by Susan May Warren that kicks off the new Deep Haven Collection! Sign up at www.sunrisepublishing.com/free-prequel.

OTHER DEEP HAVEN NOVELS

Deep Haven Collection

Only You

Still the One

Can't Buy Me Love

Crazy for You

Then Came You

Hanging by a Moment

Right Here Waiting

Deep Haven Series

Happily Ever After

Tying the Knot

The Perfect Match

My Foolish Heart

Hook, Line, & Sinker

You Don't Know Me

The Shadow of Your Smile

Christiansen Family Series

Evergreen

Take a Chance on Me

It Had to Be You

When I Fall in Love

Always on My Mind

The Wonder of You

You're the One That I Want

For other books by Susan May Warren, visit her website at
http://www.susanmaywarren.com.

Turn the page for a sneak peek of the next Deep Haven novel,
Crazy for You ...

SNEAK PEEK

CRAZY FOR YOU

The plan was easy. Bring Oreos, kiss his mother, and skedaddle.

No need to stick around and get caught in another fight.

The last thing Peter Dahlquist needed this Memorial Day weekend was another fire to put out. At least, the family relations type. A good old-fashioned barn blaze—he'd be all in.

He stood on the apex of Zimmerman Mountain and looked out on the land that had been in his family for more than eight generations. Eighty acres, about half of it developed now with log cabin and A-frame Zimmerman homes, all nestled in a valley of birch and pine forest. And sprawling out at the foot of the acreage was the glorious blue of Lake Superior, calm and barely frothy against a pebbled shore.

For the annual family picnic, all seventy-two of his closest relatives were gathered in the field behind him, in the yard of the family lodge, the first homestead—now remodeled—of Luther and Agnes Zimmerman. The fragrance of fresh cut fescue and other field grasses mixed with the smoke from the usual bonfire. Uncle Martin held camp talking politics in his grizzled voice with the dozens of other uncles and aunts, most of whom Peter didn't know.

Okay, he knew them all. But sometimes, he wished he didn't. Especially when it came to local politics.

"Uncle Pete, watch out!"

He turned just as a football shot toward his head. But instead of ducking, he reached out and nabbed it with one hand.

He still had it.

His second cousin, once removed, held up his hands and Peter chucked it back to fourteen-year-old Ben. He'd heard the kid was hoping to make the Deep Haven Huskies football team this fall.

"Wanna play with us?"

Toss around a ball and avoid getting roped into discussion? Definitely.

He opened his mouth to say yes when Elton stepped up and dropped a heavy hand on Peter's shoulder. "Sorry, Ben, I've gotta steal Pete to help unload wood for the fire. As soon as we get it going, we'll eat. Tell the others, son."

Great. See, he should've made a run for the hills as soon as he was done stacking wood for the fire. And running back to town for more ice. And after the game of hide-and-seek with his younger cousins.

Okay. Peter just couldn't find the words to say no.

Which was, of course, why he was in this mess.

"No problem," Peter said as he grabbed the wheelbarrow from Elton and followed his older cousin to the wood pile behind the family lodge, a simple one-room cabin they used for all the family events.

"So. Pete, you know which way you're voting, right? We could really use that property."

Yep. Ambushed. He knew it was coming.

If he kept his mouth shut, what were the chances of being struck by lightning? Peter glanced at the wide expanse of clear blue sky stretching over Deep Haven and the glistening sapphire of Lake Superior down the hill. Not a hint of a storm. At least not the kind he could appreciate.

"I'm still researching all the options." And a way to bring about a peaceful end to this longstanding family feud. It all started with him. He had to find a way to end it.

Elton grabbed a small log and faced him. "The Westerman Hotel should be brought back to its former glory. We can do that. We've got the Grand Moose Lodge here on the ridge and the Mad Moose Hotel down in town, but the Westerman with all that lakeshore could really help us draw in a different clientele. And it would be great for the community. We can use that big ballroom for weddings and events." He threw the log in the wheelbarrow. "Besides, we're family. What other options are there?"

Peter bent down and pitched a log onto the pile. "You know the other options. Ever since Pierre's burned down, people have been wanting a pizza place. That could be good for the town too."

"People? Oh?" Elton made a face and shook his head. "You mean the Dahlquists. Isn't it enough that they own half the county? They've got four other restaurants." He threw another log into the wheelbarrow with a violent *thunk*. "How many more does Deep Haven need?"

Everyone just needed to calm down. Peter took a breath. "El, if Dahlquists own half of the county, Zimmermans own the other half. You've got two other hotels besides the resort and Mad Moose."

"No, you're just saying that because you're a Dahlquist."

"Hey, I have Zimmerman blood. You know that—"

"Exactly. So show some loyalty, dude."

Peter took a breath. "I am being loyal. But—"

"But nothin'. Are you a Zimmerman, or aren't you?" Elton chucked the last wood into the wheelbarrow and stepped up to grab the handles. "Don't betray the blood, man."

He didn't wait for Peter as he trundled the wheelbarrow away.

Are you a Zimmerman, or aren't you?

The answer should be obvious. Apparently not.

Now might be the exact time to leave.

Except, by the time he got back, Grandma Zee and the aunts finally brought out the hot dogs, buns, and store-bought potato salad. Family units clumped together and moved through the line. His cousin Katie, first cousin once removed, handed him her shih tzu while she piled up her plate. She'd inherited the Zimmerman dark hair and tall basketball legs. He followed her to the fire pit where she sat with her husband, who held a babbling toddler.

"Peter, you don't mind watching Daisy while I feed the baby, do you? Then Paul can make a plate."

Paul Hamlin, of the lesser known Hamlin clan. He'd played football a couple years after Peter.

"Sure."

"She probably needs a trip out to the woods, but be careful. She's a fraidy-cat and might bolt if she hears any strange noises. And I forgot her leash, so you need to carry her."

If it got him out of Elton's crosshairs, he would watch the spoiled dog all night. There was no way his outspoken cousin was done with the discussion. He'd probably track him down with one of those logs.

Peter tucked Daisy under his arm, his stomach rumbling. By the time the dog did her business and he got back to the gathering, the food table was as bare as the dusky sky. He watched the teenagers start up their touch football game again. Ben and one of the older kids snuck out into the woods beyond the field.

Oh, he knew exactly what they were up to. Some things never changed. He'd probably wander over later and make them all put out their cigarettes and warn them about the current level three fire warning.

But the Zimmerman clan weren't the troublemakers in town. Well, not usually.

His mom came up to him, her smile bright. She wore her favorite purple Deep Haven Huskies football sweatshirt with white capris. "Hey, Pete." She patted his arm and handed him a Rice Krispies bar. "I noticed you didn't eat."

He took the treat. "Thanks."

"I also saw you brought Oreos again."

"If you want me to show up, you'll have to be prepared—"

She held up her hand. "It's fine." She smirked. "I'm just glad you showed up. It's hard to be in enemy camp."

"Mom, you're hardly in enemy camp—"

"I'm a Dahlquist now. Yes, your father was my first love and I married into the Zimmerman family, but I think they would've been happy if I'd *stayed* married to his memory and never looked at another man. I'm not sure that they ever got over Gary adopting you and giving you *his* last name when I remarried."

"Mom, you're not the enemy. Grandma wouldn't insist that you come if you were."

"You're right. And if I miss this, then I miss Grandma Zee's famous rhubarb cake." She winked.

Truth was his mother was his one reason for coming. This was one of the only times he got her to himself while his dad took his two younger brothers camping. Abby, his sister, had opted to stay in the Twin Cities with friends.

"Cute dog." She patted its head.

They found seats near the fire. He had to give it to his great-grandparents—when they built this cabin, they took maximum advantage of the grassy slope and the view. The firepit was in the perfect spot. The outside speaker system of the lodge pumped out country tunes. Bright colors lit the sky as the sun sank lower. If only he could relax and enjoy it like every other year.

"Dad and the boys make it to the camping site yesterday?"

"Yup, their annual trip. But they'll be at the Dahlquist get-together tomorrow evening." She rubbed her arms. "It's going to be a cold one tonight. I hope Gary packed his good sleeping bag."

"I'm sure they're fine."

"Probably. But it's a wife's prerogative to worry. And a mother's."

He saw the concern in her look, but better to pretend he didn't. He stared into the flames, watching the glowing coals burn, seeing the warm faces of his relatives as they joked and roasted marshmallows for s'mores. He didn't look at Elton, but he felt a simmer of conversation, as if it buzzed in his blood, just as Elton suggested.

"Are you doing okay, Peter?"

"Ma, I'm fine. You know me."

"I just want you to be happy."

"I am." Really. He was. He had a great job, great family. So what if, at times, it felt like something was missing?

Grandpa Zim lumbered over and plopped down next to Mom. "There's nothing to worry about, Barb. Peter's a good boy. And he's going to make the right decision in that vote next week."

And here they went again. Back into the crossfire. His mother's lips curled into a tight smile. The others probably didn't see the pinch around her mouth as anything significant, but the smile she gave Grandpa was as fake as the artificial sweetener in his pop.

Elton spoke from across the circle, where he sat on a bench, his mouth full of food. "Yeah, Peter knows what he needs to do."

The chatter ceased. And he didn't count, but nearly everyone, including Grandma Zee, pinned their attention on Peter. The dog squirmed in his lap.

Uncle Al's voice boomed from across the pit where he sat in

a lawn chair. "Of course, he knows what to do. We're counting on him. Right, Peter?"

At any time the Lord could open up those skies and bring that deluge. Or earthquake. Tsunami. He'd even take a tornado. He wasn't picky.

Instead his newly engaged cousin Ree—just an ordinary first cousin—and her fiancé, Seth Turnquist, came up from the driveway holding hands. He liked Seth. Big guy. Had saved lives last fall when a town dock collapsed. And Ree had harbored a crush on big Seth for as long as Peter knew her. Now, she glanced at Peter, a twinkle in her eye. She never had any problem mixing it up with the Zimmerman brood. "Come on, guys. Give Peter a break. This is supposed to be a family picnic, not the Deep Haven City Council Meeting."

"Thank you, Ree." At least someone understood the position he was in. Of course, she'd also asked for an exclusive interview for the *Deep Haven Herald* once he decided, so maybe she was just trying to stay on his good side.

Daisy picked that moment to rush out of Peter's lap and inspect the crumbs under the tables. He followed her. Might as well see if there was a lone hot dog bun or something left.

Vivien Calhoun, third cousin by marriage, joined her best friend Ree at the food table, scooping up the last Oreo in the package. "What's this vote about?"

Seth dropped a bulky arm around Ree, pulling her close. "The Westerman Hotel is up for grabs."

Vivien brightened. "Oh, I love that old building!"

Old was right. If Adrian Vassos had purchased the property like Peter had hoped, this wouldn't be an issue, but as soon as the place was available again suddenly everyone wanted it. And he'd regretted running for city council ever since. He couldn't go anywhere without one side or the other of the family pushing him to vote their way.

Worse, the place was a fire trap waiting to blaze over. As fire chief of Deep Haven, all he could see was a potential fire hazard sitting right on the harbor shore, vacant for the local kids to play in, get trapped, and die. Something needed to be done with the place soon. Seb Brewster, their mayor, had already called for a vote—which, of course, Peter had stalemated with a tie.

Seb expected him to break it at Tuesday's meeting.

Change of subject needed now. "Vivien, what are you doing in town? Are you back from New York for good?"

She came and sat next to him, petting Daisy while he bit into the burnt hot dog he'd scrounged up. Her wavy brown hair hung down her back, long legs in skinny jeans tucked under her. Her blue eyes gleamed in the firelight. "I am. I'm running a summer theater program."

"Where?"

"Here. In Deep Haven."

Uncle Charlie laughed from his lounger nearby. Not really an uncle—his father's cousin. But every man over fifty was monikered with "uncle." Uncle Charlie wore his typical Twins cap, a pair of jeans, and a flannel shirt he couldn't quite button over his girth. He held one of his grandkids on his knee. "Who's going to do summer theater?"

Vivien glared at him. "The kids. I started working with a children's theater back East and loved it. Kids have so much potential and they usually aren't as self-conscious as adults. Besides, what else are they going to do all summer?" Daisy shuffled over and Vivien pulled the dog onto her lap. "And how about you, Petey? Dating anyone?"

He stared down Vivie. "No. No time for that around here."

Seth smirked as he roasted a marshmallow for Ree, the skin turning a delicious golden brown. "Yeah. That and the fact that you're related to pretty much everyone in Deep Haven has put a serious damper on your love life, man."

Vivien shrugged a slim shoulder and flipped her dark hair. "Then why don't you move?"

Move? Moving wasn't the answer.

Yeah, this big crazy family drove him nuts, but he loved it here. He loved walking into the Loon Cafe and knowing every person who sat at the counter or in the red-padded booths. He loved his job as fire chief, helping people, fighting fires, running the annual Fire Prevention Week at school. Loved to see the awe in the kindergartners' faces when he brought the fire trucks to school. He loved the lake, the town, and every festival they hosted. And it was because of his love for Deep Haven that he'd run for city council. He'd wanted to give back and make Deep Haven an even better place.

No, he wasn't going anywhere. If God wanted him to have a love life, He'd have to plop someone in the middle of his lap.

Someone called his name, shaking him from his thoughts. "Yeah?"

"So you already met him?" Uncle Charlie was asking, clearly by the raised eyebrow, for the second time.

"Who?"

"The new paramedic we're getting. Cole Barrett said he was moving up here soon and taking Eli Hueston's place now that he's retired to Florida. Said the guy's name was Ross or Ron or something."

Peter stood and glanced at Seth, good friend to Kirby Hueston, the one most people in town thought Cole should've hired. Thankfully he was deep in conversation with Ree, paying no mind to the talking on this side of the fire. "I haven't met the guy. He's supposed to come next week. But if Cole knows him, I'm sure he'll be fine. Besides, it's not my choice. It's Cole's."

Uncle Charlie shook his head. "I don't know about that. Sounds like he's from the Cities. Minneapolis. You know those guys can't drive for beans. Especially in the winter. He should leave driving the rig to me and Dean. We know how to handle the ambulance on these roads."

Thankfully Uncle Chuck turned to his son, Elton, to

complain some more about all the tourists that came up and quadrupled the population of Deep Haven during the peak summer and autumn weekends, completely discounting his family's hotels' dependence on them.

Peter made a noncommittal grunt and kissed his mother's cheek. Time to escape before the stupid vote came up again.

He dropped off Daisy with her family and walked away from the warmth of the fire with a wave goodbye.

His mom followed him down the long dirt road to the field where he'd parked his truck.

"Mom, I can walk to my truck by myself, you know."

"Oh, I know. I just…uh, I wondered what you were thinking."

"About what?"

She looked back at the gathering around the fire pit and dropped her voice. "Well…the vote."

His shoulders tensed. Blitzed by his own mother.

Her hand rested on his arm. Squeezed. "I know the Zimmermans want that place for their next moose-themed hotel, Peter, but it would make your dad so happy if you would vote for the restaurant."

Aw… "But Elton and Grandpa Zim have a good point too. A family-centered hotel on the lakeshore would bring more tourists for the restaurants and other businesses."

She stilled, staring at him. "Are you serious? Honey. You can't vote against the Dahlquists. It's—"

"Disloyal?" He stopped and turned to her. "I'm in trouble either way. No matter how I vote, some family is going to hate me."

She sighed. "Not me. I'll always love you. You know that."

He refrained from rolling his eyes. Barely. "Thanks. Guess I was hoping for a bigger argument."

She laughed, a quick chuckle that had more to do with pity

than humor. "I'm sorry you're in this position." Her voice grew quiet. "I do understand."

Yeah, she did. She had once been married to a Zimmerman —Peter's biological father. After he died, she worked hard to stay connected with them for Peter's sake. Like coming to their Christmas party and this picnic every year.

But she'd remarried, had three more children, and now she had to live with the Dahlquists and the repercussions of Peter's choice.

Peter kissed her cheek and pulled the keys out of his pocket. "I know, Mom. I know."

She caught his face in her hands. "I know you'll make the right choice."

And what exactly was that?

A gust of lake wind whipped through his sweatshirt as he watched her walk back to the crowd. Then he turned, and in the wink of a sunset walked out to his truck.

How could a guy have the biggest family in town and still be so alone?

ACKNOWLEDGMENTS

One of my favorite vacation destinations has long been Deep Haven, MN. From Mona at the Footsteps of Heaven bookstore, to Pastor Dan at the Community Church, to the Christiansen clan with all their adventures, diving into a Deep Haven novel was like taking a trip to meet up with old friends.

Then I learned that instead of merely vacationing in Deep Haven, I was being invited to build a home there and to join the Deep Haven family. What an amazing opportunity for which I am beyond grateful. I pray Ella and Adrian fit seamlessly into the life of that small town.

Building a home, even if it is a fictional one, takes many hands. I am filled with thanksgiving to each one who used their talents to bring this project to life.

Susan May Warren: My mentor, my editor, my friend. Thank you for seeing potential in me and for investing so much of yourself in my journey. And Lindsay Harrel: I'm humbled by the time you have spent working on making this project a success. Thank you for all your encouragement! The two of you are a joy and an inspiration to work for.

Thanks to others on the team at Sunrise: Barbara Curtis, my

editor who asked all the right questions and fixed all my math errors; and Rel Mollet, whose unending enthusiasm for the project fueled my desire to keep going.

I want to give a shoutout to The Western Wisconsin Writer's group for letting me wax on and on about the things I was working on. Thanks, guys.

Much appreciation too for my second office, Ellie's Ice Cream in Amery, WI. Thank you for letting me use your space whenever I needed different scenery and a sugary pick-me-up.

To Rachel Russell and Michelle Sass Aleckson: Thank you for working through the hard stuff with me, even when it all turned out to be hard stuff. Just keep swimming!

With a heart full of gratitude, I say "Thank you" to my amazing family and friends. You are the best cheerleaders ever. Full stop.

Macy and Anna: Thank you for existing on sandwiches, keeping the house running, and forgiving me for being away in Deep Haven so often. You guys are the best.

Eric: What a whirlwind this year turned out to be. Thank you for being my partner on this ride. Your love and support mean everything to me. You can't buy me love, but you do buy me ice cream and that's kind of the same thing.

And, finally, many thanks to God who gave me this dream in the first place.

ABOUT THE AUTHORS

 USA Today bestselling, RITA, Christy and Carol award-winning novelist **Susan May Warren** is the author of over 80 novels, most of them contemporary romance with a touch of suspense. One of her strongest selling series has been the Deep Haven series, a collection of books set in Northern Minnesota, off the shore of Lake Superior. Visit her at www.susanmaywarren.com.

 **Andrea Christenson** lives in Western Wisconsin with her husband and two daughters. When she is not busy homeschooling her girls, she loves to read anything she can get her hands on, bake bread, eat cheese, and watch Netflix—though not usually all at the same time. Andrea's prayer is to write stories revealing God's love. Visit her at www.andreachristenson.com.

CPSIA information can be obtained
at www.ICGtesting.com
Printed in the USA
LVHW091327160222
711299LV00004B/91